The Dome Wars

a novel by Harlen West

Dedicated to Brenda West,
Velma West,
and Judy Szafranski,
for their unwavering support.

Cover Illustration
by

Ann McRann
Ann Sileas Arts
annsileas@gmail.com

© 2016 O'Neill Publications

O'Neill

Publications

ISBN 978-0-578-18710-5

Chapter 1

Dark Clouds

William Harbill, President of the Federation of Democratic States, stood in his dressing room, staring in the mirror. "Have I aged that much in just four years? I must look twenty years older." He patted the loose folds under his chin in a vain attempt to push back the sagging skin.

"Starting to show my age," he said to no one in particular. His wife had told him a dozen times that, at 62, he just looked his age and still looked pretty good to her and to quit worrying about it. It was just one of the many worries that, lately, seemed to obsess him. He glanced at the calendar on the wall. It read June 7, 4222, A. D. A knock on the door interrupted his thoughts.

"Yes, come in," he said.

A prim, middle-aged woman opened the door slightly, stepped inside and announced, "Your staff has assembled in the conference room, Sir."

"Good! Tell them I'll be right out. Oh has Doctor Steebler arrived?"

"Yes, sir. He's waiting with the others," she replied. Moments later found he and his staff with the famous Dr. Steebler, head of the Board of Science Research and Developement, seated at the conference table.

"Good morning, everybody," said the President addressing his staff. "Please, be seated. We all know why we're here. As I stated in my memorandum, we're facing a crisis and, quite frankly, right now, I don't know how to deal with it. That's why I've called Dr. Steebler to attend this meeting. He will you brief you on what he reported to me yesterday. The Doctor rose to his feet. He was an imposingly big man, well over six feet tall. His persona automatically gave him an aura of great inner

1

strength. He spoke slowly.

"I'm here at President Harbill's request to talk to you about the future. It's about the domes. Everyone knows about the domes. For fifteen hundred years we've lived under them, admired them, but mostly taken them for granted. We seldom give a thought as to their purpose. The average man on the street goes about his daily business happy, comfortable, and oblivious.

"I'd bet that nowadays hardly a person stops to think about how our lives depend on the domes; that the air we breathe, the water we drink, and the food we eat, would not be possible without them. But I'm afraid trouble lays ahead—big trouble! By Executive Order, the public, including our elected officials, have not been informed and most certainly are not aware of our problems as relate to the domes.

"To bring you up to date, the domes are seriously threatened. What we've been keeping to ourselves in absolute secrecy, is that the velocity of the storms circling in the atmosphere outside the domes has measurably increased. It's common knowledge that these storms are the major cause of the cyclones and tornadoes that constantly harass our planet, but only we few know that they're now gusting up to horrendous speeds of over five hundred miles per hour.

"As you know, the domes were constructed over the centuries by our most brilliant engineers and have withstood the test of time. However, time and constant buffeting by these fierce winds are causing irreparable damage. The moorings and pilings that basically secure the domes are slowly being uprooted. I'm very much afraid that within a few years the domes will lose their grip and be torn loose from their moorings. Each day we are witnessing more and more damage. We're working feverishly to make repairs as fast as they occur, but I'm afraid it's inevitable. The domes will, in time, be uprooted from their moorings and blown away into outer space. If we are still living under them when this happens, the results will be catastrophic! We will die! Our civilization will perish! I want to caution you gentlemen. These findings I have reported to you are not theories: They are facts."

President Harbill looked around the conference table at his staff, who sat there with mouths agape, and then asked in a low voice. "Do you have an estimate Doctor? How many years do we have before this tragedy occurs?"

"At the current rate of deterioration I would estimate about twenty plus or minus a few years. It's impossible to give you an exact figure. Of course we won't be sitting on our heels. My colleagues and I will be making every effort humanly possible to find a solution to this problem and will keep the President informed of our progress. Well, that's about all I have for you right now except to say, 'Heaven help us!'" At this earth shattering announcement, and seemingly having nothing else to say, Dr. Steebler turned and left the room, leaving his stunned and speechless audience behind.

Chapter 2

Martial Law

The Central Military Command was one of the most powerful and influential arms of the Government. It controlled all of Earth's military forces, including the Central Police Agency and the Space Fleet Command. It almost paralleled the President in authority. Its leader, a black granite-jawed giant, controlled it with an iron fist. His was the only government agency housed in an underground complex.

This complex was commonly called the Ant Colony. It acquired its name because of its resemblance to the ant colonies that had been kept in aquariums by children who were fascinated by the ants' regimen and organization. But that was many years in the past. The Office of Internal Affairs had long ago outlawed the private ownership of ant colonies, because, like most other indigenous Earth creatures, they were all but extinct and could only be studied in the government-controlled Earth Life Museum.

Nevertheless, for the Central Police Agency's home, the name "Ant Colony" stuck. It was a completely self-contained area, requiring only fresh food and water to supplement its own extensive supplies. Its maze of underground tunnels led to offices, warehouses, living quarters, recreational areas, training facilities, and large conference rooms. At his insistence, it also contained the headquarters complex of the Central Military Command's Supreme Commander, Field Marshal Franklin D. Varco.

Twenty years earlier, after he had graduated from the Police Academy, Second Lieutenant Varco began his career serving in various government agencies. Wherever he served, he did so with great efficiency, winning the support and respect of his superiors with his amiable disposition and eager-to-please, can-do attitude. He always displayed great enthusiasm, attacking any job assigned to him with an energy that was not always expected from a junior officer. Everyone wanted Franklin Varco on his or her team. Needless to say, he received the highest praise and outstanding ratings from his superiors, who saw to it that he received his promotions as soon as he became eligible. Lieutenant Varco, who some believed to be on his way to becoming General Varco, was the brightest star on the military horizon.

It wasn't long before the often-promoted Varco reached the grade of Lieutenant Colonel and attracted the attention of the President of the Federation. A vacancy had occurred in the Central Police Agency. The Deputy Commander had retired, and the President was searching for a suitable replacement. His staff had presented him with a list of candidates, each of whom had to be thoroughly investigated before a decision could be made. Even though Varco was still considered to be a junior officer by some, many of the others who talked to the President about the candidates gave Varco the highest recommendations and urged the President to promote him to the position with the rank of Brigadier General.

The President, after giving much thought to the situation, decided to give the position, on an interim basis, to a thirty-year veteran, Major General Warren Hood. He felt he needed more time to examine the credentials of the young and inexperienced officer. In the meantime, Varco was seated as a member of the President's Military Council, where he could be closely monitored and evaluated.

Varco made an immediate impact on the council. He was a fountain of knowledge and an instinctive leader who seemed to know everything from troop deployment to crowd control, from training requirements to military stratagems, yet he never ruffled anyone's feathers or bruised any egos. In fact, he was very popular with the other members of the council, who seemed to look upon him as the unspoken champion of the group. Almost all of the suggestions he presented to the council

5

were adopted. Most seemed so practical that the other members of the council wondered why they hadn't thought of these changes a long time ago. The President was very impressed with the knowledgeable, affable, but down-to-earth, hard-working colonel. He believed, given enough time, this young officer could be developed into a commander of the highest echelon. Unfortunately, due to unforeseen developments, the need to test the acclaimed skills of the young colonel came sooner than later and forced the President into a decision he wasn't really comfortable with.

After only eight months in office, General Hood died, suddenly, of a massive heart attack. He was addressing a group of recruits when he brought his arms to his chest, let out a loud gasp, and collapsed on the podium. It was a sad day for the President. He and the general were old friends. It didn't make it any easier for him to know that within just one month, he would have to appoint someone to replace his old friend as Deputy Commander. As the days passed, he couldn't bring himself to appoint someone else to the vacant position and asked his staff and advisors to recommend someone to replace his friend. His entire staff and most of his advisors recommended Lt. Col. Varco.

The President was hesitant. There was something that he just couldn't quite put his finger on that made him reluctant to give Varco the job. Rationalizing that he was perhaps being too critical because of the loss of his friend, he decided that all of his advisors who had recommended Colonel Varco couldn't be wrong and President Harbill finally gave in and appointed him as Deputy Commander of the Central Police Agency with the rank of Brigadier General. All Varco needed now was a majority vote from Congress, and the appointment would be official. To his extreme satisfaction, Congress unanimously approved the appointment and confirmed his promotion to the rank of Brigadier General.

Although he was now the Deputy Commander of the Central Police Agency and directed of all the Agency's activities, Varco had a boss. He was Field Marshal Jerome A. Lovell who,

6

as Supreme Commander of the Central Military Command, was over both the Central Police Agency and the Space Fleet Command.

As a commander, Marshal Lovell was more of an administrator than a warrior. Those under his command always had their houses in order, marched with precision, and were immaculately attired. One could always depend on the fact that all the areas and offices would be spotless, desks kept neatly, and all administrative files would be in exact alphabetical order and locked away securely as instructed by the very latest, up-to-date, Standard Operating Procedures. If the President or Inspector General's Office inspected one of Lovell's bases, they would be hard-pressed to find even one speck of dust, let alone something serious enough to warrant the issuance of a demerit.

It was common knowledge that, had the Marshal ever been called upon to mobilize has forces to ward off an enemy attack, he would have been hard-pressed to carry out a successful campaign. Since their government, for centuries, had no enemies, this never seemed to be an important issue for Lovell, therefore he never gave it much thought. Nevertheless, military exercises were routinely conducted as a matter of protocol, but Lovell remained in the background and left the running of the exercises to his two respective Deputy Commanders, the now-Brigadier General Varco of the Central Police Agency, and Commodore Sorenson of the Space Fleet Command.

It didn't take Varco long to gain the old Field Marshall's trust and respect. Lovell, who relished his free time, was quick to take advantage of the situation, and saw no problem in turning the reins of responsibility over to his new deputy, while he pursued his off-duty activities. The Field Marshall took Varco completely into his fold, and it was not unusual to see them, as of late, in each other's company socializing and dining.

After three months, the personnel of the Central Police Agency began to see a different, and not so pleasant, side of their new Commander. Without any warning, he came down on his subordinates with an iron fist. He let them know that, after observing the Agency's operations for several months, he found

7

the personnel to be undisciplined, the officers too lenient, and in his opinion, derelict in enforcing regulations. They were very good at marching, with their uniforms always neat and their shoes polished, but they were sadly lacking in every other phase of their duties. Varco called them, "parade soldiers who are good at marching, but not much good for anything else."

Varco soon let it be known that he was taking personal control of this command. He warned everyone that drastic changes would be needed to turn this agency around. There was not even a hint of the friendly and understanding commander he seemed to be when he first took over. Marshall Lovell seemed to be in concurrence with his new deputy's mode of operation, and overlooked all of the complaints coming in from the lower echelon commanders, who were becoming painfully aware that their new chief was extremely hard-nosed and controlling.

Varco changed almost everything about the agency, including their hours of operation, training requirements, and shift changes. Quite a few eyebrows were raised over his demotions of certain officers and other personnel changes. It seemed that General Varco was everywhere. Any member of the Central Police Agency, regardless of his rank or station, who didn't live up to his strict and demanding code of duty and performance, suffered the consequences.

Subordinate officers were soon to realize they had lost their authority. They no longer had control of their own precincts. All field operations, even day-to-day work assignments, had to clear through Varco's office for approval. The rate of demotions, terminations and reprimands doubled after Varco began his "cleansing" of the agency. Applications for transfers tripled; morale was almost nonexistent.

As Varco's power grew, Field Marshal Lovell's role and authority diminished. He seemed to abrogate his responsibilities and authority, giving all the reins to the ambitious Varco. Everyone, including President Harbill and the members of Congress, excused the Marshal for his inactivity and lack of leadership because of his suddenly failing health. Having always been energetic and in excellent physical condition for a man of his age, he started to lose his vitality, and slowly became more and more dependent upon his Deputy to take over his responsibilities. At first, he complained he "just didn't have the energy he once had," but his condition seemed to worsen daily, until he finally collapsed and had to be rushed to the hospital.

The Government's top medical specialists were called in to treat the Marshall; but even with their extensive knowledge and advanced testing, they were unable to diagnose what was causing Marshall Lovell's illness. Varco visited him every day at the hospital, and each day, the Marshal's condition grew worse. After six months, with no signs of improvement, the once-beloved Field Marshal lapsed into a coma, and three days later died.

Once again, the President would have to make a hard decision. He had been favorably impressed by General Varco's performance during the time he served on his Council; but the rumors about his methods of handling his command of the Central Police Agency gave him more cause to not completely trust the man. However, it seemed there was no one as capable and experienced and in face of the recommendations Varco received from so many of his advisers, he couldn't very well refuse to appoint him to the position as Lovell's replacement.

One month later, Brigadier General Varco was duly appointed by the President, and confirmed by Congress, as Supreme Commander of the Central Military Command, giving him complete authority over both the Central Police Agency and the Space Fleet Command. He was promoted to the rank of Field Marshal, making him the youngest person ever to hold that office.

Four years had passed since Varco's appointment as Field Marshal. His complete change of character from the friendly, nice guy, to the hard-nosed controlling Commander he had become, enabled him to forge his command into one of such power that it gave cause for both the President and members of Congress to sometimes wonder what, exactly, was he up to? No longer was Varco thought of as the affable, friendly, easy-going, man-of-the-hour. If at all possible, he was avoided and every effort was made by almost everyone, including the top government authorities, to not cross his path and to appease him whenever and wherever possible.

The person, who had been the most disturbed by Varco's promotion, was Admiral Sorenson, Deputy Commander of the Space Fleet Command. The chain of command had placed the overall command of both the Central Police Agency and the Space Fleet Command under Varco, as the Supreme Commander. Even Sorenson's recent promotion to Vice Admiral did little towards easing his deep concerns about working under Varco. Having served alongside him in joint exercises as his equal prior to Varco's appointment as Supreme Commander, Sorenson was well aware of Varco's harsh tactics as a commanding officer.

One morning, as Marshal Varco exited his office flanked by his personal security guards, he heard loud shouts coming from down the hall. This was unusual, because loud noise in the Colony was forbidden by law, and was strictly enforced. In a complex such as the Colony, noise had to be contained at all times, otherwise sound waves reverberating down the metal corridors would be unbearable, and any kind of communication would be impossible. Upon occasion, soldiers had even been court-marshaled for violating the Excessive Noise Laws.

The present offensive racket was coming from the main conference room, the same room in which the Marshal had scheduled a secret meeting with his top military commanders. Instant anger consumed Marshal Varco. His smoldering black eyes narrowed to little slits, his muscles tightened and twitched, and his teeth clamped tight in his jaws. He could not tolerate lack of discipline at any level; but from his top commanders? He stormed into the conference room and, with chin jutting forward, stomped up to the speaker's podium.

Everyone who had been standing when Varco slammed into the room, scrambled to find a seat. The only sound was the scraping of a few chairs on the floor as the officers vied for a place to sit, and the heavy breathing of those whose voices a few moments before, had been raised in anger. To make matters worse, Marshall Varco's entrance had been so sudden that no one

10

had called the room to attention, a breach of military etiquette that added fuel to the Marshal's anger. For long minutes that seemed like hours to those present, Varco just stared at his subordinates. The room, containing twenty-seven officers, all commanders and senior staff members, became so quiet hardly anyone dared to breathe. Finally, someone in the room cleared his throat, breaking the thick silence.

The Marshal spotted the offender. "Did you have something to say, Admiral Sorenson?" he sneered caustically.

"Err- ah- no sir. Just a slight cold," The Admiral, himself a man of distinction, stood to face his commander.

"You must have had something to say, but, since you don't seem to be able to get it out, get back to your seat and sit down!" retorted the Marshall, the pitch of his deep bass voice growing louder with each word. "You all must have something to say. I heard you yelling like a bunch of recruits all the way down to my office. For now, I'm not going to dwell on this incident, but I assure you that in some way, each of you will be disciplined for this unacceptable behavior."

Varco then loudly resumed, "First, I want it understood that everything discussed in this meeting is top secret. The material I'm going to divulge is extremely sensitive and will not be spoken of outside this room. You will not discuss any part of it with your family, or with fellow officers. Anyone violating this command of silence covering what we will be discussing at this meeting will face criminal charges. By that, I mean you could be subject to facing a military court marshal or even imprisonment. If any of this information leaked out to the general public, the consequences could be so serious and catastrophic that the devastation caused during the Last War would pale in comparison."

Marshall Varco, speaking slowly and forcefully so that each word would sink in, continued, "Before I can begin any discussions concerning this matter, any of you who feel you cannot abide by these rules or who do not have the discipline to withstand the pressure that I am certain, in the very near future, we will be expected to withstand, may leave this room and resign

11

their commission. If you decide on this course of action, I assure you there will be no harmful consequences or detrimental actions taken against you."

"I'm aware that the ruckus I heard before I came down here was probably about some rumors or hints you've heard from some of your cronies in the Capital, most probably concerning the subject of this meeting. Mainly for that reason, I want each of you to think carefully about this offer to resign before you make your decision. Whatever you decide, understand it will be a permanent decision. You will not be allowed to change your mind later on, even if you find that you can't handle the situation."

Marshal Varco continued staring around the room, looking each person in the eyes, as if to decide for himself which one, if any, of his officers would fail him, and be left by the wayside. Expressions of doubt and consternation showed on many of the officers' faces, and others seemed to be embarrassed by the idea that any of them would not stay and see this thing through, whatever it may be. Some, perhaps, would have considered resigning, but knowing their commander and his utter contempt for anyone he considered a "slacker," feared that the consequences for resigning would be little different from being court marshaled for leaking information. Not one man left the room.

After some minutes had passed, Marshal Varco, with a look of satisfaction on his face and nodding slightly, spoke to his officers. "Very well. I see you have all decided to remain and fulfill your obligations to the Federation, as I believed you would. So let's get this meeting started."

"To begin with," continued the Marshal, "I have been ordered by the President to a meeting being held in his private rooms in New Washington for a conference. The President hasn't informed me of what the conference is about but I do know who else is attending ... all of the State Representatives, the President's Cabinet, and the Federation's top scientists. This kind of conference is only called at a time of crisis or in an extreme national emergency."

12

Varco again thrust his prominent chin out, and declared, "I'm not without my own resources, and I have an informant who has given me a good idea as to what the President's planning to discuss at this meeting. He's going to declare that all the Earth's inhabitants are in extreme and imminent danger and that we all have to start making immediate plans for mankind's survival."

A clamor spread throughout the room. "What do you mean by 'survival'?" "What kind of emergency?" "How do you know all this?" Questions were erupting faster than anyone could possibly answer.

Varco held up his hand for silence. Suddenly, without warning, two squads of armed soldiers entered the conference room, locked all the exit doors and then stationed themselves around the walls of the room. The staff officers looked about nervously. Never, in their wildest thoughts, would they have imagined that conditions could be so serious as to warrant this kind of action by their commander.

Varco looked imperiously down at his officers. "How do I know these things?" he continued, ignoring the looks of consternation on the faces of his officers. "Because I make it my business to know," the Marshal sneered.

"President Harbill thinks he can keep his little secrets hidden from me? He can't! I know what's happening on every inch of this planet. My agents are in every corner of the world. Even the President's own administrative offices have been penetrated. Every day, I'm brought up to date on the latest events of every department in the Government. I'm going to this conference armed with knowledge of the White House's most confidential secrets."

"Before we go on," said Varco, "there's something each of you must do for me. I know when you received your commissions you gave a pledge of allegiance to the President and acknowledged him as the Commander-In-Chief. My military legal staff has advised me that these pledges are technically not totally binding. These pledges are not and never were meant to bind the actions of soldiers to the Executive

13

Branch."

"Even the President knows that to effectively control a police force or any military organization, officers and their subordinates must owe their loyalty to their field commanders. Without this loyalty at the field commander level there would be a complete breakdown of discipline. Therefore, as your commander and immediate supervisor, you owe your allegiance and loyalty to me and only me!"

Varco paused, eyed his officers, and then continued. "You will find letters for you to sign on the table at the back of this stage. These letters are pledges of loyalty to me and statements verifying your total support of my policies. I need assurance that our agency is strong and united. Your pledges of loyalty will be the glue that unites and binds us together."

The Marshal glowered at the generals and admirals seated before him and said, "For the last time, any officer wishing to leave the Agency and resign his commission, may do so now."

After a pause, Admiral Sorenson, the officer who unintentionally opened the meeting by clearing his throat said hesitantly, "Sir, I believe it would be in my best interest to resign my commission and return to private life."

The Marshal looked quizzically at Sorenson. "Admiral Sorenson, you surprise me. Haven't you been on the Presidential Advisory Council for the last two years and aren't you currently the Space Fleet Commander?" he asked.

"Yes, Sir. As a matter of fact, as you know, I am still currently on that staff, and have been appointed those duties," replied the Admiral.

"A man of your leadership abilities and influence would surely be missed by both the President and myself. The President will think, as I do, that your resignation is most strange," said the Marshal.

"And I will miss serving," said Admiral Sorenson. "I just don't feel that I possess the qualities or the politics to meet the total commitment you require. I think, in my present position, I am more closely associated with the President. Perhaps I may

14

continue to be of valuable service as an advisor to the Executive Branch, or in some other capacity."

"I see," murmured the Marshall. "Are you sure you've thought this over carefully, Admiral?"

"Yes, Sir. I am."

"That's too bad." For several moments Varco, almost sadly, peered down at his rebelling officer. "I think, Admiral, yours is a special case. I think that, for now, I'm going to detain you. I need time to consider your resignation. I don't believe there's a job in Washington for you."

"Detain me? Am I under arrest?" The Admiral wanted to know.

"Let's just consider you as my guest until I get back home," said Varco as he nodded to two of his security guards, who quickly marched to the Admiral's side and escorted him from the meeting room. Not another man moved but a hushed gasp echoed throughout the room. Admiral Sorenson had many friends. There was a pause. The Marshal, seemingly lost in thought, finally stirred.

"That's too bad," he murmured. "He was a good man."

The next hour of the meeting was taken up with the Marshal's top commanders and staff officers filing onto the stage and signing their Pledges of Loyalty and Statements of Policy Support. When the subdued officers returned to their seats, the Marshal resumed his presentation.

"As I stated earlier, I'm going to New Washington to attend the President's conference. I'm pretty confident that what he's going to do is give us a 'State of Affairs' speech in which he and that scientist of his will claim that this entire planet is headed for disaster! The note I got from my informant stated that they're saying the climate is hotter, the winds outside are getting stronger, and the domes are weakening and may soon give way."

Varco paused and waited for the eruption of voices that filled the room following his statement to subside. He raised his hand and was gratified by instant silence. He thought, "Now, this is what I mean by discipline and loyalty!" He continued, "That isn't the worst of it. I also think that he is going to

15

recommend that we prepare to leave our planet and colonize some other planet somewhere in some other galaxy we don't even know." Again, whispers and murmurs pervaded the room. Varco motioned for silence. "I've also been told of rumors floating around that our scientists have developed spacecraft that are capable of traveling to distant galaxies. Personally, I don't know for sure. My informants haven't confirmed this, so I wouldn't bet on it."

"What I am reasonably sure of is that those domes are secure and with a little bit of maintenance, will hold for years. In other words, I think the President is deliberately exaggerating the situation and jumping the gun. I think he's an egomaniac who envisions himself as the great savior of humanity."

"Anyway, for some reason I haven't figured out yet, he and his scientist have concocted some pretty wild theories – and that's what I think they are—theories!! When he unveils his speech to the conference about the world coming to an end and evacuating all the peoples of Earth to some unknown planet, all hell's going to break loose! Some of these irresponsible remarks are bound to leak out and when they do, there's going to be civil disturbances the like of which we've never seen before."

"This is where we come in," said Varco, shifting his eyes and emphasizing each word. "It will be the job of the Central Police Agency to prevent civil disorder." Raising his voice again he continued, "These will be your standing orders. Each of you will return to your respective states or territories. Once there, you will re-establish order and maintain security over the civilian population, tighter than we ever have before."

"I want you to ferret out all subversive activities. No public gatherings or meetings will be allowed. Individuals or groups spreading social unrest or advocating terrorist activities, anti-government propaganda, or general complaints or disturbances, will be rounded up and incarcerated. If they are unruly or resist, they may be executed. No trials will be necessary. Dissidents will be shot on the spot, the same as looters were in times of war. We will be entering an era of dangerous times and you will be dealing with dangerous people.

16

These people must be dealt with immediately and severely. Call it quick justice. The executions of a few troublemakers will set a good example and keep the rest of the populace in line, and possibly save the World from mass hysteria."

"In other words, I am declaring Martial Law throughout the World." Varco paused and looked about. "I expect my commanders to carry out these orders vigorously. Martial Law will be absolutely enforced until I return from the conference."

There was a disturbance from the back of the room. A general stood up, waved his hand, and asked, "Marshal Varco, Sir! Isn't Martial Law an order that only the President can give? I know I was gone on leave for a while, but I didn't see any presidential orders come across my desk. Did I miss something?"

The Marshal peered through the assembly. "Who said that?" he demanded.

Nobody answered. The general who had asked the question had already sat down, disappeared into a sea of faces, and was not spotted by the Marshal.

"I don't remember declaring this an open forum", sarcastically growled Varco, "but I will answer the question. I've been in contact with the President and he agrees with me that Martial Law is necessary. You all know how it is! Recently, he's been so busy he just can't find time for all his administrative details, so he leaves some of them to his department chiefs."

"In the meantime, I can assure you that as soon as I get to New Washington, orders from the President will be forthcoming. If any of you have a problem with establishing martial law in your area, I'd like to tell you that I have many good men standing in line who'd love to have their own command."

Marshal Varco looked pleased. He was sure that he had all of his commanders in line. "Gentlemen," he said, "I hope I've made myself perfectly clear. Are there any questions? – No? Good! As soon as I return, I will schedule another meeting where we will discuss the results of the President's conference and your results in enforcing martial law. We will then plan our next phase of operations."

With this, the Marshal paused, then remarked, "Well, that about covers everything you need to know: Any questions or last minute thoughts?' There was no response. "Then, commanders, you have your orders. Let us all execute our duties."

Chapter 3

Some Hard Decisions

Miles away in New Washington, President Harbill looked out of his office window and absently wondered about the fake grass and trees on the front lawn of the Presidential abode. Were they really necessary? They looked too synthetically phony to fool anybody. Lord knows it would be impossible to grow real plants on the metal plates under the White House lawn. His reverie was interrupted by a knock on the door. It was his daughter, Zorena. She swept past his secretary and seated herself on the plush overstuffed office chair reserved for her father.

"Hello, Daddy," she greeted him, looking sweetly and innocently into his eyes.

"What the – Zorena! What are you doing here?"

"Aren't you glad to see me, father?" she smiled.

The President sighed, "Of course I'm glad to see you, Sweetheart, but you're not supposed to be here. You're supposed to be in school at the Space Academy."

"I'm bored with school, bored with the Academy, and I'm bored with post graduate courses," pouted Zorena, her long blond hair swirling about her shoulders as she shook her head. "I want to do something with my life. I feel like I'm treading water, or worse, standing still; going nowhere."

"Yeah, right! At twenty, you're going nowhere? What am I going to do with you?" the President asked. He was completely frustrated with his beautiful, brilliant, but headstrong daughter. He knew why she was here, and it wasn't because she was bored.

"Daddy," she said, looking up at him. "I want to go on the project. I know all about it. I know I'll qualify, but I can go only if you give me the OK."

19

The President shook his head. "No, Zorena! You've discussed this with me before and I haven't changed my mind. You're not going and that's final! Besides, you're not even supposed to know about the project. Anyway, its three months away and you're not qualified. The Academy tells me you haven't completed your space flight or navigation training yet."

"It's not fair," objected Zorena. "I don't see why I shouldn't be considered just because I'm the President's daughter! When I graduate, I'll be qualified as a fleet pilot and an aeronautical engineer. I have one of the best records and received some of the highest grades in my class. You know that, if anyone else had my qualifications, they would be at the top of the list."

"Like I said before, Zorena," replied her father, "there'll be other things just as important you can get involved in – and, as I also said, you're not qualified for this mission."

Zorena knew her father was not happy about her showing up at his office. "Don't worry about my qualifications, Daddy. I'll be ready! Tell Mom I said hello," she quipped as she slid out of his chair, whisked out the door, and cheerfully waved goodbye.

The President, watching her depart, mused, "What an actress! Get back in school!" he called after her. He definitely did not want her on that project, but he knew the Academy would highly recommend her if she applied; just something else to worry about. The President frowned. A much more serious problem than his daughter's education weighed heavily on his mind. He was thinking about the upcoming conference.

Just prior to the Last War, a facility was constructed to protect the President of the United States, his staff, and select members of Congress from long-range missiles, nuclear bombs, and other weapons of mass destruction. It had been constructed thirty floors under the White House. It had not saved its occupants from the horrors of the Last War, but, for the last 1500 years, it had proved invaluable as a high security area for conferences.

It was quite an experience attending a conference here.

20

Once conference delegates arrived, they were assigned quarters that included all of the elements necessary for a short – or prolonged – stay. They were provided with a sparse, but comfortable room and meals that were healthy, but with no frills. A complete library, lounge area, recreation area, swimming pool, and exercise area completed their living space. Once the delegates checked into the facility, they were not allowed to leave the premises. Their working agenda was posted daily and they were restricted to the conference area until all business was concluded.

The conference room was ready. To the casual observer it seemed austere, with its bare white walls having no decorations with the exception of a bulletin board hanging next to the door. However, hidden within these walls there was a hi-tech security system with eye-in-the sky camera surveillance, ultra high definition sound systems, and a squad of security guards equipped with laser rifles and stun guns. These were extraordinary precautions that were not ordinarily required for a Presidential conference.

At 8 o'clock on the morning of June 5th, 4553 B.C., fifty state representatives, four cabinet members, and five scientists filed into the conference room and seated themselves. Accompanying them was Field Marshal Varco.

At 8:30am, President Harbill, accompanied by His Holiness, Dr. Joshua Zinn, Religious Leader of the World Church, entered the room, stepped up to the podium and faced the assembled conferees. The room was quiet. All rose and bowed their heads as Dr. Zinn blessed the members of the assembly, and prayed for their success in dealing with the difficult problems facing them. After Dr. Zinn finished his ritual, he departed. The Church would not be privy to these proceedings. The President was not yet ready to deal with the masses.

He opened the meeting and addressed the assembly. "Please, be seated," he said. After the shuffling of chairs quieted, he continued, "I wish to extend my appreciation for your attendance and ask you to pardon the short notice given for this

21

conference. I have recently received information so alarming that I felt it necessary to summon you here immediately. This will be possibly the most unusual and certainly the most important conference any of you have ever attended. Our very lives may depend on what we decide here in the next few weeks."

"To begin with," he continued, "I want to put everyone at ease. We must start our meetings with clear minds and in good spirits. The format for this conference will be casual. I don't want us to be stiff and formal with each other. It's going to be tough enough without that. It is imperative that we have a good exchange of ideas and suggestions and, for that, we need to be comfortable in dealing with each other."

"What I do not want in this conference are unnecessary issues. I know there will be many of us with conflicting ideas and that's okay, but I do not want the airing out of dirty laundry. In order to accomplish the tasks ahead of us, it will be absolutely essential that we focus on the issues at hand and not allow ourselves to become distracted."

"To begin our conference, I want to introduce Senator Maria Grazzi who, as well as being the Senator from South Euro, is our most renowned historian. I have asked her to give us a brief overview of Earth's history over the past 2000 years. Madam Grazzi, if you please."

A slight, light complexioned woman stood up, and walked to the podium. Although small in stature, her regal bearing commanded the attention of the entire assembly. Her eyes sparkled with intensity. She spoke in a low, clear voice.

"Fellow delegates, we have come to what many of us consider the crossroads of our existence. Perhaps, if our forefathers had followed a different path, we would not now be facing these most difficult times. I choose to start the overview with the Nineteenth and Twentieth Centuries. Four significant things occurred during that era. First, the Industrial Revolution and the use of fossil fuels. Second, the invention of the airplane. Third, the atomic bomb. Fourth, and probably the most important and devastating event, was that in the late 1900's, the

Earth's temperature began to rise.

"In examining the facts as to why these four events were so significant, we find that the Industrial Revolution, which started in the1800s, brought about the use of fossil fuel, mainly coal and oil products, which are now, by law, prohibited. These fuels were used for the next 250 years to produce 90% of the world's energy. The by-product of these fuels was poison gases, primarily carbon monoxide, carbon dioxide, and chlorofluorocarbons. Ignorant and greedy, the industrialists pumped billions of tons of these poisonous chemicals into the Earth's atmosphere, lakes, rivers and oceans.

"First, let's look at the chlorofluorocarbons. As everyone here knows, there is a belt of ozone gas that blankets and circles the Earth. This belt is only fifty miles wide, but it protects the Earth from the sun's ultra-violet rays. When chlorofluorocarbons were released into the atmosphere, they attacked and destroyed several layers of the ozone belt. The partial destruction of the ozone belt created huge holes and exposed the Earth to the Sun's deadly ultra-violet rays.

"Next, we will examine carbon monoxide and carbon dioxide," she continued. "As these chemicals, a bi-product of fossil fuels, were released into the atmosphere, they formed, over the years, a thick deadly haze that reached from ground level to twenty thousand feet. This haze, that in olden days was called smog, settled over the entire planet. It polluted the very air people breathed. The fumes affected over 200 generations. People could not breathe and had to carry oxygen with them wherever they went.

"This deadly haze had no place to go. It would not dissipate. It could not escape our atmosphere. The chemicals polluted the lakes and rivers. People could not drink the water. There was no relief from the poison gases. The smog also created an insidious and most serious side effect called the Greenhouse Effect. The Greenhouse Effect literally trapped heat under the smog. This trapped heat caused – and is still causing – the Earth's temperature to rise.

"As the temperatures rose – they called it 'global

warming' – our weather patterns became unpredictable. Extreme cold fronts from the North collided with equally extreme hot fronts from the South. As a result, hurricanes and tornadoes become more and more volatile. The Earth's air and water temperature continued to rise at a rate of two degrees Fahrenheit every hundred years. As the temperatures rose, the hurricanes and tornadoes grew more and more violent.

"Of course, before all of this happened man had invented the airplane and learned to fly. Flight was considered the most important discovery of the Twentieth Century. People could travel with unlimited restrictions to anywhere on the globe in a matter of hours. They could also deliver weapons of war with equal ease.

"The discovery and use of atomic weapons," she continued, "heralded the way for mass destruction. All mankind seemed to be consumed with intolerance, hate, and rage. When it became inevitable that man could not settle his differences in peaceful negotiations and with all nations, even the smaller ones having atomic power, it was time for another war to end all wars. The major difference was that this war would be fought using atomic weapons.

"Then, in 2140 to 2150, A. D., came what we call today the 'Last War', that actually only lasted for less than one year. By the time this war started, man had perfected his weapons. He had also perfected its delivery system. He could deliver a missile to a designated target with pinpoint accuracy. Missiles were launched. There was no defense.

"Under bombardment, all of the major cities and almost all of the smaller communities on Earth withered, collapsed and died, leaving only charred ruins. Most of the inhabitants also died under heat so intense it burned the flesh off their bodies until nothing was left except black ash, which was blown away by the wind.

"As devastating as this was, it was only the beginning of the Black Death. Fallout finished what the bombs could not. Radioactive material, rising as puffs of billowing mushrooms, drifted around our planet like gossamer clouds, and rained

24

radioactive dust on nearly all corners of the Earth. For nine long years, the fallout continued. Billions of people died horrible deaths, their bodies mutated, twisted and contorted. Almost all of the animals perished, except for a small number—mostly farm and food animals—that could be protected in caves and mines and other underground shelters."

After pausing to take a sip of water, Madam Grazzi started again. "The fall-out finally stopped. At the outbreak of the Last War, Earth's population numbered over seven billion people. As near as we can judge, less than two billion survived. Amazingly, the survivors, mostly from rural and country areas, were reasonably healthy, but homeless. They survived mostly because of the usable items they found in rural area stores, markets, and warehouses. They owed their lives to canned and bottled goods; canned fruit, vegetables, meats, bottled water and juice, and canned anything that was edible. Everything in cans and bottles was preserved and protected underground from radioactive fall-out. Supplies were bountiful, and underground springs were found that supplied water, but they were all coveted. Quarrels broke out among different factions that wanted control of the food and water supplies. These supplies meant wealth. Wealth meant power. Power meant greed. And, as history has taught us, greed almost always leads to conflict.

"For some two hundred years, petty kings and warlords ravaged the Earth. Over nine hundred million people, caught up in these conflicts, were killed. Finally, one strong group emerged victorious. It defeated the petty kings and warlords and formed one central benign government, which we know today as the Federation of Democratic States (FDS). The rest, you know. We built homes, started new industries, farmed our lands, planted new forests, and replenished our herds of animals that survived. We framed our constitution and established states and human rights.

"To protect ourselves from the ever-increasing heat and violent weather, we had to construct our cities and agricultural stations under gigantic domes. Throughout the new world, in isolated areas that were the least devastated, fifty cities with

25

connecting agricultural stations were erected, all covered with domes. They were called City-States, as they are called today. Each City-State housed approximately 20,000,000 citizens and became the foundation of our government. Every two years, each City-State elects its own City commissioners, who govern its affairs. Every two years, national elections are held to select one representative from each City to Congress. Every four years we have presidential national elections and every four years we elect 12 judges to our Supreme Court. All elected officials are limited to two terms in office.

"We are a true democratic nation, and have raised ourselves from the ashes of war to become a great nation," she proudly declared, "and we have lived in peace for two thousand years. However, I must conclude my brief history on a sad note. A new danger now confronts us and someone more qualified than I must report on this aspect of what appears to be the most perilous period of the entire history of our planet."

The President stood up and faced a hushed assembly. "Thank you Madam Grazzi. That was an excellent and most informative presentation. And now, before starting the proceedings, we must hear from our scientific community. They will bring us up to date about our current environmental situation and also their findings concerning mass transportation and other research. Ladies and gentlemen, we have a serious problem. Our scientists have what they believe may be the solution to our problem. Please give your full attention to a man who needs no introduction, Dr. Manns Steebler."

Dr. Steebler strode before the assembly and faced his audience. He was dressed in his traditional uniform, a white smock, which seemed rather out of place compared to the other well-dressed delegates. His bald head stood out, but his face was hidden behind a heavy black beard. He stared at the audience, his half-framed glasses resting on a large bulbous nose. He did not look like a scientist, yet he was renowned as the greatest genius of his time.

"I'm not a good public speaker," he started, "but my colleagues have appointed me to speak, so I will do my best. As

26

Mrs. Grazzi did, I too will go back in history so that you may see how the progression of events has affected our lives, as seen through the eyes of the scientist.

"After the Last War and the emergence of the Federation, scientists readily saw that weather patterns were much different than they were in the 1900's through the 2000's. Even then, temperatures on Earth were increasing almost yearly and the continents were experiencing severe droughts. Pollutants had begun to infect the Earth's waters and some species became extinct. The planet's general weather conditions, however, were still pleasant enough for comfortable existence.

"Man continued to use fossil fuels for power and scientists during that time believed the increasing temperatures were normal patterns of evolution that had occurred with regularity for millions of years. Earth had historically gone through Ice Ages, followed by years of hot, tropical heat. The scientists said this was normal evolution and nothing to worry about.

"As the years passed, however, with more and more pollutants being pumped into the atmosphere, the Earth's temperature continued to rise, and the Earth's lakes, oceans, and rivers become more polluted. It was evident that this was not normal evolution. As Mrs. Grazzi said, the time came when you couldn't drink the water, or breathe the air. Everyone had to carry oxygen bottles with them wherever they went and all water had to be processed.

"Then came the time when we could no longer sustain ourselves on the planet. The ice caps melted, causing the oceans to rise. The melting of the ice caps resulted not just because our atmosphere was polluted but also, as our measurements discovered, the sun itself was registering hotter temperatures than in the past.

"There is speculation that our sun may be entering the first stage of super nova. A Super Nova, as you know, is a condition where a star begins to burn hotter and hotter, and grow larger and larger to a point where it burns itself out and then collapses within itself and becomes a very small but dense dead star. This increase in the sun's temperature over the past 3,000 years has given us serious cause for concern. However, this is only a theory and may or may not be true.

"In any event, the increased radiation from the Sun, and the release of these pollutants, caused Earth's temperatures to rise. This, in turn, caused the ice caps to melt. The result was the levels of our oceans rose drastically. The ocean's levels rose so high that the continents were reshaped. Island nations disappeared. All lowlands were covered with water. All Earth's inhabitants had to move to higher elevations. To compound their problems, Earth's inhabitants were soon confronted with tornadoes and hurricanes whirling and gusting at speeds in excess of 350 miles an hour.

"After the populace resettled on higher ground, it became necessary to start building domes for protection. At first, the domes were small. They were just large enough to house the people in comparative comfort. However, as the winds grew stronger and more violent, it became necessary not only to protect people, but also the land, animals, vegetation, and all of our other resources.

"The domes became larger and larger until they reached gigantic proportions. We became dome-building experts. At various locations around the world, we built domes to cover our cities and agricultural stations. We could enclose the populace and all the resources we needed inside the domes and live more comfortably than we had ever lived before. We cleansed the air by pumping the polluted air out of the domes and into the atmosphere. We no longer needed to carry around oxygen bottles. We purified our water resources within the domes. We could maintain the temperature inside the domes to a comfortable 80 degrees Fahrenheit. We could also control the temperature of our farmlands and keep the ground fertile enough to reproduce four different crops per year, thereby producing a variety of crops in a much smaller area than ever before thought possible.

"Unfortunately, with the good came the bad. As we lived our lives so tranquilly inside the domes, the weather

28

outside the domes did not get any better. In fact, things have gotten worse – much worse! Temperatures outside the domes are now reaching a soaring global average of 140 degrees and it is becoming harder and harder to maintain temperatures inside the domes. Also, the velocity of the tornadoes and hurricanes is reaching over 500 miles per hour and the domes are being severely buffeted. And that, ladies and gentlemen," said Dr. Steebler, "is pretty much the situation as it is today.

"The temperature outside the domes is hovering at a global mean of 140 degrees and the winds are gusting up to around 500 miles per hour. We are closely monitoring the domes' moorings, but even considering our ability to maintain the domes, we estimate that, within ten to twenty years, the moorings will give way and will be torn loose by the winds. At that point, anything left on this planet will be swept away. The results will be catastrophic. We will not survive.

The conference room erupted with a surge of gasps and angry voices. Loud shouts of "That's absurd!", "I don't believe it!", and "This is nonsense!" could be distinguished among all the exclamations of surprise and shock at this astounding announcement.

At this point, Marshal Varco stood up and waved to the crowed for silence. When the noise subsided, he turned and addressed the President.

"President Harbill," he said in a very patronizing voice, "I think that many of us here are aware - or should I say have suspected - that you were going to threaten us with a pessimistic declaration of our situation, but many of us believe that you and the scientists are grossly exaggerating the facts." An avalanche of angry voices from the delegates echoed the General's sentiments.

The President looked squarely at Varco and spoke in a loud and commanding voice. "Marshal Varco, I must remind you that you are here only as the Chief of my Security and Military Forces. You are not an elected official. You do not have a vote! Congress promoted you to your present rank and position on my recommendation. You work for me! You will

29

report to me in my quarters when we have our first break to discuss protocol. In the meantime, sit down!"

Varco, shocked and sputtering, mumbled, "I must remind you, Mr. President, I am a Grand Marshal of this World Federation, not one of your rubber-stamped Generals!" and sat down.

The President then addressed the Assembly. "Let us please maintain order. Everyone sit down and allow Dr, Steebler to finish his presentation. Remember what I said. You are all here representing your respective States. This is a democracy! Every elected representative will have a vote. All issues will be decided on by a majority vote. I will also remind you that it would be impossible for us to have any meaningful discussions or make any decisions without first knowing all the facts." He then turned to the podium. "Dr. Steebler, please continue."

Dr. Steebler, looking over the rim of his glasses, leaned on his elbows over the podium, and looking out at his audience, continued. "My friends, I did not come here to frighten you. My intention is to inform you of all the scientific data we have been able to compile and let you know after long and intense study of this data, the conclusions that I and the other scientists have come to. The simple fact is that we must leave this planet as soon as possible!

"I am among the first to realize that the very thought of that is frightening. The logistics of moving an entire planet's population is mind-boggling, but this is why the President has brought us together in this meeting. We must decide what we are going to do and how we are going to do it. Also, remember that we don't have a lot of time to make these decisions. As for the scientists, I will tell you exactly what we have accomplished towards that end and what our options are.

"For thousands of years, man has been researching and working towards space travel. Our problem has always been that we have not developed the technology that would allow our ships to travel through space at speeds fast enough to allow us to reach a destination suitable for colonization.

"Even though we now travel among the planets in our

30

own solar system, and have even established small colonies on a few of them, with the ships we now have, it would take thousands of years to reach our nearest neighbor, the Andromeda Galaxy. The colonies we have established on our other planets can barely sustain themselves with the comparatively few inhabitants that are living there. The idea of moving our entire population to any of these colonies is impossible. We could not sustain life.

"In the last ten years, however, there have been many breakthroughs. Our researchers have recently discovered a way to harness and re-energize light fragments in such a manner that we can literally make light particles travel faster than the speed of light. As I speak, we are building an engine using this new technology and anticipate that within three months we will be able to test a new prototype spaceship. If we are successful, we believe we will have time to search for a planet or moon outside of our galaxy that is suitable for our needs. We also believe that we have time to build a fleet of transport ships that could deliver us all safely to any destination that our research indicates would be suitable for colonization.

Dr. Steebler paused, took several deep breaths, and leaned on the podium as if needing this support to continue. He looked like a man with the weight of the world resting on his shining bald head and broad shoulders that were bowed under the strain of responsibility for being forced to impart the news of this inevitable catastrophe.

After a few moments, he lifted his head and shoulders as if he was resolved to his task, reached for a sip of water, and looked out over his audience. Not a sound could be heard in the room. It was as if everyone was holding his breath. He put the glass down on the podium and continued to speak.

"We are also working on an option that we call Plan B. We have discovered a wormhole that is accessible from Earth. We accidentally discovered this in our research while working with light. Ladies and gentlemen, we have stumbled onto time travel."

At this announcement, loud gasps and emanations of

surprise and disbelief could be heard around the room. The Doctor raised his hand and, as the noise subsided, continued speaking.

"Yes. We now have the technology to go back in time and can even regulate what era we travel back to. The prospect of time travel is unlimited and we should have this project perfected and ready to go within the year. However, we will only be able to travel back in time to our own planet. Obviously, that makes this the least desirable of the two plans.

"We have no way of knowing what to expect if we came face to face, on the same plane and at the same time, with our ancestors. We should, at all costs, avoid this. But it is an option and a chance we may be forced to take."

Dr. Steebler paused, then, glancing at the President, continued with his speech. "Sir, ladies and gentlemen, that concludes my presentation. However, my fellow scientists and I will keep you apprised of all developments and will be ready to answer any questions you may have about either of these projects." With this statement, the Doctor turned and quickly left the room, leaving the shouts of disbelief and questions behind him.

President Harbill rose and, addressing the stunned and suddenly quiet assembly, began to speak. "Well, I believe that pretty much outlines both our past and present situations. If we believe our scientists – and I do – then we must make some hard and fast decisions about our course of action."

"The next phase of our deliberations will be a session of open discussions, allowing each of you to voice your opinion. I have scheduled six-minute time frames that will allow each delegate to have the opportunity to speak and ask questions. Speakers will rotate, beginning with Table 1 and continuing, in order, through Table 50. Each of you may use all or part of your allotted time.

"After the first round of talks, we will begin round-table discussions. At that time, delegates, by a wave of the hand, will be recognized by the chair, and allowed to speak. I've made these arrangements so that we can have comprehensive discussions without resorting to shouting, trying to be heard. Don't worry! I'll try not to overlook anybody!

"I anticipate there will be lots of discussions and probably many votes will be taken, but we must come to a decision on a course of action and do it promptly. Let's pray that when the decision is made, it's the right one."

The President, glancing at his watch, said, "Let's break now for lunch. We'll meet back here in one hour."

Singling out his Police Chief, the President, accentuating each word, said, "Marshal Varco, please accompany me to my office."

President Harbill sat stiffly behind his desk. He motioned to Varco, and in a stern voice, ordered, "Sit down!"

Marshal Varco, obviously very angry, plopped down in the chair, and leaning forward, said in a loud voice, "Look here, Harbill! I don't know why you're taking this high-handed approach with me. You seem to have forgotten that I am the Supreme Commander of both the Central Police Agency and the Space Fleet Command!"

At this remark, Varco paused as if he needed a moment to think. Then, his eyes narrowed and his jaws clenched even harder, as he exploded, "I'll admit you've managed to pull one over on me, especially concerning the new spaceship development and this "wormhole" thing. As head of the Fleet Space Command, I should have been kept up to date on all of this as it was happening and I assure you, some changes are going to be made and heads are going to fall because of it!

"And when it comes to the way you treated me in that meeting, protocol dictates that I receive the respect afforded me by my rank and station. You have humiliated me in front of the entire body of Federation representatives! I demand an apology and I demand that you make that apology on the floor, in front of the delegates!"

President Harbill stared impassively into the eyes of his rebellious and fiery police chief. How the man had changed! Varco was once one of his most trusted and valued lieutenants. Now, here he was, consumed with a hunger for power and trying to force a showdown with the President of the Federation!

"You're lucky I don't court martial you," replied the President in his most demanding voice. Immediately after this was said, Varco exploded out of his chair with a threatening gesture towards the President.

"Be careful!" said the President. "You have your personal bodyguards back at the Colony, but my own security guards are right here, outside this door. Sit down or I'll have you arrested!"

"On what grounds?" an alarmed Varco growled, as he returned to his seat.

"How about treason, for beginners?" answered the President. "I have in my possession a memo stating that you have declared martial law in all of the States of this Federation! That, alone, is a treasonable abuse of authority. That's one charge – and, by the way, that order has been rescinded. There will be no martial law while I am President!

"Added to that, I have another memo from a reliable source that says you advised your officers that they do not owe their allegiance to the President. That's also an act of treason and subversion. It was a blatant attempt on your part to undermine the authority of the Office of the President of the Federation. That makes two charges!"

The Marshal, sitting straight up in his seat, looking as if he were a statue carved out of stone, glowered at the President.

"Then, there's this little matter with Admiral Sorenson," continued the President, raising his voice. "You arrested him? You arrested a member of my Advisory Staff and the Commander of the Space Fleet Command? Your audacity is beyond comprehension. I could have you executed!"

President Harbill then leaned back in his chair, placed both hands on his desk, and declared, "For reasons of my own, I'm not going to arrest or court martial you. However, I am going to demote you! I think a majority vote on this matter by the Senate won't be too difficult to obtain, eh General?"

An almost imperceptible look of satisfaction crossed the President's face as he shot one more invective at the General.

"By the way—you won't be going back to the Colony! You will remain here, in New Washington, on my staff as an advisor on civilian affairs. On my orders, Admiral Sorenson has already been released from custody and promoted to the rank of Full Admiral, with duties as Supreme Commander of the Central Military Command over both the Police Agency and Space Fleet Command. He will now be your Commanding Officer!'"

Varco's jaws clenched with anger, as his hands gripped the arms of his chair so hard that his knuckles stood out like spikes protruding from a slab of ebony marble, but he said nothing.

The President continued, "Admiral Sorenson's second in command, Vice-Admiral Yamato, has also been promoted, and will replace him as the Space Fleet Commander. As for you, your role for the remainder of this conference is strictly as an observer and nothing more! Maybe you'll learn something.

"In case you're wondering why I'm keeping you around, it's for three reasons. First, you're too young to be retired and too famous for me to dispose of. Second, you're extremely intelligent. At one time, you were a great team player that I valued as one of my most astute advisors. I'm hoping that if you ever get your head out of your ass, you'll make a significant contribution to our project. Third, I just don't trust you worth a damn and I intend to stick you someplace where I can keep an eye on you."

Chapter 4

Tragedy Strikes

As the President feared, the conference dragged on and on. For two months, the Representatives haggled and quarreled. A resolution seemed impossible. There were two completely opposite sides with seemingly no compromise to be found.

One side wanted to press forward with plans to leave the planet, while the other side insisted that they wait, because they believed the domes would continue to hold. This faction wanted the scientists to concentrate more effort on shoring up the dome's moorings and less effort chasing the "impossible dream" of space travel to another galaxy.

Neither side had enough votes for a clear majority, so a deal was made. When the new prototype space ship was ready for its test flight, the Delegates would convene at the Colorado Springs Dome, home of the Space Fleet Command Center, and witness its maiden voyage. Pending the results of the test flight, the Delegates would then return to New Washington to resume their talks, vote on the issues, and hopefully decide on their course of action.

A whole year had passed; much longer than the anticipated three months announced by Dr. Steebler at the Conference. Certain designs were found to be flawed when put into production and corrections had to be made that took time, but, now, construction of the experimental space ship was completed. Two of the Fleet Command's top veteran test pilots, Lt. Commander Tom Culver and Lieutenant Arthur Agar, had been selected as the crew. They had been extensively trained for the mission and had a thorough understanding of the ship's instrumentation and new technology.

A launch date for the test flight was set. The weather

had been calculated. There would be no storms or gusts of wind around the launch site. The President, along with his Council and other dignitaries that included all of the City Delegates, were seated in their assigned places at the viewing windows. Standing in a small, enclosed area adjacent to the spectators' gallery, were a small number of students who had been chosen by the Space Academy to attend the ceremonies. Among them, and unbeknownst by President Harbill, was his daughter, Zorena, who had taken the day off from classes.

Above the windows and located on each wall were large screens that allowed all the spectators to see and listen to the scientists and technicians as they made preparations for the final launch countdown. Time seemed to be suspended, and the wait interminable, but no one showed any indications of impatience. The only emotions being expressed were those of excitement and anticipation, with possibly one or two expressing a tinge of doubt and concern. One of these was Zorena, who was being reassured by her fellow cadets that everything was going to come off perfectly as planned.

All eyes were glued to the windows and screens as they watched the two pilots approach the launch pad. They were lifted by an elevator to the top of the ship and disappeared inside the hatch. Anticipation of the imminent launch of their long-awaited deep space ship produced complete silence in the gallery. The ship was a thing of awe and beauty. The very look of it inspired confidence and pride. All eyes were riveted on the launch pad. The countdown neared the end; Five, four, three, two, one. There was not the familiar loud rumble of rocket engines that everyone was accustomed to; just a subtle movement, like a bird about to fly. Slowly, like a magic carpet, the ship began to silently lift off the ground. High above, a section of the roof of the dome retracted, leaving a gap in the ceiling just large enough for the ship to pass through. The ship, glimmering in the light, nosed higher and higher, faster and faster until it passed through the dome, into the sky. The roof of the dome closed, sealing it once again from the Earth's contaminated atmosphere.

Higher and higher in the sky, the beautiful ship rose. Suddenly, a slight shudder, like a small earthquake, shook the dome and the entire area. Everybody felt it. Startled, they jumped up from their seats, wondering what had just happened. Then came a tremor so violent that it knocked people to the floor. Panicking, they all scrambled to their feet. Suddenly, they heard a scream, and someone pointed to the top of the dome. Casting their eyes skyward, they watched in horror as fire engulfed the ship. A series of explosions rocked the atmosphere and fiery debris from the ship rained down upon the dome. Despite the explosions and the crashing of the ship's parts onto the top of the dome, the dome held. None of the Delegates or others in the Spectators' Gallery were injured, but they were all horrified by the heartbreaking sight they had just witnessed. Sobs of mourning, interspersed with mutters of cursing at the calamity they had just seen could be heard throughout the Gallery.

In the nearby area occupied by the cadets, it was Zorena who had screamed in horror and disbelief as she watched the ship explode and turn into a fiery ball of destruction. There was so much confusion, only a few of her classmates noticed as Zorena collapsed and fell to the floor. Quickly, they picked her up and carried her back to her quarters at Space Fleet Command.

Chapter 5

Secrets

Lieutenant Commander Edna Mallory, Assistant Commander of the Space Fleet Command, strode briskly along the corridor that led to the female cadet quarters at Space Fleet Command. Along one side of the long corridor was a row of windows that overlooked Space Command's administrative buildings and training facilities. The opposite side of the corridor was lined with doors leading to the cadets' individual living quarters.

This much-decorated female officer of the Space Fleet Command was exceptionally tall and lanky for a female. Her countenance announced forcefully that she would brook no nonsense from any of her subordinates or anyone else who dealt with her.

She stopped at room 19 and pressed the small glass panel activating the Personal Visi-Control Identifier located at the side of the door. After waiting several moments and receiving no answer, she again pressed the panel, this time for a longer period, indicating her impatience at receiving no response from inside the room.

Finally, with tightened lips and face disfigured by a fierce frown, Commander Mallory clenched her fist and angrily banged on the door, shouting, "Zorena, I know you're in there! Open this door this instant and let me in!"

Lifting her head slightly, and eyeing her Visi-Screen from her bed where she lay crumpled up like a tortured ball, Cadet Zorena Harbill saw the Commander standing outside her door. She did not want to see or talk to anyone, especially her commanding officer. However, she was cognizant enough to realize that refusing to obey Commander Mallory would incur consequences she was in no condition to deal with, and certainly would regret. Reluctantly, she reached over and pressed the button, allowing the lock to disengage.

Outside in the hall, a buzzer sounded, the door unlocked, and Commander Mallory stalked into the room. Zorena, hair unkempt, eyes puffy from crying and self-pity, was sitting up on her crumpled bed, arms clenched around the pillow held tightly to her breast.

"My God, Zorena! You look terrible! What do you think you're doing? What's the matter?" the Commander asked demandingly.

"Nothing," quietly answered Zorena, eyes cast down.

"Well, your 'nothing' is causing everybody around here a lot of problems! No one has seen or heard from you for ten days!" Commander Mallory paused, looked around the room, and raising her eyebrows, continued in a sarcastic voice, "I presume you've been here in bed, from the looks of things. You've been absent from your classes, you haven't answered your message machine, and you wouldn't open the door to anyone trying to check on you – not even your friends! Are you sick?"

"No," answered Zorena,

Commander Mallory paused, then said in her sternest voice, "Well then, Zorena – if that's the case, this is an order! Get up, get dressed, and report to the Commandant's office. He wants to see you immediately."

Zorena took a moment to answer, then, raising her head to look at her commanding officer, spoke in a quiet voice, "No."

Startled at this reply, the Commander raised her voice and demanded, "What do you mean, 'No.'? Are you refusing to obey a direct order?"

Almost instantly, Zorena's demeanor changed. She suddenly became enraged. She threw her pillow down to the floor; and in one swift movement, rolled to the side of the bed, and sat stiffly with feet on the floor and fists clenched beside her.

Looking defiantly at her commanding officer, she declared petulantly, "I don't care! I'm not going to see the Commandant, or anyone else! I don't care what you do to me.

I'm resigning! I don't want to be a space pilot anymore. I don't care if the domes fall apart. My father doesn't want me here. Everything's gone wrong, so why should I care?"

Despite desperately trying to control them, tears slowly overflowed Zorena's eyes and streamed down her cheeks. In a choked voice, she uttered, "Commander Culver and Lieutenant Agar are dead! The project is ruined! What does it matter what I do or what you do or what anybody does?

"Even my father thinks I'm wasting my time here! I wanted to make a difference, but no matter what I do, all he can say is that I'm not qualified!"

Commander Mallory, hearing all this, suddenly felt compassion for this young cadet. She walked over to the bed and sat down next to Zorena. "I don't really know what's going on here, Zorena, but you are wrong."

She then took Zorena's shoulders and turned her so that she could look directly into her face. "Everyone here thinks very highly of you, Zorena! I know terrible things have happened recently, and we've all been disappointed, but this is not the end! The tragic deaths of Commander Culver and Lieutenant Agar were very hard on all of us, but in this Command, we learn to accept tragedy and disappointment and move forward. For some reason, you don't seem to be able to come to grips with that, and I think you need help."

An hour later, Commander Mallory was in the Commandant's office discussing Zorena's strange behavior.

"I suppose I could accept her resignation or discharge her for some reasonable cause," the Commandant, Captain Joe Pappilos, said. "What do you think? Is she having a nervous breakdown?"

"I don't think so," said Commander Mallory. "She's always been so stable; the one you could depend on. Her presence was always so uplifting. She was an optimist who saw the bright side of everything. Also, you would be losing a very capable officer. She's near the top of her class in every category, and she's an excellent pilot. Added to that, don't forget, she is the daughter of the President of the Federation."

41

"Ten days absence without authorization is a very serious matter," mused the Commandant. "Being the President's daughter shouldn't entitle her to any special benefits or privileges. However, her academic record does."

"I'm going to have her evaluated by a Federation psychologist. If he uncovers any mental or character flaws, she's out! If she doesn't have any mental problems, then I want to know the reason for her uncharacteristic behavior. If she does have a reason, it'd better be a damn good one!"

Deep inside the walls of the Federation's Medical Facility was a door with a window containing a sign that read: "Doctor Jerome Badger, MD, PhD." Behind this door, and seated at an oversized oak desk, was a plump, middle-aged man with tufts of graying hair sticking out over his ears and deep blue eyes that crinkled at the edges, making one think that he viewed the world with a secret amusement all his own. As Chief Psychiatrist for Space Fleet Command, perhaps this benign attitude was his method of coping with all of the various problems for which he was expected to find a solution.

He awaited the arrival of Cadet Zorena Harbill with both curiosity and trepidation. He was not looking forward to the task of psychologically evaluating the daughter of the President of the Federation. It was a delicate situation. If he evaluated her as mentally deficient and was later proved wrong, it could cost him his job. On the other hand, if he gave her a clean bill of health and she had another breakdown, he would definitely lose his job.

Zorena was ushered into the doctor's office by his Medical Assistant, who seated her in a chair specially designed for patients. It was cushioned and comfortable, albeit an ominous looking thing fitted with straps, headgear, and various tools to be used by the Doctor as occasion dictated. For one who was suspected of having a nervous breakdown, Zorena appeared calm and composed.

Dr. Badger waited for Zorina to get comfortably seated, then asked, "Do you know why you're here, Zorena?"

"Not really," she replied. "I know I'm supposed to be psychologically evaluated. I don't think you're going to find

42

anything wrong with me; but go ahead. You're the Doctor."

"You seem a little hostile," replied the doctor in his soft, smooth voice.

"Wouldn't you be, if you were going to be examined by a psychiatrist to determine your sanity, and then face a group of officers who will determine if you're fit for duty?" replied Zorena.

"I have your file here. You have an excellent record," stated the Doctor

"It doesn't seem to be doing me much good now, does it Doctor? I got depressed. Is that one incident going to ruin my whole life?" asked Zorena.

Doctor Badger answered in a reasoning voice, "It could happen again. What if you were on a sensitive mission and something went wrong, and you became depressed? Who's to say you wouldn't just quit and crawl into your shell again?"

Zorena spoke sharply, "It won't happen again!"

"How do you know that for sure?" questioned the Doctor. "You told Commander Mallory you didn't care if the domes were torn apart. What about that?"

Zorena was beginning to lose her composure. "Of course I care. Of course I don't want anything to happen to the domes. I was speaking out of anger."

"You're starting to get angry now," the Doctor observed.

"I can't win! If I don't get angry, you think there's something wrong. If I do get angry, then I'm schizoid. I think you're determined to give me a negative report," said Zorena as she slumped in her chair.

"I'm not against you, Zorena," Dr. Badger said. "In fact, most of your responses have been quite normal, but I've got to find out what depressed you so deeply, to the point where you wanted to just give up. That's not like you. What you did was uncharacteristic. It goes against your entire psychological profile and that is what's worrying us."

"I've told you all I know," said Zorena dejectedly. "I got depressed, that's all. My father is against me. He doesn't want me here, at the Academy! Our new prototype space ship, which was our big hope, was destroyed! We were so confident. We thought we finally had the ship that could save everybody! Now the project is ruined and Commander Culver and Lieutenant Agar are dead. It's hopeless!"

"But you were the only one in your class who broke down. Why was that, Zorena?" asked the Doctor. "Why did it affect you more than your classmates? There must be more to it than what you're saying. There has to be a more concrete reason. I can sense you're leaving something out."

Zorena retorted caustically, "My classmates don't have a father like I do who is against them – and has the authority to do something about it."

"I talked to the Commandant about that, and he says your father told him that he's very proud of you," commented the Doctor.

Pushing his assurances aside, Zorena replied, "He didn't sound very encouraging the last time I talked to him!!"

Feeling that this subject was not supplying him with the information he needed to get to the bottom of her problems, he leaned forward over his desk, and said, "Zorena, I'm going to ask you a few standard questions. Please answer them truthfully. I am required to tell you that the chair you're sitting in is a high-tech electronically equipped lie detector, so any attempt to evade the question or answer untruthfully, will be noted immediately."

Zorena said, "This is humiliating. I refuse to submit! This is the way I would expect a common criminal to be treated."

"No, Zorena. A criminal would be strapped down! However, if you choose, you can refuse to submit to these questions. You're free to go!"

"Good," said Zorena, and stood up as if to leave.

Eyeing her sternly, Dr. Badger warned, "However, Cadet Harbill, if you leave without this evaluation, you will be discharged from the Academy as unsuitable for the military service. Future career opportunities will undoubtedly be severely limited. Most likely, you'll wind up in a civil service position somewhere." The Doctor shrugged. "However, if you want to give up your career, that's up to you!"

Zorena sat down. She was dumbfounded. This man was unwilling to reason with her. He seemingly had complete control of her life.

"Go ahead with your questions," she said. "I've got nothing to hide."

"Okay. First, sit up straight. That's better. Ready?"

"Yes."

"Do you love your mother?"

"Of course I love my mother," said Zorena crossly.

"Just answer yes or no. Do you love your father?"

"Yes."

"Do you hate your father?"

Zorena hesitated, and then replied slowly. "No."

"Do you like it here at the Academy?"

"Yes."

"Do you get along with you classmates?"

"Yes."

"Do you like your instructors?"

"Yes."

On and on went the questions, which to Zorena seemed senseless and pointless. Then the Doctor asked a question that caught her completely off guard.

"Did you know Commander Culver?" he asked.

She hesitated slightly, then replied, "Yes."

"Did you know him well, personally?"

"No."

"Did you know Lieutenant Agar?"

Tentatively, Zorena replied, "Yes."

"Did you know him well?"

Very slowly she said, "No."

At this response, Dr. Badger raised his head from the computer screen and turned to look sharply into Zorena's eyes.

"Zorena, the lie detector has indicated that your last response was not truthful. I'll ask you one more time. Did you know Lieutenant Agar well?"

Almost whispering, Zorena murmured, "Yes."

45

"Were you and the Lieutenant friends?"

Zorena sat very still, then answered in a voice so softly the Doctor had to strain to hear her answer. "Yes," she murmured.

"Close friends?"

Zorena, with a long, painful sigh replied, "Yes."

Dr. Badger suddenly turned off the lie detector controls, leaned back in his chair with his hands clasped over his ample stomach, and looked at his patient with sympathy.

"Zorena," he said, "when that test ship exploded, it was reported you fainted. After that is when you went into your depression and disappearing act. Why?

"It's time for you to come out of your shell and tell me everything," he continued. "Remember, anything you tell me is strictly confidential. The law protects the confidentiality between a doctor and his patient. Neither the Commandant nor your father need ever know what you tell me."

Zorena sat in the chair with her head lowered, trying to hold back her tears. After a long pause, she said in a quiet voice, "Arthur and I, Lieutenant Agar, we were in love. I loved him so much, and he loved me. After I graduated and received my commission, we were going to be married."

"You and Lieutenant Agar? Did anyone else know of your love affair?"

"No," replied Zorena. "Fraternization is against the rules. We kept it a secret. We were very careful. After he died in the accident, I was devastated. I lost my love, my dreams, my hopes for the future." Zorena began to cry hysterically. "We never even had a chance to say goodbye," she sobbed. "I couldn't tell anybody – I couldn't even mourn."

Dr. Badger rose from his chair, walked around his desk to Zorena, and gently put his arms around her, pulling her head to his chest. Now, he understood what so deeply troubled this young girl who was so highly regarded by everyone whom he had spoken to about her.

Zorena collapsed into the Doctor's arms, grateful to finally be allowed to express her deep and anguished feelings.

46

Dr. Badger said softly, "Go ahead and cry, Zorena. You can mourn now. Everything is going to be all right."

As he comforted the sobbing Zorena, the Doctor was relieved. His report would show that Zorena was mentally sound. His problems, and Zorena's, had been solved.

Chapter 6

Conspiracy

Senator Hans Becker, a small, wiry man with sharp bonelike facial features, was the elected representative of North Euro. He relaxed on his sofa, slowly sipping his drink. He was happy with his role as co-conspirator in a plot to change the power structure of government. He smiled inwardly at what he was about to propose. The Senator was well known as a dissident. He disagreed with almost all of the President's proposals, and stirred up controversies between his co-delegates wherever he could.

His visitor sat erectly in an easy chair across from him. A table had been placed between them and on the table were some files and a map of the world. The map depicted the locations of the fifty city-states of the Federation, and the names of the representatives of each State. Some of the states were colored blue and some yellow.

"Care for a drink, General?" offered the Senator.

"No, I don't drink," answered General Varco.

"Okay. Well, General," started the Senator, "in light of what happened at the space launch site last month, at least twenty-eight other Representatives and Governors and I are looking for alternatives to President Harbill's efforts in handling all these problems facing us in what he says is a time of crisis. We're willing to support a move that would end Harbill's coalition in the Senate and force a mid-term-national election."

The Senator continued, "We're all in complete agreement with you that the seriousness of the problems with the domes is vastly exaggerated. We believe our scientists and tech-men should concentrate on solving the problem of shoring up the dome's moorings, instead of wasting so much time on this space travel thing."

48

"If we put our combined efforts in the right place, we could have several hundred more years of peaceful existence. We'd then have plenty of time to research space travel and look for an acceptable planet to colonize. There is absolutely no need to rush frantically into an ill-conceived solution to an undetermined problem"

"What's this got to do with me?" asked the General, frowning. "I have no power or political influence."

Becker took a sip of his drink, and went on, "You have more than you think, General. In spite of your demotion by the President, our election committee feels you are still very popular with the public and would be the most viable candidate to oppose Harbill."

"What are you talking about?" asked General Varco.

"What I'm saying, is that if we could force a mid-term election, you would be our choice as the presidential candidate to oppose Harbill." smiled Becker.

Varco was stunned. He couldn't believe what he was hearing. "You mean your party would sponsor me as your presidential candidate?"

"Yes! We feel that with you running, we'd be a shoo-in to win this election. We also feel we have to disclose what President Harbill proposed to the delegates at the Washington Conference a year ago and what happened on that day when he unveiled his spaceship that was supposed to be the answer to all the world's problems."

"We intend to broadcast it on all the news outlets. Even though the President has classified this information as Top Secret and only to be given out on a need–to-know basis. Congress is ready to pass a bill to de-classify the minutes of the Washington Conference and make all of this stuff he's been keeping a secret known to the public."

"When all those people out there hear about how President Harbill tried to pressure the State Senators to vote for a bill that would force us to abandon our planet and leave our homes and everything we've worked for, especially when they hear all about that disastrous debacle at the Space Fleet launch

49

pad, we should win this election by a landslide."

Varco sat back in his chair. Putting his fingers together under his chin as if praying, he nodded his head, and smiled at the Senator. He liked what he was hearing. His imagination soared. Once he was elected and took control, revenge for past wrongs would be immediate and sweet. Through narrowed eyes, and with and a look of deep satisfaction on his face, he readily agreed to be the presidential candidate on the reform ticket. As he left the Senator's home, his stride was almost bouncing as he hurried back to his office.

As he watched General Varco hasten out the door, Senator Becker rose from the sofa and went over to the bar to fix another drink. His demeanor exactly emulated a picture of the cat that ate the canary. He was filled with the excitement of having succeeded in his mission with General Varco. "Now, let's see what that ass, Harbill, can do about this!" he said aloud, to no one in particular.

When the news broke about President Harbill's attempt to force the people to leave Earth and the fate of the ship that was supposed to transport them, the citizens of the Federation were outraged. With some expressing their anger by rioting and ravaging public property, their hostility had to be contained by force. The majority of the citizens, however, and especially those who held positions in authority, thought that President Harbill had completely lost his senses. He was obviously mentally disturbed and it was time for new blood in the White House.

It was time to put a man into office that was better qualified to lead, who was better informed on matters of national security and certainly one who had the public's interest at heart. To the public, General Varco was that man. A motion was quickly passed by the senate, establishing a one-time ballet for the public to vote to determine whether or not a mid-term election should be sanctioned. The vote was overwhelmingly in favor of the election and it was scheduled to take place in six months' time. The following months saw President Harbill's approval ratings dip to under forty percent, while General

50

Varco's popularity soared.

With the election only a week away, President Harbill sat at his desk reading the New Washington Journal. The latest figures were out. General Varco was leading all polls by a margin of 63 to 32.

Dr. Steebler, his long-time friend, confidant, and frequent visitor to the White House, sat across from him.

"It's amazing," said the President. "The people don't know what they're doing. They have no idea what they're letting themselves in for. In spite of all of our efforts to tell the public about Varco and all the things he's done – his attempt to place the country under martial law and his illegal actions towards me and other leaders, he still appears to be very popular. What do you think, Dr. Steebler?"

The Doctor looked over the rim of his glasses at President Harbill and replied, "What do I think?" He paused, then declared, "I think that electing Varco into office will be the worst possible thing that could happen to our country. It will be a tragedy. He'll be out for revenge and the first person he's going to come after is you. You know that, don't you?"

"Yes, I know," said the President.

"Then, he's going to come after the scientists and tech-men and force us to work on the domes and abandon our space flight research. I have great apprehension and fear for all of us. From the rumors I've heard, he plans to put the entire country under martial law, suspend all elections, and place Police Commanders as Governors of the States."

"Surely the state representatives wouldn't allow that to happen," retorted the President.

"Who's to stop him?" asked the doctor. "First, he'll remove Sorenson as Commander of the Central Military Command and then, as President, he'll be Commander-In-Chief of all our military, including the Central Police Agency and the Space Fleet Command."

The President, contemplating what Dr. Steebler had said, replied, "That's the one bad thing in our Constitution. They should never have put all our military under one command."

"But none of this is going to make any difference, Mr. President," replied the Doctor.

"Why is that, Dr. Steebler?"

"Because, Mr. President, when the domes give way - and they surely will – We'll all die anyway."

The President looked at Dr. Steebler and said, "It looks like the only thing that can save us is a miracle. I've never believed in miracles, but I'm praying for one now."

Chapter 7

Disaster

"Sir! Sir! Wake up!" The insistent hand of Security Agent Dan Gardner gently shook President Harbill. "Wake up, Mr. President. You have a call."

"Uh-uh, wha-what's wrong?" stammered the President, still half asleep, his eyes refusing to focus on the uniformed man leaning over his bed. He struggled to bring his mind into sharp readiness for what he was about to hear. Nobody dared disturb his few hours of sleep, unless there was a dire emergency only he could deal with that would require his immediate full attention. He shook his head from side-to-side, and nodded to his Agent.

"It's an emergency call from the Department of the Interior, Sir. Dr. Huang is calling."

The president sat up in bed and looked at his clock. It was 4 a.m. This had to be something really bad coming from Dr. Huang who was the Federation's Assistant Interior Administrator assigned to the Chinese Sector.

The Chinese had always prided themselves upon being capable of taking care of their own problems, without calling on the Government or any other outside source for assistance. They were extremely resourceful and had diligently educated and trained their citizens in every capacity that they felt was necessary to maintain the independence of the area and the welfare of their citizens. More than once during the annual City State Conferences they expressed contempt for those States who they said constantly called on the Government or other states to bail them out instead of taking care of their own problems. "Yes," he thought with a deep sigh, "this is bad!"

Agent Gardner handed him the Visi-Screen control. "Hello," he said.

The face looking at him from the screen was haggard

and drawn, with an expression of terror and grief. The always perfectly groomed and stoically composed man the President had always known and admired for his performance at his position and his professionalism when dealing with other people, was not the one speaking to him now. This man was disheveled, uncombed, and looked as if he had slept in his clothes for a week.

"Mr. President, this is Dr. Huang," the man exclaimed in a hysterical voice that grew louder and more persistent as he spoke. "I didn't mean to go over the head of my superior, Dr. Yi, but I couldn't locate him anywhere! There's been a terrible disaster! It's horrible! The world is coming to an end! They should have listened to you! We're all going to die!"

"Dr. Huang! Calm down!" commanded the President. "What's going on? What's the matter?"

"It's the South China Agricultural Dome!" cried the Doctor, trying to get some control over his voice. "Last night, a 550 mile-an-hour tornado ripped it right out of its moorings. All the people in it were swept away … dead! The livestock, the farms and all the produce are gone! Not one building was left. They were all blown away. There was no place the people could go and be safe from this horrible thing! Even the forest and all the animals in the reproduction sanctuary are gone! Billions of tons of earth were blown away into the atmosphere! There's just nothing left!"

President Harbill, listening to Dr. Huang in disbelief, and seeing him grow more hysterical with every word, interrupted him and demanded, "How do you know all this? You must have been in your home in the Metropolitan Dome, or you wouldn't be here! You obviously weren't in the Agricultural Dome or you'd be dead, if what you say is true!"

The Doctor shuddered, took a deep breath, and replied, "There were a few survivors. We rescued three young teen-age boys playing 'Army'. They were camping out in an old abandoned underground bomb shelter that was located at the opposite side of the Dome that first started to collapse. They were terrified when they saw what the wind was doing to

54

everything and ran into the shelter and stayed there until our Police Rescue Squad could get to them."

He paused, took a crumpled handkerchief he had gripped in his trembling hand, and wiped the perspiration from his forehead. "Thank God one of the boys had sense enough to be wearing his emergency chest communicator, which was a miracle. You know, kids nowadays think those things are stupid, because they've never heard of anyone who had to use them, except in minor accidents around the farm so they hardly ever put them on. This kid just happened to be one of those with parents who forced him to wear it wherever he went.

"I shudder every time I think about it! If he hadn't been wearing that communicator, the boy never would've been able to contact the Metro Police. When he finally reached them, he was so hysterical they could hardly understand what he was saying. Then, they didn't believe him! Who would? When they tried to contact the police stationed in the dome and some of the administrators, they couldn't reach anybody. That's when they decided to go over to the dome and find out what was going on. That's when they located the boys and brought them back."

The President listened to this with incredulity, then asked in a strident voice, "How do we know we can believe the stories of three young teenage boys?" asked the President.

"They were thoroughly debriefed by a team of experts from the Department," answered the doctor. "We believe them. Also, the police who rescued the boys saw much of the devastation. With the dome gone, they wouldn't even have been able to land their rescue craft if the bunker where the boys were didn't have a protected hangar located underground that was accessible to the shelter where they were hiding.

"Fortunately, our people used foresight when they equipped all of our police rescue craft with signals that would open the top of all these old hangars, just in case of an emergency like this one. We also have satellite pictures confirming the dome is gone; and the infrared lenses show no sign of life of any kind!"

"How many people are we talking about?" queried the

president.

"About 500,000, we estimate, including administrators, farmers, and laborers," cried the doctor.

"My God!" came the shocked response. "Have we sent in rescue teams to see if there are any other survivors?"

"They're searching now, Sir, as we speak. But this is even more disastrous than anyone could ever imagine. That one Agricultural Dome produced one-quarter of the world's produce, an eighth of the livestock, and about an eighth of our lumber," said the doctor. "I just don't know how we're all going to survive this!"

As snapshots of how this calamity would devastate the entire world flew like bullets through his mind, the President jumped out of bed, still clenching the Visi-Phone, and in clipped words, demanded, "Have any teams been formed to inspect all of the other domes to find out if there's any kind of structural damage that's been overlooked?"

Apologetically, Dr. Huang replied, "Not that I know of, Sir."

"Okay! I want you to contact the engineers in every state and every Agricultural Dome! Order emergency inspections and I mean inspections with a magnifier of each and every one of them! As soon you get the results of those inspections, report the findings directly to me."

"In the meantime, I'm going to order an immediate emergency session with the State Representatives. I want you and Dr Yi in attendance. If there are any domes that are damaged and need repair, get the work started immediately."

The President thought for a moment, then said, "No! Change that! Get a hold of Dr. Steebler and tell him to call me. Tell him I want him to get together a task force to get these inspections and any needed repairs started as soon as possible. And tell him not to worry about authorization. I'm going to declare a Code 9 National Emergency."

Once again, the Delegates found themselves in the New Washington conference room facing the President, only, this time, under a completely different set of circumstances. Their mood was somber and quiet.

President Harbill entered and took his place at the head of the assembly. As he stared around the room looking at each of the delegates, he could see that some of them refused to meet his eyes. They were slouched down in their seats, and guilt was written all over their faces. It was as if they wanted to disappear, rather than face this man they had only recently tried to disgrace and remove from office.

The President started to speak, "I'm sure that by now you all know what happened just 48 hours ago to an agricultural dome in the South China Sector," he began. "The deaths and devastation are horrible." The delegates nodded as he continued, "I tried to impress on you before how great our peril is. You didn't listen! Now, there's no time left. No time for political skirmishes and no time for speeches! It's time for you and I to act." He continued, stressing every word, "If we want to live; if we want our families to live; if we want to see our grandchildren grow up; if you want to see the human race survive, we must act and we must act now!"

Among the delegates, a hand was raised. It was the hand of the Senator from North Euro, Hans Becker. His bony face, thin body, and wide-eyed stare, gave him the appearance of a walking cadaver.

The President nodded towards him and said, "The Chair recognizes Senator Becker."

Hans Becker stood up and spoke. "Mr. President, there are still some of us who are a little suspicious of your motives. We realize that some kind of action is needed, but we question the need to act in the next few days. The national elections are just two days away. I believe that in these desperate times of need, we should have a president to lead us who is the choice of the people and duly elected into office by the people."

Around the room, there were sounds of agreement from a few of the Delegates. He continued, "Dr. Steebler and his crews are working night and day and have found no further trouble spots in the domes. I, for one, don't see any reason for a change in our course of action. The dome that was lost was an isolated incident that can't happen again. That particular dome's pilings were moored in soft earth. Engineers have been working for years, trying to compact the areas around the pilings, but there was just nothing really solid for the pilings to be anchored to. I make a motion that we suspend any action for the next two days, adjourn this meeting, allow the national elections to go on as scheduled, and then let the duly elected members of government take action on these very perplexing matters."

"I second the motion!" declared Senator Bristol from America North.

President Harbill spoke, "A motion has been made and seconded to adjourn this meeting and allow the elections to go on as scheduled. I must warn you that, if this motion were passed, it would cost us serious delays at a time when any delay might prove disastrous. Please cast your votes on this motion now." The motion was defeated 36 to 14.

The President mumbled to himself, "Well well, it looks like Becker's lost some of his cronies. He raised his voice and looked directly at the Senator. "You've brought up some very interesting points, Senator Becker; most of them wrong. First, I'm in contact with Dr. Steebler daily, sometimes almost hourly. We are in more danger than you think and in more danger than we were when we met here a year ago. Dr. Steebler says that by using an upgraded brand of molten steel concrete they have strengthened the pilings in some areas where they had been weakened. He says that though they seem secure for the moment, the severe windstorms are causing the pilings to rock back and forth, creating weak connections. There are so many pilings, it is almost impossible to monitor and repair their moorings as fast as they weaken."

"As to my motives," said the President, "my only motive is to save our country and our people. As for the country being led by, as you put it, duly elected officials, I must remind all of you that I am the President of the Federation of Democratic States and was duly elected into that office for a term of eight years, of which there are four years remaining!"

The President continued, "If there are no more motions

58

on the floor," he paused and made eye contact with each delegate, "I want to make the following statement. First, according to law, a President can assume total control of the Government by enacting the Emergency Powers Act. This act allows him to run the Government without restrictions and without representative concurrence in times of national emergency." There was a slight murmur from the delegates. "Our present emergency meets the required criteria to enact this law. To enforce the law, the only requirement remaining is for the Chief Justice to certify that all of the criteria as stipulated in the act have been met. He is ready to perform this duty."

Hans Becker waved his hand, was recognized, and asked, "What about the elections?"

"Elections will be suspended until this emergency no longer exists," explained the President. "However, I need everyone's support. I want to know that the Representatives of our country are behind me."

Assenting voices were heard throughout the assembly. A motion was quickly made, seconded and passed, by a margin of 39 to 11, giving President Harbill Emergency Executive Powers as provided under the Emergency Powers Act.

The President rose and faced the delegates. "Thank you," he said. "Thank you for your vote of confidence. We can all take a break now. Let's reconvene here in two hours. Dr. Steebler will be joining us. He will bring us up-to-date on his activities, including his reports on the domes and his research on space travel. I think he has some pretty good news for us at a time when we could use it."

When President Harbill reached his quarters, he was informed by his secretary of an unexpected request. General Varco was in the building, and asked for an audience with him.

'What's Varco up to now?' he wondered to himself. "Get a hold of him," he said. "I'll see him now. Tell him I can give him 20 minutes."

Within minutes, Varco was standing outside the President's office. "General Varco is here," his secretary informed him.

The President sat down behind his desk and prepared to meet this man who had become his nemesis and who had tried to usurp his position as President.

"Send him in."

General Varco entered the office wearing full dress uniform, and with precise military strides, marched to the desk where President Harbill was seated. He saluted the President and stood stiffly at attention. The President, still seated, returned his salute and motioned for him to sit in the chair facing him.

"Well, General Varco," he intoned sarcastically, "I have about 20 minutes to give you. What's on your mind?"

Varco turned, strode to the chair and squared himself in front of it. He dropped to the seat with shoulders and back held straight, as if still at full military attention. As he sat facing him, the President watched the General intently, hoping to get some indication as to what was coming, but Varco's face mirrored the tension in his body. The only telling hint of emotion the President could find, were a few drops of perspiration showing on the General's forehead.

"Mr. President," Varco began in a pleading voice as he addressed President Harbill, "Please, bear with me! What I have to say is very difficult. I have never been one to admit to mistakes or to offer apologies. I have never been a person who takes the easy way out. I've always faced up to my responsibilities and actions in a direct and succinct manner. I feel that I have always been a man of conviction, believed in what I was doing, and acted accordingly."

He paused as if to let this confirmation of his character sink into the President's mind, then continued. "I firmly believed that the people of our nation would riot when they became aware of our situation and that instituting Martial Law would be necessary for national security.

"I believed the domes, if maintained properly, would hold for another 500 years and I honestly believed that you should be removed from office before a disastrous mistake was made that would completely destroy our civilization."

President Harbill, staring at him with distaste, declared

60

in an angry voice, "You've given me a lot of grief, Varco! You've got a lot of nerve coming here!"

Shifting slightly in his seat, Varco replied, "As I said, Sir, those were my convictions."

Ignoring this interruption, the President continued angrily, "Varco, you have seriously endangered our nation! You and your conspirators have managed to set us back months in planning and research. Heaven only knows what you would have done if you had won that election! I think you would have jailed or maybe even executed me but, worse than that, you would have led this country to its doom!"

Flinching at these words, Varco said, "I'm here now to admit that I was wrong, Sir. I made mistakes in my assessment of situations and in handling administrative issues."

"Ad- Ad- Administrative issues!" sputtered the President. "Varco, I don't have any sympathy for you. I'm not a hating man, but I almost hate you! The difference between us, Varco, is that you don't have any feelings of caring or compassion towards your fellow beings and I do! You could kill thousands of innocent people or put millions in absolute misery and think nothing about it!"

"You do me ill credit, Mr. President," the General blurted out.

The President leaned across his desk, and staring straight into Varco's eyes, said with determination, "Do I? If I had the authority to hang you, Varco, believe me, I would! But I can't even put you in jail! You haven't broken any laws, at least none that I'm aware of." He shook his head from side to side, then added forcefully, "What, in God's name, should I do with you?"

Replying, Varco said, "I didn't come here to beg for mercy, Mr. President, but to admit that I was wrong. I regret my actions – even though I felt they were justified at the time – and I'm ready to take full responsibility for them."

President Harbill leaned back in his chair and answered, "Very well, General Varco! Until further notice, you will be confined to the New Washington Area Military Officers' Quarters. Consider yourself under house arrest! You are dismissed!"

Despite this command, Varco didn't move. "Sir, I still have a desire to serve my country."

The president, angry at this failure to obey his order, shouted, "General, I said you are dismissed!"

Varco appealed, "Mr. President, I – "

The President interrupted him. "Varco, I would be a fool to trust you. How do I know you wouldn't conspire against me again? I gave you one chance and I'm still paying for that decision. I am not inclined to give you another."

General Varco got up from his chair and moved to stand in front of the President's desk. "I swear, on my honor as a military officer, Sir! I would be loyal to you and would serve you and the Federation to the best of my abilities and without question!" he stated pleadingly.

The President sat silently for some minutes as he eyed General Varco. He remembered that before all this trouble had begun, the General had been one of his most valued, though not completely trusted, aides. He wondered if, after having all these retributions for his presumptuous actions land on his head, Varco had learned any kind of lesson about honorably serving the Federation and its President. If he had, he could be very valuable during this crisis and whatever they all would have to face in the future.

With that in mind, he said in a stern voice, "Report to your quarters, Varco. I'll consider your request. That will be all."

Chapter 8

A Choice of Two

Admiral Yamato sat on a hard wooden bench in the outer office, waiting for his meeting with President Harbill. The Admiral's appearance was that of the classic Oriental warrior; crisp and sharp. He was the epitome of a Space Fleet Naval Officer. Despite his appearance, the Admiral was a little nervous and apprehensive about the up-coming meeting. He glanced at his watch. It read 7:55 AM. The meeting was for eight o'clock. He knew the President would not be late. He also knew that Dr. Steebler would be in attendance. That put him a little at ease, because, of late, he and the Doctor had been working closely together on the Ranger Project. He also knew that his friend and commanding officer, Admiral Sorenson, would be at the meeting. At precisely eight o'clock, Admiral Sorenson and Dr. Steebler entered the anteroom. The three men barely finished greeting each other when the President's administrative assistant ushered them into the President's office.

"Be seated gentlemen," greeted the President. "I see, Dr. Steebler, you have all of the domes pretty well stabilized."

"Yes, Sir," replied Steebler, "but it takes constant repair to keep them minimally safe. We have engineers who perform weekly inspections on every dome and make repairs as soon as damage of any kind is spotted, but these are only short-term cures. The basic problem still exists. The constant buffeting of the domes by the wind is causing too much structural damage to the moorings. A good analogy would be like a wire. Take a wire in your hand and pull on it. It seems very strong, but if you bend it back and forth a few times, it breaks. That's what's happening to our pilings and, like the wire, they're going to break."

The President, looking for some kind of assurance, asked, "In your last assessment, you estimated that we have maybe 10 to 20 years before the domes are destroyed. Does that assessment still hold true?"

"No, Sir, I'm afraid not. We've studied and analyzed the pilings. With our new readings, we estimate we are looking at about five years to seven at the most. The President shook his head and exclaimed, "Damn! The news always seems to get worse! All right, what about the space flight research? Your reports seem to be rather vague and inconclusive."

The Doctor shuffled some documents he was holding and replied, "That's because we don't have any answers, yet. As you know, Admiral Yamato and I have worked together on space flight almost exclusively for the past several months. We've flown two unmanned test flights. One failed to return and the other didn't reach the desired speed."

"Maybe you need to put a real pilot at the controls of one of these test flights," said the President. "Perhaps a pilot could get a better response from the ship than a robot. At the least, a human pilot would be able to give you a good perspective of the ship's performance."

Admiral Yamato spoke up. "In view of what happened the last time we launched a test ship using real pilots, we're fearful of using human pilots until we have the bugs worked out, Sir."

The President, in consternation, said, "Well, that's very humane, Admiral, but considering the circumstances, I think you had better reconsider. Time is running out. Use volunteers! You must have a lot of trained pilots who would like to volunteer for these flights."

"Yes, Sir. That was our next step," said the Admiral, "and I do have a list of pilots who have volunteered."

"Good," he replied. "Send me the list. I would like to commend those brave officers for their courage and devotion to duty."

"I thought you might want to see the list, Sir. I brought you a copy." The Admiral pulled a file out of his brief case and laid it on the President's desk.

The President set the file aside. "Well, is there any good

64

news?" he asked. "Anything I can feed to our detractors? Their voices are becoming very loud and the people are beginning to listen to them. How about it, Admiral Sorenson?"

The Admiral, attempting to reassure the President, answered, "It's a very small minority of the population that's causing trouble. The problem is centered around Dr. Zinn and Senator Becker. Dr. Zinn, in his sermons, is inflaming his disciples. Some of them actually believe that he's God's anointed messenger. He's preaching in his sermons that there's no reason to worry; no reason to leave our planet and our homes; that God will provide for us and will protect us from evil. This is very heady stuff and people are starting to listen to him. Senator Becker is fanning the flames and making sure that all the major media outlets are broadcasting Dr. Zinn's messages."

"One of his sermons is on the air right now, Mr. President. I think you should hear it," said Admiral Sorenson getting up from his chair and turning on the tele-viewer.

His Holiness, Dr. Zinn, resplendent in his ceremonial robes, appeared on the screen. "Our President," he was saying, "is a weak soul, mired in a sea of doubt. His administration has divided our country; man against man, brother against brother. His apathy towards its citizens is evident. He promised us salvation but so far has only delivered chaos. Oh, God in heaven!" cried the Reverend, raising his arms toward the sky, "deliver us from our President's sinful, treacherous path! Remember us Lord. We are the chosen children of the Almighty; His cherished souls!" He looked directly at the camera and pointed his finger at the screen. "Do you believe God created us, blessed us and all things good, only to cast us into the fires of hell? No! That was never his intention."

Dr. Zinn continued, "God said, 'He who believeth in me shall not perish,' I Repeat, 'He who believeth in me shall not perish.' What God is saying is that we must have faith; faith that the Lord, thy God, will deliver us from evil! I say unto to you, 'Stay in your homes! Do not leave our cherished Earth! You will be saved!' Now, let us pray for the President's enlightenment, that he may know the truth and change his course."

65

"Turn it off," said the president. "This is treason! Why haven't you arrested him?"

"We can't arrest him yet, sir," the Admiral explained. "He's smart! He hasn't attacked you personally – only your policies."

"How are you handling it?" asked the President.

"Like I said, it's not a big problem right now. It's still a very small minority we're talking about. They're not breaking any laws, so, as of right now, I don't see anything I can do about it. However, I'm keeping my eye on the situation. I think that if we tried to silence Dr. Zinn, we'd just be adding fuel to the fire. We don't want to make a martyr out of him. I believe what the people are looking for is some kind of positive action by the government. We promised them a way out of this danger and, so far, they've seen no progress and no change in our status."

"Ok," said the President with a touch of sarcasm, "so much for the 'good news'! What about the Expeditionary Force?"

"We're right on target, Sir," said Admiral Sorenson. "We've filled the Expeditionary Force with volunteers from the ranks of our finest officers and men. We're fully staffed and equipped and ready to go! Until the time comes for deployment, they remain in a state of rigid training. I've been training right along with them, so that I'll be ready to go as their commander."

"That, you will not do, Admiral Sorenson!" the President replied emphatically. "You find and train someone else to command those troops! I need you right here! Your job is running Homeland Security and that means right here with us. You're not going anywhere!"

Trying to hide his disappointment, the Admiral replied, "I have a lot of fine officers, Sir, but as of right now, not one them is capable of leading this Force."

The President, totally frustrated, fumed, "Well, Admiral – you find one!"

After pausing for a few moments to let his boiling cool down to a simmer, he asked both of his experts, "Dr. Steebler, Admiral Yamato, can you give me an estimated time of departure

66

for our Expeditionary Force?"

Dr. Steebler was slow to answer. "Realistically, Sir, we are probably a year away from delivering a safe, reliable ship."

"That's not acceptable!" again stormed the exasperated President. "The people will riot! We will lose control!"

Both Steebler and Sorenson waited, holding their breath while the President regained his composure. Dr. Steebler, measuring his words, said, "Sir, do you remember last year at the conference? I mentioned an option B."

"Yes. I remember."

"And do you remember that I cautioned it would be unwise to consider it, because we could come face to face, on the same plane and at the same time, with our ancestors?"

"Yes."

Dr. Steebler began to exhibit some excitement as he told the President, "Sir, we have perfected time travel! We can do it! We can do it now! We can travel in time! But, as I said before, we can only travel back in time and on this planet! However, we do have one advantage."

Shocked at this pronouncement, the President asked, "What do you mean?"

Reining in his excitement, Steebler answered, "We'll be able to pick the exact date of our landing. We have the transport ships. We have the personnel transporters and equipment freighters. We can fly them through a wormhole and land at any time in the past that we choose."

Leaning forward towards the President and emphasizing each word, Steebler declared, "We have perfected time travel and tested it! We've sent individuals back to the past and brought them back! We don't have enough ships or equipment at this time to transport everybody, but we are able to send an Expeditionary Force back to the ancient past and determine if it is feasible to colonize and coexist in the conditions of that era."

There was a long pause. Silence suffocated the room. Finally, the President responded, "I didn't realize you had accomplished so much in this field. Why haven't I been kept abreast of these developments?"

67

"We were confident this option would never be needed," replied Dr. Steebler.

"I see," the President responded. "You say everything's in place to begin this operation?"

"Yes, Sir," replied Dr. Steebler.

"Admiral Sorenson and Admiral Yamato, do you both agree?" the President asked.

"Yes, Sir," both men assented.

"To ensure our readiness," Admiral Sorenson said, "we have conducted special training of our Expeditionary Forces on how to cope with the many unique and diversified situations they may encounter. To deal with any unexpected surprises, we are prepared to send along force-field and anti-weapon shields to protect our people from possible attacks by any they may encounter. As a precaution, we're sending enough material to build small domes to house our troops and enough equipment and supplies to support them for an extended period of time. We anticipate they may have trouble living outside a dome."

"Gentlemen," said the President with a sigh, "You have greatly revived my spirits. You may have just presented us with salvation. I'll have to confer with all of our State Representatives, but I'm pretty sure they'll be greatly relieved. This pressure of living on the edge is terrible and the responsibility of keeping our citizens calm is difficult. Not being able to offer them any kind of hope is devastating. Now, there is hope. I'm sure the delegates will quickly agree to go ahead with the project."

"Sir, there's still a problem!"

"And that is, Admiral Sorenson?"

"Who is going to command the Expeditionary Force?"

Chapter 9

Reconciliation

The President sat in his office staring absently out the window. Two weeks had passed since his meeting with the project planners. He had just ended a meeting with the State Representatives. The Ranger Project was a go. He felt tired. He needed rest; something he had denied his body for 72 hours. Yet, there was more he had to do before he could succumb to the luxury of sleep.

Reluctantly, he reached for the file containing the list of volunteers that Admiral Yamato had left on his desk. It was a long list; two full pages, with 32 names listed alphabetically. He vacantly read through the list, until suddenly one name jumped out at him: Ensign Zorena Harbill. He threw the list down on his desk, and reached for the office viewer.

"Yes, Sir?" a woman's voice answered.

"Miss Engle, contact Space Fleet Command immediately! I need to talk to Zorena. An hour later Miss Engle was back. "Sir, I couldn't reach Miss Harbill. She's not in her quarters. Her squadron is out on maneuvers and she won't be back until tonight."

"Okay! Miss Engle, wait a minute! Call Space Command again and tell Zorena's commanding officer that I want to talk to her!"

Within a few minutes, the President received his call from Lt. Commander Mallory. He frowned into the Visi-Phone and gave his command. "Commander, its imperative that I see my daughter as soon as possible. I don't want you to call her off maneuvers, but I understand she's due back Friday morning. Tell her I want to see her next Friday at 12 noon for lunch. I expect you to see to it that she gets here!" Without waiting for a reply, he slammed the phone onto his desk. He said to himself, "That daughter of mine is going to drive me crazy!" Then a smile began to creep across his face, as fleeting thoughts of Zorena's escapades ran through his mind. "But she sure has lots of spunk!"

On the appointed day, Ensign Zorena Harbill stepped into her father's office. He immediately recognized a difference in her. The girl that he knew so well was gone, replaced by a young woman looking very much like a self-assured, confident Space Fleet Naval Officer.

"Hello Father," she greeted him, stiff and formally.

He very much wanted to hug her, but he didn't. Somehow, the way she was holding herself, it didn't seem appropriate. "Zorena, you look wonderful! How are you? How have you been? I haven't had a chance to see much of you lately."

"I'm fine, father. How are you?" she replied coolly.

"Fine. Fine. I'm sorry I haven't been in closer contact with you, honey. I heard you received your commission. I'm very proud of you."

"Father, I received my commission six months ago."

"Ah, yes. Sorry I missed your graduation. It's been really difficult for me to get away. Oh, have a seat. I've ordered lunch. Here it comes now." A tray with soup, sandwiches, and a beverage was placed in front of them.

"I'm not hungry," she said icily. "Tell me what you want. I have to get back to my unit."

Her father looked at her with a puzzled frown on his face. "What's the matter, Zorena? You seem to be upset about something. You've acted very cool towards your mother and I ever since I wouldn't allow you to volunteer to test that prototype space ship. That's been over a year and a half ago. Besides, you were too young and inexperienced, anyway. Remember, those two officers died."

Zorena looked at her father and said sarcastically, "I guess you don't know, father, my squadron has been training for months now on a special assignment. You used your influence to order me here, take me away from my duties, and disrupt my

70

entire squadron's training routine. None of the other officers in my squadron get that kind of preferential treatment; only me! It singles me out and I don't like it."

"I know about your special assignment and its dangers, Zorena and that you volunteered."

Zorena stared angrily at her father. "So, what are you going to do? Tell me that I can't volunteer; that I can't fly the new space ships; make me sit behind a desk? Are you going to run my life for me? I'm not a child anymore, father. You can't dictate what I can and cannot do!"

The President looked at his daughter and wished she weren't so cold. "Zorena, I'm not your enemy, I'm you father. You know I love you and wouldn't do anything to stop you from doing whatever you set out to do, but I can and will stop you from doing certain things if I think it will be in the best interest of our family."

Pleading for her to understand, her father continued, "You may think that you are entirely independent, Zorena, but you're not! And yes, you do get special treatment. You get it whether you want it or not. You're the daughter of the President of the Federation! Wherever you go, and whatever you do, you represent me and this Government and people give you special treatment because of that! You'll never be able to shake that off, Zorena, any more than the rest of us can!"

Zorena's cold and angry attitude didn't change as she listened to her father. It was the same lecture she'd heard from him many times over.

"So," she replied, "is that why I'm here, father; to be told that I can't be a part of the new space fleet project, so that you can keep your own little circle of friends and family secure, when everybody else has to make sacrifices?"

"No, Zorena, that's not the reason," he said. "After Admiral Yamato briefed me on how dangerous those test flight programs are, I decided I had to see you. I think I realized, for the first time, that you're not a young teenager anymore. I realized that you're an adult, a person to be respected and admired. You're well educated and highly trained and you have most certainly excelled in the field of your choice."

The President took a deep breath and continued, "Now, you have volunteered to fly experimental test flights. Most of these flights have failed. Some have ended in disaster. Your mother and I would have chosen an entirely different career for you, certainly not Space Fleet Command! However, if testing space ships is what you want to do, then your mother and I are behind you all the way!"

Her father reached over and took both Zorena's hands in his. "But we do have to face reality. It occurred to us that once you get deeply involved in this project, it might be a long time before we ever see you again. It occurred to me, being fully aware of the dangers, it's possible that we might never see you again! I couldn't stand the thought of you, out there, putting your life on the line, serving your country with you, your mom, and I having a strained relationship. I had to see you; to talk to you; to tell you how much I love you, and how very, very, proud I am of you. I couldn't tell you these things over a viewer. Zorena, I wanted to see you in person. I'm sorry about the way I had you sent here, but you and I are both so busy that we have very little private time."

Zorena's hard expression melted. "Oh, daddy," she sighed, "I'm so sorry! I know I've been acting badly. I feel so guilty. You have no idea how happy this makes me. I hate it when we quarrel. Until I went away to school, we were always such a close family. I guess I've been pretty selfish, thinking only of me and my career and what I want." Tears were beginning to puddle in the corner of her eyes as she looked at her father and said in a small voice, "Now, look what you've done. You've made me cry."

The President gently squeezed her hands and said, "It's not all your fault, honey. I've been pretty selfish, myself – trying to control your life ever since you were a baby. I just never knew when to let go."

Father and daughter sat together in a comfortable silence, until the President interrupted, "By the way, it was I who suggested to the Admiral that he use volunteers, instead of robots

72

as test pilots. He was a step ahead of me, though. He already had a list of volunteers! I'll admit, I was shocked and just a little bit perturbed when I saw your name on the list."

The President sat up straight in his chair, looked into his daughter's eyes, and said, "Zorena, what you have accomplished at the academy is truly outstanding. What else can I say?"

"Daddy, I told myself that no matter what you said, I wasn't going to cry. I love you, too," she smiled, as she wiped away a tear and hugged her father.

"Zorena, I have one last request. You must see your mother."

Zorena looked up at her father and asked, "How is Mom? When I talked to her about two weeks ago, she seemed so weak. Yes. I want to see her as soon as possible."

The President replied with a sigh of relief, "She's doing much better. Thank God! Pneumonia is so rare, nowadays, that specialists had to be called in to treat her, but the doctors say she's almost completely recovered."

"Oh, that's wonderful!" exclaimed Zorena. "When can I see her?"

"You can see her tonight," said the President, smiling broadly. "It's supposed to be a surprise. We're having a State Dinner, honoring Space Fleet Command's test flight volunteers. Admiral Yamato, Captain Pappilos, you, and your commanding officer, Lt. Commander Mallory will all be there. So will all of your comrades. I told Admiral Yamato I wanted to commend the volunteers and I couldn't think of a better way to do it than to give each one my personal thanks and recognition for their courage and devotion to duty at a White House dinner, and you, young lady, are ordered to be there."

Chapter 10

The Arboreium Tunnels

Dr. Jonas Friedman, the brilliant physicist and inventor of the Reflective Magnifier, presented himself at the entrance to Dr. Steebler's laboratory, where he was met by a security officer and escorted to the Doctor's office.

Sitting behind a huge desk that was covered with stacks of papers and files, some so high and in such disarray that they threatened to come tumbling down any minute, was Dr. Steebler. He looked up and saw his friend at the door. "Come in, Jonas," he said as he tried to find a free spot for his friend to use. "Come in and join me for a cup of tea."

The two men, sitting at the desk, sipped their tea in silence. When they finished, Dr Steebler, with a touch of a button, summoned his secretary who whisked the saucers and cups away. "Well?" began Dr. Steebler, when she had left.

"The project is a go, Sir. The personnel transporters and equipment freighters are on the launch pads, ready for take-off. All we're waiting for is a weather clearance," said Friedman.

Dr. Steebler was pleased at this piece of good news. "I was beginning to despair. For a while, I thought this day would never come. If it hadn't been for your Reflective Magnifier, it wouldn't have."

"Yes, Sir. The Magnifier does, at least, allow us to go twice the speed of light. That's not enough speed to get us out of our galaxy, but it was enough for Professor Arbore to discover the spatial tunnels that made time travel possible."

"An amazing man, Professor Arbore," said Dr. Steebler. "Imagine, living in almost complete isolation for ten years, working on his theories of relativity in relation to Earth. When he came to me with his theories, I was shocked by his appearance. He looked terrible! Nothing but skin and bone, all stooped over, his hair almost gone, his skin wrinkled. He was only forty five, but he looked eighty!"

Steebler continued, "His theories, though, were pure genius! He said he had heard about your Reflective Magnifier and he figured that if he had a vehicle that could travel twice the speed of light, he could prove that time travel was possible. Then, you installed your Reflective Magnifier in an engine and the designers and engineers went to work and built our first faster-than-light probe."

"Yes, Sir," said Dr. Friedman, "a probe with unusual dimensions, if I may say so: 400 feet in diameter by 700 feet long."

"Yes, I remember," said Dr. Steebler. "Well, the Professor got his probe and sent it into space. I was skeptical, but he proved his theory. Professor Arbore found his wormholes. He called them tunnels in space, or spatial tunnels, and claimed you could return to any date in the past by accessing a tunnel at a specific point. He insisted on making the first test run himself!"

"So, what did you do?" asked Dr. Friedman.

Dr. Steebler smiled. "I let him go. He was a qualified pilot. When he was a young man, he attended the Space Academy's Flight School. He never graduated, due to illness, but he did finish his flight training. All he needed was a little brushing up."

"Yes. I remember the crash training," observed Dr. Friedman.

"Well, why shouldn't I have let him go? He was qualified, obsessed, and quite mad, you know? Why risk an Academy pilot?" queried Dr. Steebler, in defense of his decision.

"But what about the time and money we had invested?" Friedman asked.

"So, what? We were looking for any kind of solution, clutching at straws, really," answered Dr. Steebler.

"Well, it's all history, now," reflected Friedman.

"Yes," mused Dr. Steebler, "The Professor flew his mission, stayed in very close radio contact with us, penetrated a tunnel, and found himself flying over Earth's continents.

According to the ship's clock, it was September 12, 1955, A. D. He said it was the most beautiful thing he had ever seen. He was shocked. There were no domes, anywhere, just blue skies, blue water, brilliant green terrain, and magnificent cities, which sprawled over the landscape. He then noticed what looked like four small flying machines, coming towards him. We advised against any confrontations. He turned his probe around, re-entered the tunnel, and returned to our time zone."

Staring at the ceiling, Dr. Friedman wondered aloud, "Isn't it ironic that within two weeks after his great accomplishment, he died? His heart couldn't stand the strain, he was all excited, pumped up like a young kid, but he had an old body. He died from a heart attack. I don't know if he realized, before his death, that his theories might save mankind. However, a grateful nation mourned his death and named the tunnels the Arboreium Tunnels, in his honor. I think it's a well-deserved tribute to the man and his genius."

Timeline: January 5, 4555, A. D.

Chapter 11

The Appointment

Dr. Steebler and Admiral Sorenson sat stiffly in their chairs. President Harbill sat behind his massive desk and looked questioningly at the two men. That they were disturbed was obvious.

A frown of disapproval clouded the face of Doctor Manns Steebler, while Admiral Sorenson simply stared down at the floor. They could not believe that President Harbill had not only reinstated General Varco to active duty, but also appointed him as commander of the Expeditionary Force.

"Mr. President," Dr. Steebler was saying, "I strongly object to this appointment. To give General Varco this command is a grave mistake. How many times are you going to allow yourself to be bitten by this snake? If he had had his way, you would be in jail or lying in your grave. He's not trustworthy and I guarantee he'll find some way to turn on you again. Look at Admiral Sorenson. His unswerving loyalty helped keep you in office. Varco threw him in jail. All these years, I have been your staunchest supporter. Admiral Sorenson and I stood by you in your darkest hour. Are you going to repay us by rubbing our faces in the dirt and promoting our worst enemy?"

The President held up his hand, "Enough old friend. Enough. I am fully aware of Varco's past transgressions."

"Then, why on earth?"

Again, the President raised his hand to silence the agitated scientist, then looking to his navel chief, he asked, "How do you feel about it, Admiral?"

"If you want to know, I hate him and I feel betrayed. However, I have not come here to discuss your decision. You are my Commander-In-Chief and I have to abide by your orders. However, I don't believe it would be possible for me to work with or have anything to do with Varco or any organization he is assigned to." The Admiral then handed the President an envelope.

"What's this?"

"It's my resignation, Sir. Regretfully, I'm submitting my resignation, effective immediately. I feel I can no longer fulfill my duties. The hate and rancor I have for General Varco would inhibit my judgment. I believe that my feelings toward the General would make it impossible for me to execute the duties of my office in a fair and impartial manner."

"I'll be damned!" exclaimed the President. "You come to me with your resignation and your prettily prepared speech and expect me to let you weasel out of your responsibilities. Months ago, I ordered you to find me an officer to lead the expedition. I already informed you that I needed you here for our homeland security and you were not going to be the commander of the Expeditionary Force. All I ever got from you was that none of your officers were qualified. I took you at your word. So, don't blame me. I had to find someone competent enough – no – brilliant enough to handle the job."

"But I didn't think." started the Admiral.

"Now you two listen to me," said the President controlling his anger. "Nobody had more reason to hate Varco than I did, but the man came to me. He admitted he had been wrong and apologized for his actions. I believe he was sincere. He said he still wanted to serve his country. He swore an oath of loyalty to me and vowed he would serve me well. There is no finer field officer in the world, present company included, than General Varco. I picked him because he is the best man for the job. We all have our jobs to do. Let's set aside our pride and hurt feelings and press on with the more important task of saving mankind! Admiral Sorenson, your resignation is not accepted. You will remain as Chief of Military Operations."

Dr. Steebler and Admiral Sorenson were not the only ones who objected to General Varco's appointment. Nearly half the elected officials also voiced their objections. The President simply told them that General Varco was the best man for the job. He knew that General Varco was a man with an iron will; one who would strive to complete an assignment regardless of the obstacles. He also believed the General when he swore an oath of loyalty to him. The oath was sworn to, witnessed, and recorded by Chief Justice Hardin, at a private hearing in the Justice's chamber.

On January 10, 4555, A. D., General Franklin D. Varco received his commission and assumed command of the 1st Federal Expeditionary Force. It didn't take him long to make his presence felt. Being the ultimate perfectionist, the general inspected every facet of his command, personally interviewed his commanders, and replaced those who did not meet his criteria. He ordered more field training exercises, so he could, at first hand, evaluate his personnel under simulated combat conditions. All his men knew him to be a hard driver and strict disciplinarian. Despite his aloof and stern demeanor, they instinctively trusted him. If there was to be a fight, they wanted Varco on their side. Many a man was heard to say they would follow "Old Granite Jaw" to hell. The additional training took four months. Time was growing short and the President was getting edgy. Finally, on May first, General Varco declared, "The Expeditionary Force, one hundred thousand strong, is ready for deployment."

The final briefing before departure was being held in the Space Station's Planetarium Auditorium. All the leaders, planners, fleet commanders, and pilots were in attendance. The keynote speakers had addressed the assembly and the newly constructed Command Center Communications System had been synchronized and thoroughly tested. Nothing had been overlooked.

The last to speak was President Harbill. "Gentlemen," he spoke, "the moment is here. This is what we have waited for; have strived for. May God bless us with good fortune. Our hearts, our souls, and our prayers go with the Expeditionary Force. There is nothing left to say, except, 'We'll be waiting for you, with great hope and anticipation. We'll be waiting."

In the evening hours of June 5, 4555, General Varco

exited Earth. All eyes watched as his small shuttlecraft disappeared through the Dome's opened ceiling panels. The General relaxed as the pilot steered the little shuttlecraft towards its rendezvous with the Expeditionary Force flotilla, waiting in orbit.

Chapter 12

Enlightenment

Vice Admiral Vladimir Kukov, the Fleet Commander, was apprehensive about meeting General Varco and having him aboard his fleet flagship, the FDSS Trailblazer. The General's reputation as a hard commander that brooked no questioning of his decisions and demanded immediate execution of his commands, regardless of the possible consequences, was well known throughout all the services. The Admiral was also aware that General Varco had little respect for his fellow commanding officers, even though they were experienced and had earned their positions of command.

"Welcome aboard, General," greeted the Admiral with a salute, as Varco stepped aboard the Trailblazer.

Returning his salute, the General said, "Let's dispense with the familiarities, Admiral. Get your staff together. I understand there is a party of civilians aboard, some representatives and scientists, who are expecting a briefing outlining the mission and a tour of the fleet."

"Yes, Sir. They came aboard this morning," said the Admiral. "We've already taken them on the tour. They were very impressed. As soon as the briefing is over were ready to take them back to Earth. Their transporters are in the launching pad. We were waiting for your arrival before we started the briefing."

"You could have given them their briefing and sent them on their way as far as I'm concerned," said the General. "Get them assembled in the Ready Room. I want this briefing finished as soon as possible. I know the President authorized it, but their presence is disrupting the crew and delaying our departure. Just give them a short dissertation on the flight plan, stuff like the distance to the tunnel and the estimated time of arrival, nothing too elaborate. Then assure them about the welfare and morale of our troops; that is if anybody has bothered to check on them."

"Of course, but I'm afraid we'll not have much input or say about the briefing, General," said Admiral Kukov.

"What do you mean? Why not?"

"Dr. Friedman, Sir ... Dr. Jonas Friedman, is going to give the briefing," said the Admiral.

"Dr. Friedman, the physicist?" questioned the General. "What's he doing here?"

"He came aboard with orders signed by the President," replied the Admiral. "He'll be going with us as a part of the crew. According to his orders he is our acting science officer and ambassador-at-large. The President has given him privileged status. He is his own entity and not under your or my command and is to be given access to all operations including security."

The General's face flushed with suppressed anger. "He's a watchdog! The President's put him aboard to watch over me. We'll see about that! I'm not going to have a spy snooping about and reporting everything he can dig up back to the Whitehouse. Either the President is going to trust me or he's not, but this scientist is not going with us. As soon as the briefing is over pack up Dr. Friedman and send him back with the others."

"That's defying a Presidential order Sir!" said the Admiral and thinking to himself, "This man's paranoid."

"You send him back. That's an order, Admiral! I'll take the responsibility."

"I'm sorry, Sir, but I can't do that. You are exceeding your authority. You may be in command of the Expeditionary Force, however where the fleet is concerned, and while en route, I am in command and have the final authority on all issues. I will not countermand a Presidential order. Dr. Friedman stays," said the Admiral.

The General was stunned. "I see. Very well, Admiral," hissed the General. "I see you're going to be difficult. Have it your way, but I'll give you some good advice. Be careful. Don't cross me too many times. It might not work out to your best

82

interest. Now, you may be in command of the ships, but I can dictate time schedules. You get these celebrities and your key staff members assembled in the Ready Room. I want this briefing started in one hour."

Admiral Kukov, while anticipating something unexpected from the General, was astounded at this almost contemptuous attitude he displayed.

Clenching his jaws, the Admiral hesitated, and then looked the General straight in the eyes and replied through his teeth, "Sir, all of my staff and some of our visitors are not aboard this ship. Some are on other ships in the fleet and will have to be transported here. If normal protocol had been followed, as it should have been, and had I been notified in advance, my staff would have been aboard and everything would have been ready for your arrival. As it is, it will take more than one hour to assemble the staff, our visitors, and all the data needed."

"Well how long will it take you?" asked the General, giving the Admiral a searing look.

"At least three hours," replied the Admiral.

"All right, Admiral. I'll give you your three hours, but be advised, I will be ordering some drills and emergency exercises in the near future in which I will need the cooperation of your staff and men. I sense a lack of urgency on this ship and that's a situation that's going to be corrected. Now, show me to my quarters."

"Very well, Sir," said a quietly fuming Admiral.

Turning to a young and attractive female officer standing at attention behind him, the Admiral said, "Ensign Johnson. Will you please show General Varco to his quarters?"

"Aye aye, Sir. This way, General," replied the Ensign, as she turned and started to lead Varco away.

"Hold it there, Ensign," ordered Varco. Then turning to Admiral Kukov, he said, "I need an attaché. Mine is ill and couldn't make this mission. Since she's here, you can assign Ensign Johnson to me."

The Admiral, hiding his anger said," She's not available, Sir. She's the ship's Personnel Coordinator. I will assign you another officer."

"Are you suggesting that Ensign Johnson is not qualified?"

"Ensign Johnson is an exceptionally skilled officer in the field of personnel administration," retorted the admiral.

"Then she should do nicely as my attaché," replied the General. "I need an attaché and I need one now, Admiral! You can assign someone else to take care of your personnel."

Completely frustrated by the General's remark, the Admiral said, "I have others who are trained in military protocol who would be more suitable as your attaché."

Raising his eyebrows, the General remarked, as if not believing what he heard, "You mean you have officers on this mission who have no specific duties?"

At this point the Admiral almost sneered, "Everybody aboard this ship has specific duties, General, but, among other things, I hadn't anticipated that you'd need to have someone assigned exclusively as your attaché. Whoever I assign will have to pull double duty and, considering everything, that may not be exactly what you'll require."

"Well the job of personnel coordinator doesn't sound like a fulltime job to me, Admiral. You make whatever arrangements you need to make, but Ensign Johnson stays with me."

Astounded at the General's insistence on having Ensign Johnson assigned to him, the Admiral could only reply, "Very well, Sir!" in an almost surly voice.

General Varco, replying to the Admiral's tone of voice, asked in a very condescending manner, "Do we have a problem here, Admiral? You seem very concerned over such a trivial matter!"

"There's no problem, Sir," answered the Admiral.

Then turning to the very perplexed and embarrassed young officer, the Admiral said, "Ensign Johnson, you are immediately assigned to General Varco as his attaché. Please show him to his quarters, then report back to me for your orders."

"That won't be necessary, Admiral! She won't be

reporting to anybody but me! Any officer assigned to me belongs to me! I hope you understand that."

Then turning on his heels, he said, "Ok Ensign, lead the way and I hope I'm more satisfied with my quarters than I've been with anything else that's happened on this ship so far."

With that parting remark, General Varco followed Ensign Johnson across the deck away from a seething Admiral Kukov, who was left thinking. "How in the hell am I and my men going to be able to tolerate being around this ass of a commander, much less work with him and satisfy his outrageous demands. And why was he so insistent on having this particular Ensign as his attaché?"

Chapter 13

A Glimpse Ahead

It had taken closer to four hours than the three Admiral Kukov had promised to get all of the personnel situated and prepare all of the documentation needed.

The Trailblazer's Ready Room was not large enough to accommodate all of the visitors and personnel considered essential for this briefing, therefore only the visitors and certain key fleet officers were in attendance. Viewscreens had been set up on the other ships in the fleet to accommodate the other officers and civilians who could not be present, but who were considered essential to the mission. This allowed them to not only watch the proceedings, but, if they wished, to participate in the discussions.

Dr. Jonas Friedman, the brilliant physicist and inventor of the Reflective Magnifier, stepped up to the podium to address General Varco and those assembled. He had volunteered for this assignment, a gesture that was greatly appreciated by President Harbill. Dr. Friedman would be acting not only as the science officer to the mission but also as the official emissary and negotiator for the Federation.

"Ladies and Gentlemen, officers of the fleet," began Dr. Friedman. "We all know why this mission was initiated and the necessity that it be carried out to a successful conclusion for the benefit of all surviving mankind. Therefore, I won't burden you with a long dissertation on this subject, but in laymens terms will stay, as much as possible, with the scientific aspect of our endeavor. I request that you hold any questions or comments until I have completed the briefing. I will then respond to any questions or comments.

"As you know, our Expeditionary Force consists of 100,000 men, including forty personnel transporters, 20

86

equipment freighters, a hospital ship, two battle cruisers, and peripheral support ships. If you follow the maps and charts I have displayed on the stage you will see our route to the Arboreium Tunnel. Using the slower speed, standard hyper-drive engines, we will be traveling through space at 150,000 miles per hour. The twelve-million-mile flight from here to the Arboreium Tunnel will take 80 hours. This data, plus our course, and the coordinates to where we will be accessing the tunnel has been programmed into a master computer installed on the flagship. The computers on the other ships are slaves to the master computer, ensuring that all the ships in the armada will be traveling at the same rate of speed and at the same configuration. As we reach the tunnel, our ships will be traveling at a speed of 150,000 miles per hour. At an exact time, and to match the speed of the tunnels and traveling counter-clockwise to the planet's rotation, we will accelerate to warp two or twice the speed of light. At some point, as programmed by the computers, after circling the planet for an undisclosed number of times at light speeds, the ships will enter the tunnel.

"The flight has been programmed for the armada to enter and exit the tunnel at the precise coordinates that will shift us back to the time considered by all of our expert consultants to be the least damaging to the planet and its inhabitants, while being most advantageous to our civilization. After the armada exits the tunnel our rate of speed will automatically decelerate back to 150,000 miles per hour; it will then take another 80 hours to reach Earth.

"Once we reach the planet, we will have to penetrate the Earth's atmosphere. Before we make this penetration, to avoid burning to a crisp, we will again have to decelerate our speed from 150,000 miles an hour to 700 miles per hour. This braking action will require about 100 orbits around the Earth. After the deceleration is achieved, we will be able to enter the Earth's atmosphere. At this time, each ship's pilot will override the flagship's master computer and make his own descent to Earth. Using voice communications, the landings on the surface will be directed by a landing control officer stationed aboard the flagship. Gentlemen and ladies, if all goes well, when we get out to stretch our legs, we will be standing on Earth in the year 6000 B. C.

"I will now take your questions and comments." The Doctor then acknowledged a woman who raised her hand for attention. It was the representative from Africa East.

"Dr. Friedman," she asked. "Why was the year 6000 B. C. selected and do we expect to encounter people of that era and if so how do you think they'll react to our presence? Do you think they'll be hostile and if they are how will we handle it?"

"We picked 6000 B. C., because that was the time in history that was considered to be the dawn of civilization. The Earth at that time was ecologically stable and sparsely populated. We felt we could find an area we could comfortably colonize without confronting or interfering with any existing cultures or civilizations, thus avoiding any forceful or military solutions," replied the Doctor.

"Are we prepared to use force?" someone asked.

"Well, that is really General Varco's call, but the answer is yes, but only in self defense," replied the Doctor.

For an hour Dr. Friedman chatted with the visitors and officers fielding their questions while General Varco fumed. He wanted Friedman to end the ceaseless yakking and get those civilians off the ships.

Finally the General stood up, interrupted Dr. Friedman, and addressed the audience. "Ladies and Gentlemen," he said. "While I know Dr. Friedman could go on and on and while we would like to accommodate you, I have to bring this briefing to an end. We are coming close to our programmed departure time and must finalize our preparations. At this time, I must ask you to please return to your transporters. Upon your departure we will provide an escort to ensure a safe trip back home. I thank you for your cooperation. I hope you enjoyed the tour and briefing."

Chapter 14

Second Thoughts

For the members of the Expeditionary Force, there was nothing glamorous or romantic about space travel. As their ships hurtled through space, they found themselves in cramped quarters, eating unappetizing meals, and forced to participate in unrelenting training drills. The General was true to his word. He was apparently going to keep the pressure on everyone for the entire 160 hours it would take to reach their final destination. Many of the soldiers and sailors, being true to tradition, turned to old solutions to escape their misery. The ships' sickbays suddenly found themselves inundated with personnel complaining of every ailment in the medical library. In some cases, the medics were faced with illnesses never heard of before. The relief they sought ,though was almost always short-lived, as they were quickly diagnosed and immediately returned to duty. In the event someone did turn out to be seriously ill and beyond a ship's sickbay capability, they were transported to the hospital ship, which was a fully operational medical facility.

Other than knowing the hospital ship was necessary to the mission, General Varco had little interest in it. He had, therefore, not availed himself of any of the details concerning the staff or the ship's operation. Had he done so, he would undoubtedly have objected to the person who had been assigned as the ship's co-pilot. It was Lt. JG. Zorena Harbill. As far as General Varco was concerned he was already encumbered with two unwanted crewmembers, Dr. Jonas Friedman and a historian, Professor Helen Mercer. He would have been totally aghast had he known that a member of his crew was the President's daughter.

To Zorena, this assignment was the fulfillment of one of her life's dreams; to be a part of something so dramatically and historically important. Her squadron commander back at Space Fleet Command had accepted her voluntary request for space duty with the Expeditionary Force and forwarded it to headquarters with his recommendation. President Harbill was notified and did not disapprove. Zorena received her orders of assignment as co-pilot on the hospital ship and promotion to Lieutenant on the same day. It was the happiest day of her life and nearly erased some of the emptiness of her past.

Zorena, to establish herself as a good officer, volunteered for extra duties, which the ship's captain and pilot, Captain Corky Edmunds, was happy to oblige. She was soon to find out that what she asked for was more than she expected and found herself working tirelessly 12 and 14 hours a day. She got little sleep. What sleep she did get was just in fitful shifts of three or four hours at a time. When not piloting the ship, relieving the Captain while he slept, she found herself in charge of several details which included arranging transportation of patients to and from the hospital ship, monitoring and maintaining the ship's life support systems, and, due to a lack of qualified officers, occasionally assisting Commander Tuttle, who carried the titles of Ship's Adjutant and Operation's Officer.

With great enthusiasm and without complaint, Zorena carried out her duties. Captain Edmonds soon realized his co-pilot was a gem and was very appreciative of her excellent performance. On the other hand, Commander Tuttle resented the way the captain took to her and trusted her judgment and supervisory skills. He also resented the fact that she rebuffed his overfriendly advances and treated him in a cool, business-like manner. He now considered her an upstart who bore watching. Tuttle's actions towards her were that of a superior looking down at an incompetent underling and when not in the company of the Captain did not try to hide his feelings of dislike. Outwardly, he patronized her. To her face and in the company of the Captain, he praised her lavishly for the great job she was doing. To her back he condemned and criticized her. When dealing with him, Zorena gritted her teeth and grimly carried out his orders.

90

Chapter 15

The Zimmerman Incident

Seaman Perry Zimmerman, Machinist 1st Class of the Engineering Section, stared at the impenetrable glass bubble which housed the hospital ship's hyper-drive. He was only into his first hour of an eight-hour watch and, as usual, time just seemed to drag by. To him, a minute seemed like an hour.

The duty of the watch was not difficult. He had merely to observe and make hourly recordings of the engines gauges and ensure that all readings stayed within their correct operating ranges. The only other task of the watch was the maintenance of a hyper-drive bearing which had to be cleaned and greased every 12 hours. For a trained technician, it wasn't a particularly difficult job. The hyper-drive engine utilized dual drives, which operated independently of each other. Cleaning one bearing at a time on alternate shifts ensured there to be a fully operational drive, ready at all times. This was a double safety feature, designed to circumvent any hyper-drive failure.

As Seaman Zimmerman stared into the noiselessly whirling abyss of the hyper-drive engine an immense sense of serenity came over him. He found himself aimlessly daydreaming about different things. Often his dreams involved his immediate supervisor, Petty Officer, 3rd Class Oran Hickel. He hated Hickel with a passion and blamed him for everything that went wrong with his life and particularly for putting him on the midnight shift. His dreams of late took a more pleasant turn. He dreamed about his own impending promotion to Petty Officer 3rd Class. What a pleasure it would be to tell Hickel he was no longer his boss and to take his orders and stuff them. It was a comforting dream. He smiled to himself. He was tired. He sat down in front of the control panel. He felt so sleepy. His head slumped over. He fell into a deep sleep.

91

Meanwhile, another member of the ship's company was straying down his own path. Commander Tuttle, the unpopular Ships Adjutant and Operations Officer, when not in his office, could invariably be found in the Officers Break Room. His attraction to this area centered around a Lieutenant Nora Peterson, a nurse who, conspicuously, also spent an inordinate amount of time there. The two thought they were being discreet with their clandestine meetings but were actually the focal point of many jokes among the officers. The talk around the ship was that Tuttle, with his big hooknose, bony frame, and high whiney voice, and Peterson, with her droopy eyes, double chin and huge posterior, were made for each other.

Thinking they were safe from prying eyes Commander Tuttle smuggled Lt. Peterson into his quarters. Zorena, who happened to be walking by Tuttle's cabin just as he was closing the door, was positive she heard a high feminine giggle followed by a, masculine "shhhh".

Meanwhile, in the engineering section Petty Officer Hickel was shaking Seaman Zimmerman, trying to wake him from a deep sleep. "Damn it Zimmerman, wake up!" shouted Petty Officer Hickel. "What do you think yer doin'?"

"Ah – ahh, what's the matter? Get your hands off me," growled Zimmerman, shaking Hickel's hand from his shoulder.

"You've been asleep! You've slept through your whole damned shift, you dumb – !"

"Oh – ah, no, I didn't. I was just resting my eyes," said Zimmerman, with a start.

"Did you clean the hyper-drive bearing?" asked Hickel.

"No. I guess I didn't have time," retorted Zimmerman.

"I know you didn't clean it. I had to switch to the alternate drive while you slept! This is serious, Zimmerman."

"It's no big deal," said Zimmerman.

"Dereliction of duty is a very big deal," retorted Hickel.

At that moment, Seaman Donovan, Zimmerman's shift relief, came into the room.

"Hey, Donovan," shouted Zimmerman. "I didn't get a chance to clean the number one hyper-drive-bearing. You'll do it

92

for me won't you?"

"What? What are you talking about? My job's the number two bearing. Right, Hickel?" asked a puzzled Donovan.

"You'll have to clean that one that too, when its time," said Zimmerman.

"That's not going to happen!" interjected Petty Officer Hickel. "You're going to clean that number one bearing before you go off shift Zimmerman. It's your responsibility. You're lucky I don't bring you up on charges."

"My shifts over Hickel," growled Zimmerman. "Donovan said he'd do it."

"I didn't say anything," interjected Donovan. "Hell no! Why should I do your job?"

"Zimmerman!" said Hickel in a commanding voice. "You change that bearing now! That's a direct order!"

"Screw you, Hickel! You're not an officer. You can't give me a direct order," said Zimmerman and stormed out of the room.

Petty Officer Hickel, visibly disturbed by the blatant disregard of his authority by Zimmerman, reported the entire incident to his superior, Chief Petty Officer Yeager who, due to the seriousness of the situation, brought it to the attention of his section chief, the Engineering Officer, Lt. Commander Lewiston.

Lewiston, a no nonsense type of commander, was not one to bridge insubordination in his section. He immediately dispatched Chief Yeager to pick up Zimmerman and bring him to his office.

Upon arrival, Zimmerman, with head bowed, stood in front of his commanding officer. "Seaman Zimmerman, reporting as ordered, Sir," he mumbled.

From behind his desk, Commander Lewiston, wearing a frown of disapproval, took a moment to look Zimmerman over. What he saw was a huge round-faced sailor wearing a surly but submissive expression. Finally, he spoke. "I have here a report that says you have violated several naval regulations. Charges have been brought against you for insubordination, sleeping on duty, and dereliction of duty."

"No, Sir! Them charges ain't true," declared Zimmerman.

"There was a witness who corroborated the charges."

"They're lying, Sir! It's Petty Officer Hickel. He hates me and he's out to get me and he's getting Seaman Donovan to lie for him."

"Hickel says that when he went to check up on you at the end of your shift you were sound asleep and he had a hard time waking you up," said Commander Lewiston.

"No, Sir! That ain't true, either," responded Zimmerman. "The truth is, I wasn't feeling good and when Hickel came in I was just resting my eyes, but I was wide awake. Hickel snuck up behind me and started shaking me for no reason."

"How are you feeling now?" asked the Commander.

"Oh. I feel much better now."

"Petty Officer Hickel reports you did not service the hyper-drive bearing on your shift."

"Sir, I was just getting ready to do that when Hickel sneaked up behind me and grabbed me."

"Hickel said he gave you a direct order to clean the bearing and you refused. He said you told him your shift was over and for him to, and I quote, 'Go screw yourself,' and then left the work area."

"That's another lie. My shift was over, but I was going to change the bearing, but then to my relief, Seaman Donovan came in. Donovan knew I wasn't feeling too good so he said he'd change the bearing for me. Hickel said it would be all right and that's when I left. Looks like Hickel got Donovan to change his story so he could make these charges against me. He's out to get me. You can see that, can't you, Sir?"

Commander Lewiston looked at Zimmerman in amazement and then called out, "Chief Yeager, would you come into my office for a moment."

The chief entered the commander's office, saluted and said, "Sir?"

"Get two security guards down here and have them escort Seaman Zimmerman to the brig. Seaman Zimmerman, you are under arrest and will be held in confinement pending court martial." Two security guards arrived, handcuffed the protesting sailor, and marched him towards the ship's confinement facility.

Commander Lewiston, not one to put anything off, had one of his administrative assistants type up Zimmerman's confinement orders.

Commander Lewiston called Chief Yeager to his office. "Chief," he said handing him a file. "Take these confinement orders to the Ship's Adjutant. Before we can legally incarcerate Zimmerman, the Adjutant has to sign them. Tell him I said we'll be filing formal charges tomorrow, but we want this guy confined tonight."

"Aye, aye, Sir!" said Chief Yeager, who saluted, turned on his heel, and headed towards the Adjutant's office.

By the time the Chief made it to the Adjutant's office, it was 1700 hours. Petty Officer, 2nd Class Bradley Threet, one of the adjutant's administrative night clerks, was in the office sitting behind a desk when Chief Yeager arrived.

"Hi, Chief. What's up?" queried Threet.

"Got a little problem we need taken care by Commander Tuttle," said Yeager.

"Gee, I don't know. He's gone for the day; left about two hours ago. Anything I can help with?"

"Not unless you can sign a confinement order," said Yeager.

"Oh. No. I can't do that. He's probably in his quarters."

"Look. All I want you to do is take him this file. Tell him it's urgent. Ask him to look it over and sign the confinement order. Tell him we want this guy confined tonight."

Threet looked over the confinement orders. "Yeah, this looks pretty serious. I'm sure Tuttle would want to sign these."

A loud rapping on his cabin door startled Commander Tuttle, who was busily engaged in the delightfully stimulating activity of entertaining a certain Lt. Nora Peterson. "Who the hell?" he murmured to himself. "What is it?" he asked aloud.

"It's Petty Officer Threet. Sorry to bother you, Sir, but

95

there's been a nasty case of insubordination in the Engineering Section that needs attention."

"What is it?" asked an annoyed Tuttle sticking his head out his cabin door.

"A Seaman, while on duty, working in a critical area, refused a direct order from one his superiors. They want him charged and incarcerated tonight. Commander Lewiston wants you to sign the confinement order. Here's the file," said Threet handing it to Tuttle

Tuttle opened his cabin door just enough to grab the file, glanced briefly at the order, glanced around the room, but could not spot a pen, then cast another glance back in his cabin to Lt. Peterson who was looking at him with questioning eyes. Sticking his head again outside the cabin door Commander Tuttle said to Petty Officer Threet, "Tell Commander Lewiston this can wait. This appears to be just an argument between two enlisted men. Tell him I said to have the two men shake hands and forget it. I'll look at this in the morning. And, Threet, don't bother me any more tonight. Do you understand?" With that said, Tuttle closed the door.

Chief Yeager reported back to Commander Lewiston and told him what happened.

Commander Lewiston swore under his breath. "Okay, Chief," he said, "turn Zimmerman loose. We can't keep him locked up without orders."

Seaman Zimmerman was released from custody and allowed to return to his quarters. However, instead of going to his bunk he searched out the whereabouts of Petty Officer Hickel, who was still down in the engine room assisting Seaman Donovan cleaning the hyper-drive bearing.

Hickel looked up and saw Zimmerman coming. "What are you doing here?" he asked. "I thought you'd be in the brig by now."

"Look. Hickel, I'm sorry for what happened, okay? How about dropping the charges? Hey. They let me out of the brig. Let's just shake hands and forget it."

"I'm not forgetting anything!" said Hickel. "You were

sleeping on your watch, disobeyed a direct order, jeopardized the safety of the ship, and disregarded my authority. As far as I'm concerned, the charges stick. How about you getting out of here? How about I'll visit you in the brig?"

Zimmerman's face turned red. He clenched his fist and started shaking, "You sorry excuse for an idiot, how about I beat your brains in?" he said menacingly.

"Don't make it any worse than it already is!" said Hickel rising to his feet.

Grabbing a large wrench from a tool rack on the wall, the enraged seaman lunged at Hickel wildly swinging the wrench at his head. Hickel could not fend off his murderous attack and fell to the ground in a bloody heap from smashes to his head and face.

"You crazy bastard!" screamed Seaman Donavon, who scrambled to hit the emergency alarm button.

Moments later, marine security guards arrived and escorted Seamen Zimmerman, whom they had tightly bound, handcuffed and chained, from the area. The medics came and placed Petty Officer Hickel on a gurney, covered his body with a sheet, and rolled his lifeless corpse towards the ship's morgue.

Chapter 16

Aftermath to Murder

Zorena was awakened from one of her short naps and ordered to report to Captain Edmonds, immediately. Worried about such an unusual order, she quickly dressed and hurried to see what was going on. Having just gotten off a 12-hour shift, she couldn't think of anything that would precipitate the Captain calling her back to duty so soon. She arrived only to see what appeared to be a normal situation with Captain Edmonds at the controls in the cockpit. She entered and seated herself beside him in the co-pilot's seat. "You sent for me, Sir?" she queried.

"How are you feeling, Zorena?" he asked. "I know you haven't had much sleep and I'm sorry I had to call on you so soon."

"I'm ok," said Zorena. "Is something wrong?"

"I have to ask you to take the ships controls for a while," he said, ignoring her question. "A situation has come up which I'll not go into right now, except to say it has nothing to do with the ships operation."

"I understand, Sir," she said.

"Thanks, Lieutenant. I'll be back to relieve you as soon as I can." Having ensured, in his mind, that Zorena was awake and alert, he got up from his seat, exited the cockpit, and hurried to his office in the Command Center. Commander Lewiston, as ordered, was already there waiting for him.

The first words out of the Captain's mouth were, "What the hell is going on?"

Commander Lewiston, in full detail, told the Captain what had happened concerning the night's activities and the events leading up to the murder of Petty Officer Oran Hickel.

"This Zimmerman, where is he now?" asked the Captain.

"He's incarcerated, Sir, in the brig," answered

Commander Lewiston.

"Alright, Commander. Why wasn't he put in the damn brig after he committed all those crimes? It doesn't seem like it would be very difficult to figure out that's where he belonged. This Petty Officer Hickel would still be – should still be – alive, if people were doing their jobs."

"According to regulations, to incarcerate a serviceman you have to have confinement orders. I held Zimmerman while I had the confinement orders typed up. As you know, Sir, all confinement orders have to be signed by the ship's Adjutant. The Adjutant reviewed the orders and said they were not serious enough to warrant Zimmerman's incarceration and would not sign them. Under Naval Law, I had to return Zimmerman to duty."

The Captain asked for a copy of the confinement orders, which were handed him. He read them over thoroughly. "Are you sure Commander Tuttle read these orders?"

"Absolutely, Sir. In fact, he kept the originals. Still has them in his quarters. He said it wasn't serious enough; that it was just a quarrel between two enlisted men and to have them shake hands and forget about it."

"Does Commander Tuttle know what happened? Does he know about the murder?"

"No, Sir. I don't think so, except for Chief Yeager and me, you're the first to know. Do you want me to send for Tuttle?"

"No," said the Captain. "Get me two security guards down here. We're going to pay Commander Tuttle a little visit. I want to see if those confinement orders are in his quarters."

Flanked by two burly guards, Captain Edmonds led the way to Commander Tuttle's quarters and loudly banged on his cabin door.

"What is it this time?" came the loud whiney voice of Commander Tuttle. "If that's you Threet, I thought I told you I don't want to be disturbed!"

"Commander Tuttle! This is Captain Edmonds. Open the door!"

"Oh - ah - give me about ten minutes, Captain. I'm not dressed."

"Open the door now, Tuttle! That's an order!"

Rustling and scraping noises could be heard inside the cabin. The Captain made a motion to one of the guards who produced a key and unlocked the door. With one intrusive shove Captain Edmonds and Commander Lewiston forced open the door and pushed their way inside Tuttle's cabin. Tuttle was truly not prepared for visitors. "How dare you?" he sputtered.

The Captain and Commander Lewiston were amazed and agape; dumbfounded at the sight that lay before them. Commander Tuttle, totally nude, was hopping around trying to insert, without much success, his legs into his trousers. A rather large, wide eyed woman was sitting up in Tuttle's bed, likewise totally nude, trying to cover her breasts with what looked like an enormous pair of women's panties.

Captain Edmonds looked around and spied a file on Tuttle's desk. "Is that the confinement order?" he asked.

"Yes, Sir! That's it," confirmed Commander Lewiston.

Trying not to look at Tuttle or the woman, the Captain grabbed the file and then said, "You two get something on and meet us outside right now." The Captain, slamming the door behind him as he and Lewiston exited the cabin, turned to Lewiston and said, "That stupid son-of-a-bitch! Now I've seen everything!"

Casting their eyes about, Tuttle and Peterson, frightened and distressed, finally emerged from the cabin. Instead of facing the Captain and Commander Lewiston, they were greeted by two security guards, who put them in handcuffs and marched them to the lower decks to the ship's confinement facility.

Zimmerman's court martial was not prolonged. He was found guilty of endangerment, insubordination, dereliction of duty, and murder, and ultimately given the death sentence by an unsympathetic court. Time and space are valuable commodities aboard a space ship. Within three hours of sentencing, Machinist 1st Class Perry Zimmerman was executed by lethal injection and his lifeless body unceremoniously shunted into outer space.

100

Lt. Peterson, who faced only the minor charges of fraternization and conduct unbecoming an officer was transferred to duty aboard a troop ship's sickbay. She was reduced in rank to Seaman 3rd Class and reclassified a nurse's aide. Seaman Peterson would no longer be hanging around the officer's lounges. However, she did gain a popularity of sorts with some of the enlisted men. It seems, much to her chagrin, her reputation as a femme fatale followed her to her new duty assignment where she found herself constantly having to fend off the advances of indiscriminate lust-filled soldiers and sailors.

The court martial of Commander Tuttle was not handled as expeditiously as Seaman Zimmerman's or Lieutenant Peterson's. Tuttle, being a senior officer was entitled to certain rights and therefore due to his rank and the seriousness of the charges brought against him, would be tried by a higher court with no less than General Varco himself presiding over the trial. The trial itself of course was to be held aboard the flagship the SSFDS Trailblazer. Tuttle had been transferred to the Trailblazer and confined to quarters. The quarters assigned him was a five by eight foot cell. Tuttle was a very frightened man. He was particularly frightened of Varco. It was well known that Varco despised anyone who displayed weak character and this was doubly true of his officers.

Tuttle was found guilty of gross negligence, dereliction of duty with consequences leading to the death of a non-commissioned officer, fraternization, and conduct unbecoming an officer. He was stripped of his commission, discharged from the Navy, transferred to a forward combat-unit with the Expeditionary Force; a unit that often came under the critical eye of General Varco, and reduced in rank to Private. From now on, life was going to be very difficult for Private Tuttle. Many of his ex-shipmates aboard the hospital ship doubted that he would be able to survive in that environment.

Zorena was given a temporary spot promotion to Lieutenant Commander, which carried with it the additional duties of former Lt. Commander Tuttle.

Chapter 17

Anomaly

While Admiral Kukov did not particularly like General Varco, he certainly did admire and respect him. He had to give the General credit. His judgment in dealing with his men was an extraordinary example of extolling maximum effort from his soldiers while maintaining a high level of morale and loyalty.

When the General finally stopped the exhaustive, intensive drills, which the men seemed to have blamed on Admiral Kukov for not having the fleet fully operational, they cheered and rallied around the General. After the drills ended, the General made a speech and spoke of the pride he felt for all the members of the Expeditionary Force and the confidence he had for the success of the mission. Each man's chest swelled with pride and a sense of bonding with their Commander. They were consumed with camaraderie and a great sense of esprit de corps. They credited the General for ending the drills.

What the troops didn't know was that the only reason the General stopped the drills was because the fleet was nearing its rendezvous with the Arboreium Tunnel. They were only five hours from entry. This was undoubtedly the most critical maneuver of the entire journey. Absolute vigil and attention to detail were essential.

General Varco, Admiral Kukov, and Doctor Friedman were seated in the Trailblazer's Command Center. The ship's pilot and co-pilot sat rigidly in the cockpit. There was really nothing for any of them to do except watch the controls. All of the maneuvers from here until they exited the other side of the tunnel had already been programmed and would be executed by the ship's computers. The last hour seemed like an eternity. Anticipation was high. Only one other man, Professor Arbore, had ever experienced anything like this before. They were very nervous. Their adrenalin was flowing with no physical way to release it. They dared not look at their hands, which shook uncontrollably.

Thirty seconds from entry into the tunnel, all was quiet. At that point in time, the Trailblazer, which led the armada, automatically accelerated to warp 2 in preparation for the penetration. Suddenly, without warning, there was a violent shudder. The ship rocked back and forth and then started tumbling through space. The ship's computer went off the line and the navigational controls locked up. As hard as they tried, the pilots could not override the computerized systems and manually bring the ship under control. Radio contact from the rest of fleet came pouring in. Everyone was trying to call in. All the ships in the fleet were experiencing the same phenomenon; their ships out of control.

"Get off the radio!" screamed the communication's officer. "You're jamming the airwaves. We'll let you know what's going on as soon as we can determine what happened."

Confusion and pandemonium reigned. Everyone was lashing out, screaming, and on the verge of total panic when all at once the violent tumbling, as suddenly as it had started, stopped. All the fleet's flight systems came back on the line. The ships righted themselves and then calmly continued their flight paths with no evidence of what had caused the strange and terrifying condition. By some miracle none of the ships had collided.

"What the hell?" Admiral Kukov rushed forward to the cockpit. "What was that? Did we hit something?"

"No, Sir!" said the pilot, "None of our sensors indicate we hit or run into anything."

"Check the gauges. Do they show any abnormal readings?"

"No, Sir! Everything looks normal. Hold it. Wait a minute. The navigator indicator light is flashing. Brace yourselves! We're only a few seconds from entering the Arboreium Tunnel."

The admiral retreated to his seat and buckled himself in.

Everyone was fearful of more tumbling and violence. Five seconds went by. The men inside the Command Center barely had time to collect their thoughts when they felt, this time, a very slight vibration which, within a short period, stopped.

Doctor Friedman was the first to understand what happened. "We're in the tunnel!" he blurted out excitedly.

The news of the entry was communicated to the other ships. Everyone who had access to a view screen peered into the outer void to see what the tunnel looked like. It wasn't exactly as they pictured it. For some reason they had envisioned the tunnel to be like a translucent bubble; something that was there but couldn't be seen. They imagined it would be like flying through a magic mirror and on the other side of the mirror was fantasyland. It all seemed so unreal.

Instead, what they encountered was near darkness. The dazzling, always-present stars and galaxies were blotted out. In all directions, the only thing they could see was dark, ominous looking blue-gray walls.

A momentary feeling of claustrophobia and near panic again enveloped the entire fleet. Silence prevailed as the armada, for what seemed like an eternity, but was actually only about twenty minutes, plowed through the murky tunnel. Then they experienced another slight vibration and this time they did not lose control of the ships' flight control systems. Suddenly, without fanfare, the entire fleet burst through the tunnel. They were greeted by a view of the universe that was far different from the one they had left behind. The stars came out again but somehow, this time, they seemed closer together and shined more brightly than they had remembered. Everyone cheered and shook hands except for General Varco, who maintained a scowl of skepticism.

"We made it! We're ok!" shouted a jubilant Doctor Friedman.

"Ok," said an obviously relieved Admiral Kukov getting to his feet. "But we still don't know what happened and we're still eighty hours away from Earth. If anyone wants me, I'll be in Damage Control. I'm going to find out what the hell happened.

I want a complete check and inspection of the entire fleet's computer network and flight control systems."

General Varco remained in his seat unsmiling and apparently in deep thought. "Dr. Friedman," he asked, "What do you make of all this? As our Science Officer, surely you must have some thoughts on what caused the ship to tumble so violently just before we entered the tunnel. Is there any danger? Are we truly out of the woods and on our way towards a safe landing on the Earth's surface?"

"Well, General, I believe that a thorough inspection of all of the ships' systems, including instrumentation, computer programs, flight controls, and even the ships' hull, is warranted, but I don't think we'll discover anything wrong. I believe what we experienced was an anomaly; an unexplainable event that happened in space. If I had to explain it, I would probably theorize that we ran into something undetectable to our instruments, like cosmic dust, just as we were about to enter the tunnel. In any event, I don't believe it caused any damage or will in any way interfere with the mission."

"I hope your right, Doctor," said General Varco sounding unconvinced. "In the meantime, we had also better go to Damage Control. I have to check on the Expeditionary Force and I'm sure the Admiral will need you to analyze and head up an inspection team."

When the General and the Doctor arrived at the Damage Control Center, they saw Admiral Kukov talking excitedly to another officer. It was Commander Mohamed Jamul, the fleet's Chief Engineering Officer. "So how soon do you think it will be before we get a status report from the rest of the fleet?" the Admiral was asking.

Jamul, an experienced veteran of the Space Academy was known throughout the fleet as a man you could count on in times of crisis. He was always thought of as being level headed and not prone to making quick decisions. "Admiral, this is a most unusual and unprecedented incident. Under normal conditions, just a preliminary investigation would take two weeks."

"Commander, we don't have two weeks! We don't have one week! In three days, if all goes well, we will be orbiting around the Earth in what we believe will be the year 6000, B. C. We have to know if we have the capability to continue towards that objective. We want to know, will we be able to make the orbits and make successful landings on the surface? In two days, we'd better have some answers."

"Then, I think we had better trust our instruments and our computers, Admiral. We've been in constant communications with the rest of our ships. Sixty percent of the fleet has already reported in. They all report the same thing. All systems are a go and functioning normally. Everything's fine." The Commander then seemed to lose his concentration and looking vacantly right through the Admiral said. "There was something very peculiar though."

"What?"

"Every ship has reported one thing that's a little disturbing," mused the Commander.

"What's that?" asked the Admiral.

"It's probably nothing. Our time clocks must have had trouble resetting after we went through the tunnel," said Jamul.

"What are you talking about, Commander?" asked Admiral Kukov, who was starting to get a little exasperated by the Commander's evasiveness.

After a pause the Commander said. "All the ships' clocks read, 'June 8, 1932, A. D.'"

"Well, can't you reset them?" asked the Admiral.

"We've tried. They won't reset".

Dr. Friedman, who had been listening intently to the conversation between Admiral Kukov and Commander Jamul, broke in on their conversation. "Admiral," he said, "I'm afraid Commander Jamul's assessment is correct. I believe, in fact, we are exactly where and when the computer's clocks say we are. The anomaly that we experienced must have disrupted our computer's programming configurations and caused us to enter and exit the tunnel on the wrong date."

General Varco, who had been standing in the background

106

stepped forward. He felt he was being slighted. He was the one they should be addressing their remarks to. After all, he was the Commander of the Expeditionary Force. The ultimate responsibility of establishing the colony would rest on his shoulders. "Gentlemen," he said, "I must inform you that I, above all, have the utmost interest in what is being discussed here."

"Oh. Sorry, General! We didn't mean to leave you out of the conversation," said Dr. Friedman. "I was just telling Admiral Kukov that I believe the anomaly was responsible for us exiting the tunnel on the wrong date and ...."

The General cut Dr. Friedman off. "I heard every word that was said. I'm not sure I was supposed to, but I did. From now on, you will address your remarks to me and keep me fully informed of all ...."

"No one was keeping you out of anything," interrupted the Doctor, annoyed at Varco's insinuations. "You've been here as long as I have and know just as much about what's going on as we do. You got any opinions? We'd like to hear them."

Chapter 18

Out of Control

The Hospital Ship, UFS Nightingale, survived the anomaly of the Arboreium Tunnel and the ship's staff experienced the same feelings of near panic and terror as the rest of the fleet had. After they exited the tunnel, Dr. Friedman gave a briefing to all the Fleet Commanders and told them what he knew about the situation. After that, everything settled down. Everyone accepted their plight and realized they would be attempting to land and establish their colony in a much later time zone than they had anticipated. In the meantime, life and the functions of day-to-day duties continued, as usual.

Zorena was stunned and a little frightened by the rapidity of events that had left her with a field promotion to Lieutenant Commander. Because of the lack of personnel, she had also inherited additional duties as the Ship's Acting Chief of Operations, and Adjutant. She realized her promotion was temporary and her new duty assignments were on an interim basis until a suitable replacement for Tuttle could be found. She felt honored that Captain Edmonds had enough confidence in her abilities to recommend her for this opportunity to prove to the entire complement of officers and enlisted personnel that served under her that she was a competent and experienced officer. However, these feelings were mixed and she found it a constant struggle to keep from feeling overwhelmed by all of the positions she was expected to fill.

Zorena hadn't had much time to reflect on these turns of events, when she was called to duty. An ambulatory shuttle had been given clearance to land aboard the hospital ship. Zorena rushed to make preparations for its arrival. Aboard the shuttle, was an enlisted man suffering from severe abdominal pains that had been diagnosed by his ship's medical officer as an acute attack of appendicitis. A crew from the Hospital was standing by to rush the soldier to the operating room for surgery.

Zorena cleared the ship for docking and stood by as it came to a smooth landing in the bay. The sick corporal was quickly removed from the area. Zorena stood watch as a maintenance crew arrived, performed their post-flight inspections on the shuttle, and secured the bay. After she assured herself that the ship and the bay were secured, she dismissed the maintenance crew and her detail of guards and headed for her quarters.

Unfortunately for Zorena, the area was not as secure as it appeared. The last chore on the maintenance crew's checklist was to secure the shuttle. To accomplish this, they used retractable tie-down cables. However, tonight, one of the overhead cables was inadvertently left lying on a ceiling beam. A mechanic had lowered the cable, but forgot to secure it to the ship. An automatic time-delay mechanism malfunctioned and extended the length of the cable, rather than retracting it to its overhead socket. This unfortunate chain of events caused Zorena to become the victim of a freak accident. Just as she started to exit the bay, the loose tie-down-cable slipped off the ceiling beam. Unnoticed by her, the cable swung downward in a perfect arc and, with full force, its metal buckle struck her on the side of her head, just above her right ear. She let out a short scream, collapsed in a heap, and did not move. One of the guards heard the scream, ran back to the bay, and saw her lying unconscious on the deck. In a panic, he called for the medics, who quickly responded and rushed her to the medical emergency ward.

Zorena opened her eyes. She was vaguely aware that she was lying on a hospital bed. As she started to regain consciousness, she was suddenly overpowered by unbearable pain on the side of her head, followed by an accompanying excruciating, throbbing headache. Two men were standing over her, talking. They were not aware that Zorena had awakened.

"Is she going to be alright, Doctor?" Captain Edmonds was asking.

"You're looking at a very lucky girl," the doctor replied. "If that buckle had hit two more inches to the right of her head, she'd be dead."

Captain Edmonds shook his head. "That's all I'd need. If anything else goes wrong, I might as well shoot myself and get it over with. But is she going to be alright?"

"She's had a nasty blow – suffered a concussion. I'd say she's going to be ok. However, I want to keep her here in the hospital ward for the next 48 hours, under observation. She could experience any number of symptoms; dizziness, drowsiness, loss of co-ordination, or fainting. I want to make sure she's ok, before I release her back to duty."

"Ok, Doc. I get the point, but get her back to me as soon as possible. I really need her. She's my right arm. She does everything. I can't get along without her," said the Captain.

Zorena looked terrible. Her eyes were blackened and bloodshot, her face swollen, and of course the back of her head was wrapped in bandages. She opened her eyes and began to moan softly. "My head hurts. I'm in so much pain," were her first words.

The Doctor looked intently into Zorena's eyes. "Hello, Zorena," he said. "I'm Doctor Menes. I know you're hurting. The nurses gave you a painkiller about ten minutes ago. It should be taking effect any moment, now. Try and relax."

Zorena grasped the handrails of her bed and squeezed. Tears ran down the sides of her cheeks. "Please, Doctor! Can't you do something, now? Put me to sleep or something?" she implored.

The Doctor took one of Zorena's hands, held it in his own, and talked to her soothingly. "It's going to be alright. You're going to be ok. For your own good, you have to stay awake. We don't want you to sleep, right now."

Little by little, as the Doctor talked, her pain began to subside. The frowns of agony that had wrinkled her forehead began to disappear. She laid her head back on her pillows, closed her eyes, and relaxed.

"Now, don't go to sleep on me," said the Doctor.

110

"I won't," she said faintly.

"Hi, Zorena. It's me, Captain Edmonds," said a blurry face in the background.

"Oh. Captain. I'm so sorry! I really messed things up. Didn't I?"

"Hey. It wasn't your fault."

"I don't even know what happened. What did happen, Captain?"

"You were hit in the back of the head by the buckle of a malfunctioning tie-down cable. It did you in pretty good. You were lucky. Doc says it could have been worse."

"Good thing I've got a hard head," said Zorena, in an attempt at humor.

"I'm just glad …. Doc say's you're going to be ok. Hey. You didn't do this just to get a full night's sleep, did you? Just kidding," he jibed.

"Don't make me laugh," she said, smiling weakly. "It hurts too much."

"Ok! That's it! That's it!" interrupted the Doctor. "Sorry to break this up, Captain, but visiting hours are over. I'll have Zorena back to work, soon enough, but, right now, I have to ask you to leave. I need to run some tests on her and she needs her rest."

"Ok," said the Captain, then to Zorena, "I have to go now. I'm so relieved you're going to be ok. Let me know if there's anything I can do for you."

After Captain Edmonds departed, the Doctor turned his attention towards Zorena. "Well, I'm glad to see you're still awake. You seem to be in better spirits than when you first woke up. By the way, I'm Doctor Menes – Doctor Faro Menes. You can call me Faro."

Chapter 19

Dr. Menes

Doctor Faro Menes, an up-and-coming neurosurgeon, surprised everyone in the medical community by volunteering for a very dangerous special assignment. His adventuresome spirit and his desire for space travel led him to volunteer his services to the Federation's Expeditionary Hospital Ship. At the young age of 30, he was already renowned as an excellent surgeon. His real calling, he always thought, was that of an adventurer. The Chief of Hospital Administrations was very pleased to land a doctor with such credentials and immediately accepted him to the staff.

Life aboard the ship had been dull, not the romantic adventure he had imagined, and his patients, so far, were practically non-existent. When he heard that a ship's officer of the line had been injured and coming to his ward, he was almost happy that he would have something to do. However, when he saw Zorena laying there, how serious her condition was, and how much pain she was in, any elation that he had felt quickly vanished.

As his only patient, Zorena received the full benefit of his professional care. He catered to her needs and hovered around her to the point of annoyance. She wished he'd let her sleep. Laying on a hospital bed and not being allowed to sleep was a very frustrating experience. She could not get comfortable. First, she'd lie on one side and then, the other. Laying flat on her back was the most uncomfortable position of all. Worst of all, every time she tried to close her eyes, Dr. Menes was right there to make sure she didn't go to sleep. Finally, fully frustrated, and with the doctor momentarily out of the room, she was determined to walk right out of the ward. She defiantly sat straight up, swung her legs over the side, and

112

pushed herself off the bed to a standing position on the floor. Dr. Menes was there to catch her as she fainted and slumped in his arms. He put her back in bed. However, this time, he allowed her to sleep. She slept for seven uninterrupted hours and, upon awakening, felt refreshed and stronger. She amazed the young doctor with her recuperative powers. Within twenty hours after the accident, the swelling around her face receded and the bruises were almost healed. It was Zorena who was now doing the annoying.

"Dr. Menes," she implored, "you can see that I'm almost fully recovered. I don't see any reason why I can't return to duty."

"You just fainted a few hours ago. Do you really think you're ready? And call me Faro."

"I'll call you Dr. Mean Person, if you don't let me go. The only reason I fainted was because you kept me up so long, I couldn't stay awake any longer."

"Maybe," he conceded. "But what if I released you and you passed out on the job? The consequences could be pretty serious, couldn't they? While you were asleep, though, I had some x-rays taken. Everything looks ok. Still, I want to make sure. You only have to stay another twenty-eight hours. You can stand me for that long. Can't you?"

Zorena looked at the Doctor for the first time. She found him very attractive, in fact very handsome. "All right, Faro, I guess I'll be your prisoner. But what am I going to do? I can't just lay here for twenty-eight hours. I'd go crazy."

"You're right. Tell you what we'll do. I'll bring in a chair for you to sit in. That will be more comfortable than laying in a bed. I'll keep you company, if you want. We can play board games, watch a movie, or, if you want to be left alone, I have a nice set of history books."

"Doctor – I mean Faro, what about your work; your other patients?"

"Zorena, you're my only patient."

"Oh. That explains it. No wonder I'm being tortured," she quipped.

"Ha ha. Very funny. I can see you're feeling much

better."

During the next twenty-eight hours, the doctor and the patient became acquainted. They conversed easily and, once they spent some time together, they discovered they actually liked each other and had a lot in common. Zorena had to admit to herself she did enjoy his company. Her natural charm and beauty on the other hand had completely captivated the poor doctor. Although he wouldn't admit that such a thing could happen in such a short time, he thought he was falling in love. She had become much more to him than just a welcome diversion to an otherwise boring excursion. Reluctantly, when the time came, Doctor Menes released her back to duty. "Zorena," he said as she departed.

"Yes?"

"You will come back and visit me. Won't you?"

"Sure. You can't get rid of me that easy. You are my doctor. Aren't you?" And, with a smile, she turned and walked away.

Chapter 20

Planning Stages

Aboard the flagship, Admiral Kukov was conferring with General Varco. They were discussing, with great emotion and agitation, their options concerning how to proceed with the mission. Their ideas drastically conflicted with one another's and tempers flared as each man stressed his point. Each man was positive he had the right answers and thought he should be in command. Dr. Friedman aloofly stood aside, listening to them argue.

"In accordance with my standing orders and military protocol," Admiral Kukov was exclaiming, "I am in charge of this fleet until we orbit Earth, launch the Expeditionary Force, and deliver it to a safe landing site. Your command, General, starts after your forces are on the ground. Of course, to ensure a smooth transition, our two forces will have to work together, in a combined effort. I, of course, will coordinate the transition."

"Not so! You are in clear violation of military protocol", said Varco. "Your authority ended when you brought us through the Arboreium Tunnel. I now formally declare that I am taking total command of this mission. The right of command now reverts back to me. It is my responsibility to determine when and where we'll land and also my responsibility to ensure the safety of the Expeditionary Force."

"Enough of this! You're both wrong," broke in Dr. Friedman. "I will be in charge of the mission, including the fleet and the Expeditionary Force."

"You? By God, you're out of your mind! I'll have you arrested!" fumed the General.

"I don't think so," said the Doctor, quietly. "President Harbill had anticipated there might be a chain-of-command problem. I have sealed orders from the President that supersede all standing orders. If an emergency arises that is so serious as to endanger our mission and if these differences cannot be resolved, I am empowered to take full charge of this operation and you gentlemen, with your quarreling, seem to have created an emergency." The Doctor produced a file from the folds of his jacket and held it out. "Here is a copy of those orders. I suggest you and the Admiral read them over, carefully."

"What emergency? I don't see any emergency. What makes you think I'm going to worry about a piece of paper way out here in space, anyway?" said Varco, belligerently.

"You may not be worried about that piece of paper, but the Admiral is and he's in charge of security. When this mission is over, we will all have to face the President and Congress. They still execute men for treason. We are still able to communicate with President Harbill and others from our time with a communication system which lets us send and receive messages through the Arboreium Tunnels. I've been in daily contact with the President, reporting everything that's happened on this voyage. The President knows of our present situation. And, General, the President asked me to remind you: don't forget your oath of loyalty."

"Why are you exercising the power of these orders, now, Doctor?" asked admiral Kukov. "I agree with General Varco on this point. I don't see any great emergency, either."

"For two reasons. One: you two can't resolve your differences. Two: we have not resolved the question of what happened when we went through the Arboreium Tunnel nor why all of the ships' time clocks are reading 1932. Gentlemen, I am the only one qualified to study and analyze these problems. My first order is we are not making any landings until after I have determined that it is safe. In the meantime, Admiral, go ahead and establish an orbit around the planet. As soon as I can, I'll let you know what I find. And, General, I have no desire to undermine or usurp your authority. As soon as I know what's going on and I feel it's safe to resume the mission, I will transfer command back to you and Admiral Kukov. By the way, General, Admiral Kukov is right. Legally, under normal conditions, he is

116

in command until the Expeditionary Force is safely landed."

So, there the fleet waited, circling the planet, five thousand miles above the Earth. Dr. Friedman had ordered that high an orbit to avoid detection. In his quarters he had set up a makeshift laboratory. For hours, he studied the computer readouts of the ships movements from the minutes before they entered the Arboreium Tunnel to moment they exited it. He played the videos over and over again, looking for clues that might lead to a logical explanation of what happened. He sifted through research and other data communicated to him from the home planet by Dr. Steebler. No one at Space Fleet Command had ever encountered anything like the anomaly the fleet had experienced. Dr. Steebler did have a theory about the ships' clocks. It was the same theory Dr. Friedman had come to. They concluded the ship's clocks were not malfunctioning. When the fleet exited the tunnel it was not in the year 6000 B. C., as hoped. The clocks had accurately recorded the year. It was 1932 A. D.

After three days work, Dr. Friedman was no closer to finding out what had caused the anomaly than he was on the day it happened. He held a conference with Kukov and Varco and admitted to them he could not find any scientific facts that suggested the mission was imperiled and that the President instructed him to relinquish his authority.

"Gentlemen," he said, "I apologize for the delay, but I had to make sure of the facts. After an intensive research, I have come to the conclusion that on the day we encountered the anomaly the ships' systems did not malfunction. Like Commander Jamul said, let's trust our instruments. However, that does leave us with a very serious problem. Landing and establishing a colony in 1932 is an entirely different situation than landing in 6000 B. C. I recognize that you, Admiral Kukov, and you, General Varco, are the experts in handling the landings and establishing the Colony, so I will leave those decisions in your capable hands. However, I do recommend that you work together as a team and rely on each other's areas of expertise and not get so wrapped up in egotistical debates about who's in charge."

117

And so, a truce of sorts came about between the Admiral and the General. Together, they surveyed the planet, studying the terrain for the locations of the densely populated areas, which they intended to avoid. More importantly, they looked for areas that were isolated, but still contained the natural resources they needed; namely, fertile land and water. They finally settled on a site that looked to be the most promising. Nestled in the northwest corner of an area the ancients called The United States of America, was a spot that seemed perfect for their needs. A wide river ran east to west from the plains to the ocean and the land on the north side of the river abounded with fertile fields and forests.

The plans were made and the landing sites identified. The next night, after the sun had set and darkness settled in, with engines muffled, scout ships would make tentative landings. Once the landing site was determined to be secure, the landing coordinator aboard the lead scout ship would signal for the assault branch of the armada to begin their descent. The hospital ship and most of the armada would not land. They would remain in orbit until the colony was satisfactorily established.

Now, the last and most critical piece of information they needed was exactly who these people who inhabited this country were, which was identified on their maps as The United States of America. They wanted to know if the natives who lived here were peaceful or hostile, what kind of armament they would be facing, if they were hostile, and were they even likely to wage war? General Varco also wanted information about the landing site, itself. The site bordered the southeastern edge of a state called Washington. According to their maps, a river, the Columbia, ran through the state's southern border and would provide the water they needed. He wanted reassurance that the area was isolated enough so they could reasonably expect to land without being detected.

There was a person on board who could answer these questions; the Historian, Helen Mercer. Varco, at first, rejected the idea of consulting Miss Mercer. He did not like civilians and particularly female civilians. He felt they had no place and

118

would certainly have nothing to offer in the planning stages of what he considered an invasion. However, he had to concede, they did need the information. She was summoned and joined Admiral Kukov, General Varco, and Dr. Friedman in the Command Center.

Admiral Kukov and Dr. Friedman thanked her for coming and motioned for her to join them at the conference table. General Varco said nothing. Maintaining a scowl, his usual countenance, as of late, he unsmilingly looked at her and nodded his head.

Helen Mercer had desperately wanted to go on this mission. She considered it the most important historical event, ever undertaken. Helen was considered by her peers to be the best. She was brilliant, beautiful, and had the personality to match. She was a unanimous choice by the Historical Societies Selection Committee for the job. However, she was not here to charm an audience. These men wanted information.

"Miss Mercer," began General Varco. "I understand you are well acquainted with the history of The United States, as it was in 1932?"

"Yes, Sir. I believe I'm well versed in that time of history. Plus, to prepare myself, I have just concluded further in-depth researches of that era."

"Good," continued Varco, with eyebrows arched. "What we want to know, Miss Mercer, is what weaponry the enemy possesses, how they would stage an assault against us and, if they did choose to attack us, the approximate size of their military force? I won't be surprised if you can't give us that information. You're probably not familiar with this area. I could understand that. Perhaps, being a woman historian, you might have thought it unnecessary to study that phase of history; the military, that is."

"Of course I researched this information!" retorted a rankled Miss Mercer. She sensed an immediate feeling of dislike for the General and was not about to let this not-so-subtle insult slide by. Nor was she was going to allow this obviously male-chauvinistic tyrant intimidate her. She didn't know him well

119

enough to realize he treated everybody in a rude manner. With a frown and looking Varco straight in the eye, she said, "But one thing I'm a bit confused about, General. I didn't know that our ancestors were considered the enemy."

General Varco lifted up his head and glared at her. He did not like being criticized, especially by a civilian woman. "I think it may come to that", he said. "Put yourself in their shoes. How would you feel if an alien army suddenly invaded our country? Wouldn't you consider them the enemy? I'm hoping it doesn't come to that, but I have to prepare for all contingencies. If we have to, we will defend ourselves. I would regret spilling any blood, but we will do what we have to do. So, if you are knowledgeable, as you claim, give me a breakdown of their military capability."

Swallowing her anger and the uncomfortable cloud of Varco's scrutiny, Miss Mercer began her briefing. "For a country of this size, with a population of approximately one hundred forty million people, they have a relatively small army and a not too serviceable navy. I doubt that, in this section of their country, they could muster more than five thousand men. They just came through a war about twelve years ago and are scaling down the military. Presently, the country is struggling from a financial depression and their government seems helpless and unable to spur the economy. If they discovered our colony and decided to attack us, their ability to do so would be severely limited. They do have cannons. The largest can fire up to nine-inch shells that explode on contact. I doubt any of these could penetrate our shields. They also have mortars. When mortar shells explode, they send pieces of shrapnel in all directions. These are very effective against soldiers out in the field. Their soldiers each carry a weapon, called a rifle, which can be very deadly and accurate from a range of about up to three hundred yards. Also, they have rapid-fire weapons they call machine guns. These guns, while not very accurate, shoot out projectiles at an amazing rate, about 700 rounds a minute. When hidden from sight, the machine gun can be very deadly, especially against advancing soldiers. Then, there are the tanks.

These are clumsy armored vehicles. Each is equipped with a small cannon, mounted on a turret, on the top of the vehicle. One small hit on the side of this vehicle usually knocks it off its tracks and renders it inoperable and, almost always, kills the occupants. Lastly, they have flying machines. These machines are crude, with very poor maneuverability. They use them to fly over enemy territory and drop crude bombs on enemy positions. They pose no threat to our barriers. As to the number of men they might send against us, maybe a division; two thousand men, including infantry, a battery brigade, an armored brigade, and a squadron of bomber flying machines. Gentlemen, I see no threat from these poor people. I would think negotiations might be a more favorable solution than making war on defenseless natives. As to your other question, I seriously doubt you will be able to land without being detected. As I said, you might try peaceful negotiations before you bring out your," her voice dripping with sarcasm, "ray-guns."

"That will be all, Miss Mercer. Please, do not surmise or portend to advise us as to how we should conduct our strategies. That is not why you were summoned here and I do not appreciate your cynicism. You are dismissed." Varco did not like being lectured to, especially by a woman. He did not hide the fact he did not like her and made it perfectly clear she was no longer wanted at the conference table.

She looked to Dr. Friedman and Admiral Kukov. They responded with insipid smiles. That they were embarrassed was obvious, but they said nothing.

"You are all so very welcome," she said, her voice laced with mockery and, as she departed, she directed a scornful grin at them and half under her breath, but loud enough for them to hear, murmured, "What stupidity! What a pity!"

"What did she mean by that? That woman has a bad attitude," growled Varco after she left.

"Well, I don't think we made a very favorable impression on her, either, especially when you referred to our ancestors as the enemy," retorted Dr. Friedman.

Chapter 21

The Landing Site

The soldiers of the Expeditionary Force were eager for action. Three weeks aboard the transporters in cramped quarters, eating tasteless food, and forced to endure endless hours of drills left them jumpy and agitated. They wanted nothing more than to charge out of the confinement of their transporters and into their new environment, no matter what the consequences. However, the way was not clear. The landing site had to be checked. The General was adamant. He wanted the landing site sterile. That meant he wanted it to be absolutely devoid of any human inhabitants. A close look at the landing site had to be made. Three scout ships, under the command of Lt. Commander Crow, the landing flight coordinator, were assigned the task. As twilight approached, they boarded their small ships. "All right boys, light em up," radioed the Commander as he blasted out from the flight deck of the mother ship into black starlit night. The two other ships followed suit and quickly joined him in formation. Throttling back their engines, they silently guided their crafts downward, in an ever-widening spiral. A thin layer of clouds gave them perfect cover, making their small crafts all but invisible to anyone who might be looking up at the night sky from the planet's surface. At two thousand feet above the surface, they emerged through the clouds and looked down at the Earth. They were the first men in 2,500 years to see the planet up close, as it was before there were domes. The sight of ancient Earth, even at night, was overwhelming, and brought lumps in their throats.

"Ok, boys," said Commander Crow, choking back his emotions. "Let's take 'em down and check it out," Slowly, the three ships descended to tree-top level and began a systematic patrol of the landing site area. They could fly at very slow speeds and, for closer, longer looks, hover over any spots they chose.

After enough time had elapsed for them to complete their reconnaissance of the area, Commander Crow radioed his two scouts. "Charlie Two and Three, what do you guys see out there? Report in, Two and Three."

"Charlie Two to Charlie One. My sector looks clear, Boss. No sign of any kind of human life, anywhere. It looks like virgin territory, to me."

"Charlie Three, you out there? Check in."

"This is Charlie Three. Commander, I didn't see any people, either. No kind of movement, at all. However, I did see what looked like an old wooden structure."

"What?"

"Yes, Sir, an old building, like an old house or something. It's empty; seems to be abandoned."

"We'd better check it out."

The three scout ships landed at a safe distance from the old building. The pilots emerged from their ships and stealthily crept towards what appeared to be a door in the side of the building. They assumed this must be the entrance. Only the silence of the night greeted them as they made their way along the structure's side. With weapons drawn, they cautiously inched toward what now just looked like a hole in the wall. That it had been a doorway was evidenced by the fact that an old door lay broken and rotting on the ground. They stood at the doorway, trying to peer in. Suddenly, they were startled by a rustling noise around their feet and jumped back in alarm as something brushed by their legs, rushed out of the darkened room, and vanished into the night.

"What the hell was that?" yelled the Commander.

"Just an animal of some kind," said one of the pilots. "I saw it go. It wasn't human. It was running on four legs. From what I've read, these woods are full of all sorts of wild animals."

"Yeah, I guess you're right. Well, this is obviously just an old abandoned house that hasn't been lived in for years. Let's get back to our ships. I'm going to call the command ship and

123

give them the all clear. This site is clean. It looks good to me."

Within two hours, after receiving the all clear, the landing party began its descent. General Varco had decided he would begin the landing operation on a small scale. He would only utilize eight troop transporters, one supply ship, two battle cruisers, and his flagship for his first excursion onto the Earth's surface. The rest of the fleet was to remain in orbit until the landing site was secured. With precision, Commander Crow, now assuming his role as ground control officer, directed the ships to the designated landing area. For forty-eight hours, the area was a beehive of activity. Quarters, administrative buildings, and supply warehouses were assembled. Defensive battlements and impenetrable shields were erected and the water purification plants set up at the edge of the adjoining river. Domes were quickly raised and soon covered the entire area. The soldiers seemed much more at ease, once they found themselves under the familiar protection of the domes.

Chapter 22

Not Welcome

Billy Bob Morris was a homeless man. One couldn't call him a vagrant. Since his birth he had lived in the small town of Walla Walla, Washington with his parents. The family was well respected, but Billy Bob was a troubled boy. He was different from the other children and always strayed down the wrong path. He failed in school and dropped out in the third grade. After his parents died, Billy, unable to manage his affairs, lost their home. He became a drifter and beggar. He was completely undependable and therefore couldn't hold a job. By the time he reached twenty years of age, he was a homeless vagabond who wandered around the streets of Walla Walla. Everybody avoided Billy and would even cross the street to avoid coming in contact with him. You couldn't blame them. Billy was dirty. He stunk. He probably never took a bath and his clothing was torn and filthy. To say that he was miserable and wretched looking would be an understatement. Billy was thirty five years old now. The older he got, the more he disliked the townspeople and they him.

Some thirty miles from the town, on the edge of the woods by the river, Billy found a deserted farmhouse. It was a homestead once owned by an old homesteader by the name of Denver Johnson. Denver died in 1880 and the property, never claimed, went into disrepair and ruin. In 1931, Billy Bob moved in. It was a place to sleep. He never tried fixing up the house. He just slept on the filthy old rotten floors with the rats, fleas, and ticks. But, on this night, June 17, 1932, something different and very scary was happening. Billy was awakened, not by a rat or snake crawling over his body, but by a loud whirring noise. At first, he thought it was the wind blowing. He got up and peeked outside. He thought maybe some of the boys from town came out to pester him again. What he saw startled him and sent him scurrying back into the house where he cowered down and hid in a dark closet. It wasn't the bullies from town. What he had seen at the edge of the woods were three very strange looking vehicles and three menacing looking man-like-creatures walking toward him. Trembling with fear he listened intently as they came closer and closer. They approached the doorway and looked in. Billy couldn't contain his fear. He dropped to all fours and running as low and as swiftly as he could, scooted out between their legs and disappeared into the woods.

For two days Billy, hiding by the edge of the woods, observed the man-like creatures. With bulging and disbelieving eyes he discreetly watched them land in their enormous spaceships. He also couldn't believe how many there were and how quickly they had erected what seemed to be an entire village. He decided what to do. He knew he had to report what he had seen to the sheriff. Billy was sure that what he was witnessing was an alien invasion. This was the work of Martians. He started running as fast as his feet could carry him in the direction of town, thirty miles away.

The people of Walla Walla were startled when, on the morning of June 20, 1932, they saw a dirty, disheveled, Billy Bob Morris running down the main street of the town, wildly waving his arms and hollering at the top of his voice. They hadn't seen him in several months and, as far as they were concerned, his actions clearly indicated he had gone completely mad. They watched him in amazement as he made his way to the jailhouse and began pounding on the sheriff's door. Two of the sheriff's deputies opened the door and dragged him inside. Once they had him inside the building, and the door closed, an overpowering stench pervaded the entire jailhouse.

Sheriff Karl Huggins came out of his office, gagging and coughing, his burley figure tense and has face distorted with rage. "What in the hell's going on and what's that gawd awful smell?" he demanded to know.

One of the deputies, holding Billy Bob at arm's length by the collar answered, "It's Billy Bob, Sheriff! He was outside, banging on the door."

126

"What does he want?" asked the Sheriff holding a handkerchief over his nose.

"We don't know. We ain't had a chance to talk to him yet."

"Well take him around back and hose him down. Christ! He looks awful! See if you can find some clothes for him and burn them rags he's wearin'. Find out what he wants, then throw him in jail."

"Sheriff, you gotta listen to me! The Martians is comin'," yelled Billy, as the deputies dragged him outside.

"Crazy as a hoot owl," murmured the Sheriff as he sprayed lilac water around the room, trying to rid the jailhouse of the stench left by Billy Bob.

Finally, after he was cleaned up, his beard trimmed, and wearing some clean clothes that another prisoner had left behind, Billy was brought back into the jail.

"Ok, Billy!" said the Sheriff. "I don't know what the commotion is all about and I don't know why you're in town, but if you think I'm going to throw you in jail just so you can get some free meals, you're sadly mistaken. Just git yourself up and git out of this town and stay out. I know you've been stayin out at the old Denver place. I don't care about that. You can stay there for all I care, but the people of this town don't want you here and I don't trust you. If I catch you hangin' around I'll have my deputies bust you up real good. You understand? We'll throw you back in that rotten old farmhouse and let the rats eat you. Understand?"

"But, Sheriff, you gotta listen to me," whined Billy Bob.

"I'm warning you, Billy, for the last time."

"The Martians is comin'! Thousands of 'em!" blurted out Billy. "I saw 'em with my own eyes! They got ships like you ain't never seen before. They built a whole town in two days!"

"You're crazy."

"I can't go back there! We're bein' invaded! They'll kill me!" cried Billy Bob, now groveling on the floor.

"Where'd ya say you seen this?"

"Out by the old Denver farm, at the edge of the river. I

watched them from the woods. As soon's I saw what they were up to, I came here as fast as I could. "

With disgust, the Sheriff looked down at the groveling misfit. Then he looked up at his two deputies. "Joey, throw this crazy bastard in jail. You and Jerry take the truck and drive over to the old Denver place and check it out. Just in case there is somebody out there you better take some shotguns and take the back roads."

Within a few hours, the deputies were back and, babbling almost hysterically, verified Billy Bob's story. There were some very strange things going on out there. The Sheriff wisely decided this was out of his realm of responsibility and called the Army Base at Fort Lewis. The Army, of course, reacted to the Sheriff in much the same way as the Sheriff had reacted to poor Billy Bob. As far as the Army was concerned, the small town sheriff was suffering from some kind of hallucinations, perhaps a case of the DTs. These small town sheriffs were known to be heavy drinkers.

The sheriff wouldn't give up. To state his case, he drove two hundred miles, all the way to the west coast, to Fort Lewis. It took him three days of talking to administrators and underlings before he was able to get an appointment to see the Commanding General. In attendance at the meeting were the Fort Commander, Brigadier General Harold Starling, his Adjutant, Colonel Stark, and a very nervous Sheriff Huggins.

"And just what do you think you and your deputies saw?" asked the General with a patronizing smile. He still wasn't too sure that the Sheriff was not exaggerating something out of proportion that in all probability could be easily explained, like the starting of the new highway construction job the government had planned.

"Sir, I know reporting an invasion from Mars sounds crazy. When it was first reported to me, I had the man who reported it thrown in jail, but my deputies and I made a thorough investigation and we all came to the same conclusion. Some kind of intelligent life has landed on the edge of the Columbia River and constructed some kind of large complex; a complex far more

128

advanced than anything I've ever seen."

Finally, the general, though unconvinced and still very skeptical, sent a reconnaissance patrol to investigate the alleged invasion with strict orders to not contact or engage anyone or anything. They were ordered to just, "see what the hell is going on" and report their findings back to the fort. After three days, the patrol was back making its report to General Starling.

"That Sheriff was not lying or seeing things, Sir," said the leader of the patrol. "They've built up what looks like a very formidable base and it looks like they apparently intend to stay."

"How big is their force?" asked the General.

"I don't know exactly, Sir, but I would have to say there were thousands of them out there, and they have airplanes, if you could call them that – huge, enormous things. I think they're – ah – I think they're space ships. I counted eleven of them at the edge of the forest."

"Just exactly what do you mean by enormous?"

"Ah, Sir, you know how big a battleship is?"

"Yeah. They're pretty big."

"They're bigger than that."

"Horseshit! That's impossible! How about their men? You say you saw troops. Are they armed?"

"I didn't see any weapons, but I would have to assume they are. They have amassed an enormous army and covered their entire encampment with some kind of what looks like barriers or shields. Also every building they constructed has a peculiar looking dome over it."

"You haven't brought me back enough information, Captain. There must be some evidence of what they're up to. Did you see any of them? What do they look like?"

"We didn't have a chance to find out, Sir. They spotted us and began chasing us. We had to get out. They have small little airplanes that can fly very fast or very slow. They chased us at tree-top level. In fact it seems like they can even stop in mid-air and watch you. They dart around like flies. They followed us all the way to the edge of the fort before they turned around and went back. For a while, I thought they were going to attack us."

"What? What do you mean? You mean they actually followed you all the way to the fort?"

"Yes, Sir."

"They know our location?"

"I'm afraid so, Sir. We couldn't help it."

"God help us!" said the General.

Chapter 23

Basic Errors

In July, 1932, the United States of America was in the middle of a depression that was tearing the country apart. Banks failed, prohibition prevailed, and people were starving. Even so, life and politics in Washington D.C. went on and the President of the United States was attending to his politics, hosting a group of women representing the National American School Board Association. Standing on a podium, set up in the garden on the White House lawn, he addressed the elegantly dressed, broadly smiling ladies.

"Welcome, ladies. I am pleased to meet you. Let us commemorate this day, July 28, 1932. It is an honor and a privilege for me to present the Women's Society for Better Schools in America this beautiful trophy and a check for five thousand dollars. Your Society has led the way in – ah," his voice began to trail off. What sounded like gunshots, followed by the voices of screaming men, distracted the President. The distinct smell of gunpowder drifted over the garden party. This outburst of noise seemed to be coming from the front of the White House in the area of Pennsylvania Avenue. The ladies, suddenly alarmed, were craning their necks and turning their heads in the direction of the noise. There was another commotion. The Secretary of Defense arrived on the side of the garden looking very agitated and headed straight for the President. The Press Secretary intercepted him. They whispered something, which nobody could hear. The Press Secretary then stepped aside and made way for the Secretary of Defense who joined the President on the podium. More whispers.

"Ah, ladies," said the President, "an urgent matter has been brought to my attention. I give you my sincerest apologies, but I must leave. Please, allow my Press Secretary to take over the ceremony. Again, my apologies and our appreciation of your undaunted work towards better schools in America, and ah-er-ah- thank you." That said, the President turned about and quickly followed the Secretary towards Pennsylvania Avenue.

The ladies were almost too dumfounded and disappointed to applause. This was to be the highlight of their entire year's work.

The President, on the heels of his Secretary of Defense, ran to the gate in front of the house to see what was going on. The sight horrified him. He couldn't believe what he was witnessing. Soldiers with fixed bayonets were charging a group of unarmed civilians, hurling tear gas, bayoneting them, and firing their weapons at them. The civilians were in full retreat, some falling in the street as the soldiers continued to strike them down from behind. Their leader with blood in his eyes kept shouting. "Shoot to kill!"

"What the hell's going on?" screamed the President.

"Our soldiers!" yelled the Secretary. "They're attacking protesters!"

"What protesters?" asked the President.

"They're those two thousand World War One veterans who claim they're starving. They were protesting their deplorable conditions and claimed that even though they had served and fought valiantly for their country, their country has abandoned them. They were also requesting that Congress honor the money certificates that were given to them after the war. Congress refused. You ordered the Army to disperse them."

"Good god! They're veterans! I said disperse them, not kill them! Tell the soldiers to stop! Order them to return to their barracks. This is terrible! We'll never live this down! Damned elections are coming up in four months. Don't those stupid veterans realize we're in the middle of a depression? There is no money. I'm not even sure I'm going to get my raise this year, besides those certificates aren't redeemable until 1945. Shit! The Democrats are going to blame me for this."

The following day the Secretary of Defense requested a special meeting in private with the President. They met in the

132

Oval Office.

"What is it, Mr. Secretary?" asked the President after the two were seated. "If it's about that little incident yesterday, I've already decided on what to do about it. Err- ah- how many of those veterans were killed yesterday anyway?"

"Colonel McArder's soldiers killed 22 men, Sir."

"Goodness gracious! Ahh yes. I'll have to do something, I know, for punishment and to get McArder out of the headlines, I'll promote him to Brigadier General and send him to the Philippines. We'll give him a little title like Commander-in-Chief of Pacific Theater of Operations. Nothing's going on over there. People will soon forget.

"I think that's an excellent idea, Mr. President, however, that's not my reason for requesting this meeting," replied the Secretary.

"Oh."

"Sir, something's come up. It's so peculiar, I hesitate to bring it to your attention."

"Is it so serious that it can't wait? With the elections coming up, I have very little time for anything that can't be taken care of later. I have to get out and campaign. I'm lagging in the polls. Roosevelt is taking advantage of the depression and turning it into a campaign issue."

"Sir, this is something that may or may not be serious, but it is so bizarre that it must be looked into."

"Humph. Well, what is it?"

"There's this General Starling. He's currently the Commander at Fort Lewis. It's a small fort located on the West Coast, near Tacoma, Washington."

"Yes. I know the General. He's a good man."

"He called me. He made an official report. He said we're being invaded by-ah-Martians."

"WHAT?"

"He said aliens have constructed a base on the Columbia River near some little town. Walla Walla I believe was the name of it."

"This is all I need! Some crackpot general seeing

boogey men."

"Exactly what I thought, Sir."

"Well? What do you think it is?"

"Probably nothing serious; maybe some rowdies are trying to make a land grab. I understand there's some old abandoned property around there just waiting to be taken. Either that or maybe some Indians are on the warpath, staging a little uprising."

"Alright. I'm sure it's something like that. Here's what I want you to do. Get a hold of this General Starling and tell him to get his head on straight. Tell him to get out there and, whatever it is, put it down, take care of it, and, if I hear any more about aliens or Martians I'll have his head. He'll be looking for a new job. And another thing: have him put a perimeter guard around the whole area. I don't want any outsiders or reporters out there. I want this incident completely hushed up."

Chapter 24

My Ancestor, My Enemy

General Starling was an unhappy man. He anticipated that nobody in Washington would take him seriously. In their eyes, he looked like a fool. However, he had his orders and was determined to carry them out to the best of his ability. He devised a war plan. First, as the President ordered, they would set up a fifteen mile perimeter circling the alien's base. Then, he would amass his army and advance on the base with a frontal assault formation. The Infantry and armored brigades, with the soldiers and tanks, would form the first line and would, if necessary, lead the attack. Behind their lines, backing them would be three battery battalions ready with cannons and mortars. However, before resorting to battle, the General was going to approach the alien's base under a flag of truce. If possible, he wanted to avoid a battle. He would try to negotiate first.

General Varco, who had now formally taken command of the Expeditionary Force, planned his strategy. He was disappointed that they had been spotted so soon. However, their discovery by an enemy patrol was inevitable. He acted accordingly and sent scout planes to follow the American patrol back to its fort. He now knew the size of their force and the distance it was from his base. The General smiled to himself. How primitive they were. There would be no difficulty squashing this crude army if they chose to attack him. Knowing human nature for what it was, Varco was confident that even facing certain death and superior might, the American troops would attack. He surmised men would fight to the death against all odds to defend their homeland.

On August 2, 1932, General Starling marched his troops to the front of the aliens' main gate. General Varco, with bemused interest, watched their advance from behind the safety of his impenetrable shields. He was at ease, curious to see what kind of move the Americans would make. It came as a great surprise to Varco to see one of the enemy soldiers walk towards them waving a white flag.

"What's that?" Varco wanted to know.

"I don't know! It's some kind of a signal," one of his commanders answered.

"I know what it is," came a voice from the back of the lines.

"Who said that?" demanded Varco.

Helen Mercer stepped forward. "I did."

"What are you doing here?"

"As the Ship Historian, it is my right and my duty to observe the events of our mission."

"Really? Okay! What's that flag for? What are they doing?"

"That's called a flag of truce. They want to negotiate."

"Negotiate? Negotiate what? All I have to do is drive them out," said Varco.

"You said you wanted to avoid spilling any blood. All they want to do is talk," said Helen.

By this time, Dr. Friedman, realizing what was taking place, had worked his way up to the front of the lines and approached General Varco.

"It's time for me to do my job, General," he said. "As the President's envoy and Ambassador-At-Large, my assignment to negotiate a peaceful agreement and afford an honorable settlement with the citizens of this generation is paramount to any other action. We must, at all cost, try to avoid any military conflict with these people."

"Why," Varco sneered, "are you afraid?"

"Yes," answered Friedman. "Quite frankly, I'm very much afraid. Not of their military might, but of the consequences. Dr. Steebler cautioned us to be very careful in dealing with these people. To put it bluntly, what happens if you kill your great, great, grandfather 1,000 times removed."

136

"Quite simple," said Varco. "He's dead! But go ahead. Go out and talk to them, but remember, the only thing we will settle for is enough space for us to colonize our entire populace."

"You don't have to tell me my job. I'm well aware of our needs."

So it was that Dr. Friedman found himself walking towards General Starling's defiant small force. On his signal the compound's shields were lowered and the gates opened. Waving his own white flag, he walked on until he found himself at the very front of their lines face to face with General Starling's flag bearer. "We come in peace," he said.

General Starling, standing to the side, but near enough to observe the proceedings and close enough to hear, said to his aide Colonel Stark. "His uniform is weird. Other than that, he looks human enough. I couldn't understand him. What did he say?"

"I couldn't understand him, either. He must be speaking Martian," answered Colonel Stark.

General Starling grabbed a microphone and spoke. The loudspeaker, which he had placed before the gate, blared out his message. "This is Brigadier General Harold Starling, Commanding General of the Third Army at Fort Lewis, Washington. You have landed on and are occupying territory that belongs to the United States of America. We consider your seizure of this territory a hostile act and demand your immediate withdrawal. You will retire back to the country, state, or area from which you came. If you do not withdraw, we will consider it an act of war and will act accordingly. You have twenty four hours to vacate these premises. If you do not comply with these terms, we will forcibly remove you."

Doctor Friedman, who had not understood a word said, waved his white flag, and speaking as loudly as he could, repeated, "We come in peace!"

Colonel Stark said, "I still can't understand him, but I thought I heard the word peace. I don't think he's a Martian."

Standing in formation and facing the strange looking aliens, the only word the rank and file soldiers heard was

Martian. The word was quickly whispered through the ranks, "My God! They really are Martians."

Dr. Friedman had feared that they would not understand him. Although he was speaking English, the language had evolved so much over 2,200 years that they could not comprehend his strange dialect. To circumvent this problem, he had researched the writing of that era and had composed a letter asserting their peaceful intentions, which he now attempted to deliver. He reached into his pocket.

A soldier, just out of basic training and very nervous, misunderstood the Doctor's actions. "He's goin' for his gun!" he yelled.

Before the Doctor or anyone could react, the young undisciplined and untrained soldier shouldered his rifle and shot Dr. Friedman, striking him in the chest. The Doctor slumped to the ground. The shot spurred an epidemic of fear among Starling's untried soldiers who began firing indiscriminately at the vanguard of thirty soldiers Varco had sent as Friedman's escort. Several of them dropped to the ground, dead or wounded by this unexpected act of aggression.

"Cease fire! Cease fire!" General Starling was screaming. His orders were unheeded and too late. He watched in dread as the alien base's gates closed and the protective shields surrounding the encampment rose into place. His awe changed to terror as he saw small portal openings appear in the shielded walls. From within these portals came a loud crackling humming noise followed by intense, scorching, beams of light, which swept over the front lines of his soldiers. Horror was the only word he could later use to describe what happened. After one sweep of those terrible white beams, three hundred seventy five of his finest soldiers died screaming, their bodies burned, the carnage was devastating.

"Retreat! Retreat!" screamed General Starling. The order fell on deaf ears and was too late. His army was already in full retreat, fleeing from the aliens as fast as they could, screaming, and dropping their weapons as they ran.

General Varco also broke off the engagement and

ordered a cease-fire. When order was restored he inspected the battlefield. Fourteen of his expeditionary soldiers lay dead. He recovered the corpses of his fallen soldiers and buried them the following day with full military honors. He wanted the memory of their deaths and why they died burned into the minds of his men. Dr. Friedman was found alive and sent to the field hospital. His wound turned out to be not too serious. The bullet had passed through his body luckily missing any vital organs.

General Varco visited Doctor Friedman in the field hospital. "Well, Doctor, what do you think now? Do you still want to negotiate with these people? What do they call themselves? Americans?"

"Absolutely! I still think it's essential that we establish friendly relations."

"Look, Doctor, I was being facetious, not serious. These American's have proven to me that they are treacherous and without honor. They shot you and attacked us under their own flag of truce. You're lucky to be alive. They obviously thought they could launch a surprise attack and defeat us while we had our shields down."

"No, General. I don't think that's what happened. I saw their faces. They were frightened. I think just a few of their soldiers panicked. I don't believe their commander intended for this to happen."

"Fortunately for us, Doctor, I am in command. My experience and my understanding of a fighting man's psychology tell me differently. They see us as invaders and will do anything in their power to get rid of us."

"Tell me, General, how many men did we lose in that skirmish?" asked Dr. Friedman.

"Fourteen dead and sixteen wounded."

"General, I deeply regret the loss of our fourteen men. How many men did they lose?"

"We killed between three hundred fifty to four hundred of those treacherous bastards before they got away," snorted Varco.

"If Helen Mercer's estimates are correct, that's about a

139

tenth of their force," said the Doctor.

"Don't worry about that. Before I get through I will annihilate their entire force and level their fort."

"I implore you, General," said Dr. Friedman. "Don't do this. Those people are terrified. Let me have one more chance to negotiate peaceful terms."

"Doctor, you tried. It is now out of your hands."

General Starling was grateful for the reprieve. He had fully expected the aliens to take full advantage of their rout of his forces. Since they did not, he used the delay in time to reassemble his army. Five miles back from the enemy's camp, he had his forces dig in. Using the latest textbook strategies, learned from their experience in World War I, he had a series of trenches dug for protection and manned them with infantry riflemen and machine gun crews. One hundred yards behind the trenches, he set up his artillery, bringing in his biggest cannons from the fort.

Finding his soldiers almost completely demoralized, he knew he had to find some means to lift their spirits. He spoke to them of great sacrifices of heroes of the past: how the Spartans with only three hundred warriors held off the entire Persian Army of one hundred thousand. He then assured them that, as long as they stayed under the cover of their trenches, the beams from the enemy's ray guns could not harm them. Lastly, he spoke to them of retribution and how the big cannons he brought in from the fort would demolish the alien's base and blow it off the face of the Earth. Whether or not his men believed all that they had been told, their state of mind was elevated enough that they no longer seemed to think that their situation was hopeless and were able to carry out their duties with renewed vigor.

General Varco watched their efforts through the eyes of surveillance cameras, which he had installed on the outer perimeters. What they were doing truly amazed as well as amused him. Never before had he ever seen such a clumsy attempt at setting up a defense. He knew at any time he wanted he could completely and utterly destroy them. He thought about Dr. Friedman and his desire for a peaceful resolution. Maybe the

140

Doctor was right. Maybe he shouldn't just slay these people without giving them a chance. Varco aroused himself from his deep thoughts, quickly dismissing any feelings of sympathy. It was time for war. He met in council with his commanders to outline their strategy for the final onslaught against the enemy forces.

Seated before him, the commanders rested easily, most of them comforted with their feelings of superiority and knowing that this campaign would be an easy victory. What General Varco had instilled into the thoughts of his commanders was the belief that this campaign was a war against a treacherous, barbaric enemy. Any thought of compassion because they were their ancestors had been driven from their minds. Dr. Friedman's pleas of, "Don't kill your grandfathers," went unheeded.

"Alright," said Varco. "Before we get to our next step, I want to go over our casualties again from that last fiasco. I know we killed about three hundred seventy five of their soldiers, but exactly how many did we lose? I keep hearing conflicting reports. We only had Section One in the front line, yet I keep hearing reports of men dead or missing from other sections. So what the hell is going on? I'm going to start with Section One. The commander of Section One will give me an exact casualty report. Then, we'll go on to the next section and so on and so forth. Section One, report."

"Sixteen hundred fifty-three dead or missing and sixteen wounded, Sir," reported the section one commander.

"What do you mean, sixteen hundred fifty-three dead or missing? Your men were on the front line. Sixteen were wounded. Fourteen were killed. I counted them myself. We picked them up and buried them!" exclaimed Varco.

"Yes, Sir, but I have sixteen hundred fifty-three men I can't account for."

"You have sixteen hundred fifty-three men who are hiding from you Colonel. I suggest you put out a search party and find your little nest of cowards."

"I will continue to search, Sir. I've been searching for two days."

141

"Section Two, report," said a disgruntled Varco.

"Seven hundred twenty-three unaccounted for or missing, Sir," came an uneasy answer.

"WHAT?" bellowed General Varco, "Seven hundred twenty-three? How can you have seven hundred twenty-three men unaccounted for or missing? Your men weren't even in the skirmish."

"I don't know, Sir. We're searching for them, now."

On the ground, Varco had a fighting force of 20,000 men. The force was divided into ten sections, each led by a field commander. After polling each section for casualties, the results came to an astounding eight thousand seven hundred sixty-two men missing and unaccounted for.

It didn't seem possible. Varco and his commanders were positive that, except for the fourteen men who were buried, the rest of those men were not killed in combat. It seemed very unlikely that they deserted or were in hiding. Where could they hide? Finally it was decided that the search for the missing soldiers would go on and the war against the treacherous and barbaric Americans would recommence.

General Starling's spotters were the first to notice the small enemy airplanes coming towards them and quickly sounded the alarm. This time, he did not hesitate. This time, there would be no attempted negotiations. The distance to the alien's base was calculated and the targets zeroed in. The General gave the order, "Fire at will!" The loud reports of cannon fire echoed through the valley. With surprising accuracy, the shells struck the alien base's domes and exploded with resounding thunder.

Inside the walls, Varco and his company watched as the shells harmlessly expended themselves. As far as Varco was concerned, the enemy had made the first move. Now, it was his turn. He ordered Admiral Kukov to launch one of his battle cruisers into the fray.

Out of the blue, over General Starling's defensive positions a flying airship came into view. Nothing like this had ever been seen or even imagined before. Its sleek torpedo

142

shaped body and the gun-ports that extended gracefully from its hull instilled stark terror to General Starling and his small force. This was a nightmare! It couldn't really be happening, but this was no dream. He knew of nothing he could do or say that would be of any benefit to his heroic but out-manned troops. The cruiser silently lowered itself into position. General Starling grimaced and closed his eyes. A distinct crackling humming sound reached the ears of those on the ground. The highly feared white beam, which had caused so much devastation before, blazed out from one of the ship's gun ports and swept the trenches from one end to the other with horrendous results. All of the soldiers who had manned the trenches were incinerated. They died screaming. The cruiser then turned its attention towards the artillery's battery emplacements. Gun crews on the ground were seen abandoning their stations and running to the rear. Another beam of light from the alien cruiser swept over the artillery pieces and turned them into piles of molten metal and cremated the retreating soldiers as they ran.

General Starling ordered a full retreat. Utterly defeated and grief- stricken, his remaining troops stumbled their way back to Fort Lewis. Upon arrival back at the fort, the General called for a general muster of his troops. He was desperate to determine his losses in manpower. He was equally anxious to learn about his arms and ordered his Quartermaster to make a complete inventory of all their remaining equipment. His losses were not good, but, on the other hand, they had not sustained nearly the amount of casualties he had feared. There were a total of eight hundred thirty soldiers dead or missing and three hundred ninety-seven wounded. He was greatly relieved. He had thought his losses were much greater than that. However, his loss of equipment was devastating. They had lost almost all of their weaponry. His cannons were completely destroyed, as were his tanks. Most of their small arms had been dropped as his soldiers fled in panic from the battlefields. All that remained of his once proud division was a rag-tag army of hopelessly demoralized men.

Chapter 25

Change of Command

In the Mojave Desert, Lt. General Nathan Ridgley had America's best combat-ready troops, the 1st Cavalry and 2nd Infantry Divisions, on maneuvers. For the General, the maneuvers were proceeding exceedingly well. He was about to employ his forces in a particularly intricate phase of the operation when he received a call from the Secretary of Defense in Washington D.C. It was an urgent call ordering him to, with all haste, stop the maneuvers, take his two divisions, move out to Fort Lewis, Washington, and relieve General Starling of his command. Ridgley was furious at being interrupted. He was a personal friend of General Starling and knew him to be a not only competent, but also excellent commander. Such a change of command would be a slap in the face, not only to the officers' corps, but, particularly, the elite general staff. He calmed down after he was filled in on the details of the defeat of General Starling's army at the hands of a few renegade Indians or white bandits. It was very hard for Ridgley to understand how a band of land-grabbing renegades or a brigand of marauding Indians could defeat a well-equipped modern army. Be that as it may, the General, known for his organizational skills, assembled his men and within twelve hours had them fully operational, loaded in trucks, and on their way to Washington State.

In three days, General Ridgley and his army divisions rolled into Fort Lewis. What they saw dismayed and shamed them. The fort didn't appear to be damaged. It had obviously not been under attack, but there seemed to be a complete lack of any kind of discipline or organization. Debris and supplies were sloppily strewn all over the grounds. Shirtless, hatless, and slovenly dressed soldiers, in complete disarray, were seen lying or slouching around their barracks. They paused to gawk at the new troops as they drove into the compound.

General Ridgley's first order to his commanders was to, "get those lazy bastards cleaned up! Get them into some semblance of a military formation and get this fort cleaned up!" Having seen to the restoration of the fort and some kind of order, Ridgley went looking for General Starling. "From the looks of things around here, it's no wonder Starling couldn't fight," he thought to himself. "A bunch of piss ants could have whipped this army."

He found Starling in his headquarters slumped over his desk, head in his arms. He looked, if anything, worse than his soldiers. General Ridgley strode into the office and stared unbelievingly at the sight before him.

Colonel Stark who was standing beside General Starling came to attention and saluted Ridgley who returned his salute. He then bent down and gently shaking Starling said, "It's General Ridgley, Sir. He's here."

General Starling raised his head up and, bleary-eyed, looked at the ramrod figure of General Ridgley. "Hello, Nathan," he murmured listlessly. "Still quite the martinet, huh? - And now the hatchet man. I've been expecting you."

"Are you drunk?" Ridgley demanded to know.

"No. I'm not drunk. I wish I were," said Starling, partially sitting up in his chair.

"I'm placing you under arrest."

"Oh? On what charges, may I ask?" asked Starling without emotion.

"How about dereliction of duty and cowardice in the face of the enemy?!"

"You are wrong, Nathan. I was neither derelict nor cowardly."

"My God, man, what's the matter with you? Look at you. You're a wreck! Look at your fort. It's in shambles!"

"You have no idea."

"All I want from you Starling is who did this to you and where can I find them?"

"Nathan, you mustn't go out there! They'll kill you!

145

While we're sitting here talking, the enemy is probably on its way here to finish the job they started on me. We've got to get away!"

"I don't believe what I'm hearing. You really have turned cowardly haven't you? I can't believe you'd let a bunch of renegades or Indians do this to you."

"They're not Indians and they're not renegades Nathan. They're aliens from outer space. They have weapons so terrible and so powerful we have no way to defend ourselves against them. They turned my weapons into piles of rubble. Their base is impenetrable. The shells of our most powerful cannons bounce harmlessly off their shields."

"Aliens, huh? Brother, I've heard everything now. How about it, Colonel Stark? Did you see aliens from outer space too?"

"I don't know what I saw! But I saw something; something that I don't want to face again."

"Okay. You're both under house arrest. You stay here and cool your heels. I'll deal with your renegades or whatever. When I get back, I'll deal with you two."

Chapter 26

Revenge of the Ancients

General Varco was in a foul mood. His war briefings of late seemed more like sermons of ill bodings rather than the cheers of men after a victorious campaign. Once again, he faced his commanders in the conference room. However, this time, instead of an atmosphere of confidence and light-heartedness that had once pervaded their briefings, their countenance now appeared to reflect gloom and pessimism. A feeling of desperation seemed to have settled in. General Varco was seated at the head of the assembly, but it was Dr. Friedman who was standing on the podium addressing a downcast audience.

"Gentlemen," he began, "we have come to a situation .... No. Let's call it a crisis; a tragedy. Never in my wildest dreams would I have thought or could I have imagined the events that have transpired over the past ten days. Let me recap. We engaged our ancestors in two battles in which we killed approximately 800 hundred of them and wounded another 400 hundred. We destroyed their weapons and drove them back to their fort. It was an easy victory; easy for us. We knew they were weak and couldn't defend themselves against us. Yet we chose to attack and kill them. We knew it was the wrong thing to do. I knew it in my heart and I know most of you must have, deep down, felt the same way. But the wolf on the trail of blood has no conscience or pity, nor did we. We killed our ancestral fathers, without pity, without remorse, and without thinking about the consequences.

"Well, let me tell you," continued the Doctor. "We are now beginning to see the consequences of our actions. We killed approximately eight hundred of our ancestors. Then, much to our amazement, we discovered seventeen thousand one hundred and fifty six of our soldiers and sailors, not only those on the ground, but also those still aboard the ships that had not even landed, were dead or missing. The enemy, as General Varco calls our ancestors, killed them without firing a shot, except for that short volley in the beginning. Yes. The Americans have killed seventeen thousand one hundred fifty six of our men. That's only the beginning. Back at home, they have reported seven hundred ninety-seven thousand people dead; just vanished from the face of the Earth. President Harbill is thunderstruck. He's having a very difficult time keeping the people under control. The whole country is in mourning. How could this happen? How could we have possibly lost that many people? Our forefathers must have done it. How did our forefathers kill all those people? They killed them when they, themselves, died. How did they die? We murdered them! We did not pay heed to Doctor Steebler's warning. He told us to be very cautious when dealing with anybody from this time period. We ignored him. Well, we can't ignore this! For every person we kill while in this time period approximately ten thousand of our citizens, either here or back home, will die; just vanish from the Earth like they were never born. The figure will vary, depending on our genealogy, but the equation works out fairly accurately."

Varco spoke up, "Are you blaming me? I don't like your inferences."

"I'm not blaming anybody, General, but …. Hell yes! I am blaming you! I'm also blaming the rest of us. I did plead with you to let me talk to them, but you were so dead set on a military victory that you wouldn't even consider any other solutions."

"You were wounded. You couldn't talk to anybody," Varco grumbled defensively.

The look Doctor Friedman gave Varco emphasized the utter disdain and contempt he felt for the General. "Like I said, I'm not specifically blaming anybody. We all had a part of it. However, by presidential order, I have been placed in charge of this Mission and I intend to see us out of this mess. Our only job right now is to salvage what we can and continue in our quest to find someplace where we can establish our colony."

148

At that moment, Admiral Kukov entered the briefing room and approached Doctor Friedman. "Sir, I think you and General Varco had better come with me."

Doctor Friedman motioned to Varco and the three of them departed. "Where are we going?" asked Friedman.

"To the nearest observation post." said Kukov.

In the observation post, Varco's and the Doctor's attention was directed to a view screen. The screen portrayed images projected from front line surveillance cameras, previously installed by General Varco.

"What the ...?" exclaimed Varco.

What they saw in the view screen was a fresh build up of American arms. A wall of new huge cannons and batteries of mortars and howitzers lined the entrance to their gates. Thousands of uniformed armed men surrounded their entire complex. Crude looking tanks patrolled the perimeter. Overhead, equally clumsy looking flying machines flew directly over and around the buildings.

"Where'd they come from?" queried Varco.

"Moved in fast, didn't they?" answered Friedman.

"I'll take care of this little problem," said Varco.

"Varco, shut up!" ordered Friedman. "Evidently you didn't hear a damn word I said. We can't do anything. We can't fire one shot. We must not kill even one more person, soldier or civilian."

"What are we going to do?" asked Admiral Kukov.

"All right. It's going to be touch and go but here's what I propose," said Friedman. "We will have to get out of this time zone. I believe what our goal should be is to reprogram our ships' computers to take off from here, re-enter the Aborium Tunnel, and make our way back to 6000 B.C. For the moment, as long as we have our shields up, the Americans can't really do much damage to us. I don't know how long it will take for the computers to be reprogrammed, but we have plenty of supplies to last us for any number of months. Hopefully, it will not take that long."

"Look!" interrupted Varco, pointing at the screen,

149

"They've started. They're firing at us." As Varco said, the American batteries began dropping shells on the base's structures. As before, the shells exploded but failed to cause any damage due to the protective shields covering the entire base. The lack of effectiveness of their cannon-fire did not seem to dampen the enthusiasm of the artillerymen as they repeatedly expended a seemingly never-ending supply of shells on their invincible targets.

"I don't know how long they can keep this up, but I do know one thing for sure," said Admiral Kukov.

"What's that?" asked Friedman.

"When we get ready to fly out of here, we're going to have to dismantle this base. That means we'll have to take down our shields. During the interim, between the time when we take down our shields, dismantle the base, pack our equipment, and prepare for take-off, if they continue this bombardment we will be unprotected, vulnerable to their attacks."

"You're right," said Friedman, "and we can't leave anything behind."

Kukov frowned. "Their guns could cause us a lot of trouble. They're reasonably accurate. They could destroy us before we got off the ground."

"The problem is how to quiet those guns without killing anybody while we dismantle our base?" pondered Friedman.

Chapter 27

Unauthorized

Helen Mercer was the Ship Historian. It was a job she had relentlessly pursued, relished, and worked hard at. However, she was not quite satisfied. Something was missing. Something else was challenging her. Besides being a researcher and collector of facts, she had the heart and soul of a reporter. She sensed she was on the verge of witnessing one of the greatest moments of history and saw this as an opportunity to see the World in the 20th century as it was before there were domes and a chance to actually meet and talk to the people of that era. Helen Mercer decided she was not going to miss this once-in-a-lifetime opportunity. She knew Doctor Friedman, who was now in charge, would not give her authorization to leave the base, so she began planning on ways to leave secretly, without permission.

Three things she had in her favor; her looks, her brains, and a scheming mind. She had studied and mastered all of the major languages of that era and could speak the English of that era almost flawlessly. She also had a wardrobe collection she had brought along, just in case, and, luckily, some of the dresses were in the fashion of the day. She enlisted the aid of her staff, a secretary, an editor, and a researcher. They were thrilled to be part of the conspiracy and vowed to keep her mission a secret. They helped her assemble her wardrobe and coached her overall appearance. They were excited about her quest and wanted to go with her but realized it would be unwise. It was just too dangerous.

The big problem was how to get out of the compound without being seen. Access to most of the work sites and restricted areas were no trouble. The beautiful historian had been seen all over the compound and was well known to all of the site supervisors. They had seen her credentials and assumed she, in pursuit of her job, could go just about wherever she pleased. In fact, most of them were so flattered when she singled them out for interviews that they eagerly escorted her around and gave her all the details of the their areas of responsibility and the importance of their jobs.

Regrettably for Helen, the one area that she was most interested in was not under the supervision of any of those so easily charmed men. Helen had heard rumors about the compound's water supply system. According to unsubstantiated reports, it was believed that the compound's water supply was pumped all the way from a purification plant at the edge of the Columbia River to holding tanks inside the compound. The rumors were that the engineers had constructed a water system with a tunnel and pipeline, all underground, and camouflaged it so well it could not be seen at ground level. It was also believed that, for maintenance purposes, there had been a catwalk constructed alongside the tunnel all the way to the edge of the river and that there was a secret exit to the outside at the end of the catwalk. Helen believed these reports were true, not just rumors, and was determined to leave exactly that way. There was no doubt in her mind that, once there, she could find the secret exit. But to get into that tunnel and on that catwalk she would have to get by security.

Unfortunately, Max Bower barred her way. Max was a Major in the Security Sector and was in charge of the security of the compound's water system. He was a very tough, rough talking, sixty-year-old career soldier. He wouldn't even give Helen an appointment to see him. To do so she stopped and confronted him in a darkened hallway. He could not be charmed and was not impressed by a pretty face. After Helen's attempts to talk to him in a friendly manner failed, she tried the straight business approach.

"Major Bower," she said, "perhaps you don't know me. Let me introduce myself. I am Helen Mercer. I am the officially appointed Ship Historian and an official representative of the Federal Government. I have been commissioned by the

152

government to publish an historical record of all of the events concerning the Expeditionary Force. I have a top-secret clearance and I am authorized access to any and all of the facilities of this compound, including the water supply system. Here is my identification card. I am certainly not a foreign agent plotting some evil scheme. Surely you can see that."

The Major, without even the courtesy of an acknowledging glance, took the proffered card, looked at it briefly and handed it back to her. "Look lady," he said. "I don't give a damn a who you are. I ain't talkin to you and you ain't goin' down in the tunnel, so just peddle your ass back to wherever you came from and quit botherin' me."

"You don't have to be rude! I find you attitude very offensive! As a security officer, don't you have some kind of guidelines to tell you who has secret clearances and who is and who is not authorized? I'm going to report you for abusing your authority to Dr. Friedman," said Helen.

"Get off your high horse, lady and quit tryin' to bullshit me. You can report me to whoever you want. If Friedman tells me you can go down there, then I'll let you go. Until then, you ain't goin' anywhere near the water system. Now get your butt outta here!"

Helen left the major and returned to her quarters. She had to think. She had never been one to let a little adversity stand in her way and she wasn't about to let this boorish, senile, ill-mannered bully stop her. She would have to go about this in a different way. Perhaps the major would see things a little differently if the orders came from a slightly higher authority and then maybe a little sleight of hand.

Helen's next stop was Dr. Friedman. She had no trouble arranging a meeting with him. At the appointed hour she was escorted to his office, a make-shift-laboratory, where she found him slumped over his desk, studying what looked like a mound of paperwork. "Come in. Have a seat," he said gesturing towards an empty chair, the only one left that didn't have a pile of paperwork in it. Dr. Friedman was obviously not a good housekeeper.

153

"Thank you for seeing me, Doctor," she replied, "I won't take up much of your time. I see you are very busy."

"That's quite alright, Miss Mercer. I'm very glad to see you. I was going to send for you, anyway. First, I want to apologize for the way you were treated at that planning meeting you attended with General Varco, Admiral Kukov, and I. I'm sure you remember. I've thought about you ever since then. You briefed us about the capability of the Americans' armed forces. The information you supplied us was one hundred percent accurate. Also, your statement that our ancestors are not the enemy and your suggestion that we negotiate were excellent recommendations, but, unfortunately, not well taken. You advised us. We ignored you. You showed courage, standing up to us like that. Then, you were insulted and dismissed. Even though I was aware and did not approve of the way the General was conducting the meeting, I did not interfere. For that, I truly apologize."

"That's quite alright, Doctor," said Helen, a little flustered and embarrassed. The Doctor's apology was totally unexpected.

"No, it's not alright and not that easy. Failing to negotiate and the subsequent waging of war against our ancestors was a terrible decision; a decision that brought attention to us and, even worse, caused over nine hundred thousand of our own people to die. For this, General Varco has been relieved of duty. I have been placed in charge of the Expeditionary Force."

"I had heard. Congratulations on your promotion," said Helen.

"We cannot undo what's been done," went on the Doctor, ignoring her congratulations. He derived no pleasurable thoughts regarding what he didn't consider a promotion. "However, you can rest assured there will be no more bloodshed. I want you to understand, though, the colony must still be established. We have to fulfill our mission. Plans are being made. We are going to leave this time zone, go back to 6000 B.C., and finish the job we set out to do."

154

"That's wonderful news, Doctor! Ah, how long will it be before we leave?" asked Helen.

"There are some details that have to be worked out," said the Doctor. "Maybe between two and three weeks. I hope I've answered your questions. This is the reason you wanted to see me. Isn't it?"

"Yes. Doctor, you've filled me in on most of the details and I thank you for being so straight forward with me." Actually Helen was stunned. She was getting information she hadn't even asked for, but not what she wanted. She pressed on. "However, there is one more little matter I wanted to talk to you about."

"Oh."

"Yes, Sir. I am at the stage of my writing where I am detailing the inner workings of the colony, the mechanics of it, if you know what I mean."

"No. I don't know exactly what you mean."

"You know, the details of the day-to-day workings; the soldiers, how they are quartered how the food is prepared, their daily regimen. Then there are the different jobs of supervisors and engineers who oversee the vast array of little but necessary jobs that need attending to. None of the things that I'm looking into are sensitive as far as security is concerned, but they are important as far as history is concerned," said Helen.

"So, I don't understand your problem," replied the Doctor. "You have a clearance to go anywhere in this compound you want, except the most secret areas like the weapons center and the ships computers. The only people allowed in those areas are operators with a need-to-know clearance."

"Oh, – I don't want to go in those areas, Sir, but I would like to see the working of our water supply system. I understand it's quite a marvel."

"No. I'm sorry, Miss Mercer. That's another one of those areas that's off-limits."

"Oh, I don't want to go down into the water system, Sir. If Major Boyer would just give me a little briefing …. That's all I want, but he won't even give me a chance to talk to him."

Doctor Friedman chuckled, "the major's a pretty tough

nut to crack, isn't he? But, if that's all you want, I'll give him a call and have him set up an appointment with you. Mind you, I won't guarantee his manners."

Helen, thinking furiously, made her way back to her quarters. Phase one was completed. Now, she was about to put phase two of her plan into action. Ellie Christie, her best friend and secretary, a girl who almost matched Helen in beauty, was about to be called into action. She was a perfect choice. Helen was about to ask Ellie to play a bigger role in her scheme; a scheme that was not without its elements of excitement, danger, and risks. Only someone with nerves of steel and completely trustworthy could be asked to do what Helen was going to propose. Ellie appeared to be eager and ready.

"So, what's up? What are we going to do?" she asked.

"You are going to be me," replied Helen.

"You mean I'm going to go with you?" said Ellie excitedly.

"No Honey, but you are going to help me get out of the compound. Let me explain to you what's going on. I can't get permission to go in the tunnel. The closest they'll let me get to the tunnel is at a briefing inside Major Bower's office. Major Bower is in charge of the water systems security. His office overlooks the tunnel's entrances and exits. His only job is to watch those entrances with his eyes and his surveillance cameras. He is there sixteen hours a day. A sergeant, who's just as surly as he is, relieves him for eight hours every night. Outside that, he's always there on constant watch."

"Wow! He sounds almost impossible to get by."

"It's *almost* impossible, but not quite. Just a few feet from his office, in the direction of the exit, is a sharp bend. If I can get by his office and around that bend, he can't see me. I'll be out of sight of his eyes and the surveillance camera."

"He'd have to be very unobservant not to see somebody trying to sneak by him," said Ellie.

"Not if his attention was diverted," replied Helen, looking very intently at Ellie.

"Divert his attention? Is that what you want me to do?

156

"I can only ask. It's up to you."

"How?"

"Ok. Here's the situation. Tomorrow, at three P.M., I have an appointment to see Major Bower in his office. He has promised to give me a good briefing outlining the all the functions of the water supply system. He said it would be a detailed briefing. I think Doctor Friedman must have said something to him about the way he talked to me. He's probably feeling just a little bit guilty. Anyway, if you're up to it, I want you to dress up like me and attend that meeting."

"He'll know it's not you. He's seen you and talked to you," said Ellie.

"No. He won't know the difference. We were in a dark hall when we met and he didn't even look at my face. We look enough alike to be sisters and our voices are about the same pitch. I guarantee you he will not question your identity."

"What if I get caught?" asked Ellie dubiously.

"If you get caught, I get caught. I'll take care of you. They can't do too much to us. I do have some influence around here. Are you game?"

After a slight hesitation, Ellie looked at Helen, shrugged her shoulders and said, "Okay. Let's do it."

"Alright," said Helen, "here's the way we'll set it up. At two fifty-five tomorrow afternoon, you show up at Major Bower's office with a visi-recorder. Smile and be polite. Don't try to sweet-talk him. You'll only turn him off and make him angry. Once you're in his office, start plying him with questions. Get him thinking about the water system. Whatever you do, keep yourself between him and the glass windows in front of the tunnel exit.

As soon as he takes you in the office, I'll sneak up and hide right outside his office. Then, crouching as low as I can, I'll make my way towards the bend in the tunnel. This will be the most critical time for us. It will take me about two minutes to reach the bend. During this time, you must keep in front of him. I don't care how you do it, but don't let him look past you. Drop your visi-recorder if you have to. Maybe he'll stoop down to

157

pick it up. If you can keep his eyes off the tunnel for two minutes, I'll be gone; out of sight. After that, you can thank him for his time. Tell him his water system isn't the big deal you thought it was and you're not really that interested in it anymore. I'd love to see his face when you tell him that," laughed Helen.

"I don't think I'm going do that," said Ellie, frowning.

"Whatever." said Helen, still laughing at the thought of seeing Major Boyer rant and rave when he was told that his little job was so insignificant and unimportant that it wasn't even worthy of her time.

"I don't think I want to get on his bad side."

"I was just wishfully thinking. I'd like to see someone puncture that big Neanderthal's balloon, though."

"Helen, I didn't realize you were so vengeful."

"I'm sorry. Ellie. Ordinarily, I'm not, but he really got nasty with me. Of course, you're right. Be nice and let him finish the briefing. Who knows? Maybe he'll tell you something that's worth recording. Anyway, after the briefing, go back to the office. You and the staff stay there until I get back. I'll try to be back in seven days. You'll have to cover for me. If I'm not back in eight days, you can assume something has gone wrong. You'll find a sealed letter in my safe. Give it to Doctor Friedman."

"Helen, you're scaring me! Do you think we can really do it?"

"Honey, don't you worry. I believe we girls can do most anything we set our minds to."

Chapter 28

Unexpected Company

Getting by Major Bower was much easier then Helen expected. When Ellie, disguised as Helen, showed up for the appointment, she was greeted by the major, who was all smiles, and politely escorted into his office. Once in the office, he seated her at a table already prepared with refreshments and, with exaggerated aplomb, sat down across from her with his back to the window. He was the perfect gentleman. Despite his prior conduct, he apparently could conduct himself in a civilized manner and, perhaps, even enjoy the company of a beautiful woman. He dominated the conversation and conducted the entire briefing in his office without either of them ever moving from the table.

Helen, who had no way of knowing what an easy time Ellie was having of it, had little trouble sneaking into the tunnel and disappearing around the bend. From there, she began her long trek following the tunnel's catwalk as it wended its way toward the river. She knew, from her research, that it was about a five mile walk and estimated it would take two to three hours for her to reach the end. She carried a bag for her accessories and change of clothes. It seemed to get heavier and heavier with each mile. She was beginning to have doubts about her ability to carry out her plan. Lack of exercise back home had not exactly prepared her for this type work. On and on she went, one foot in front of the other until she became mesmerized by the monotony of her motion. Finally, numb of mind and body, the tunnel came to an abrupt end. She stopped and sat down. She had to rest and collect her thoughts. Slowly, she regained her strength and her resolve. She took a glow-wand out her bag, which lit up the entire end of the tunnel. Getting to her feet, she made her way to the end of the catwalk and began to look around for the exit. Her examination of the area proved to be fruitless. "Well," she said to herself, "they said it was a secret entrance. I'll just have to try harder."

For hours, Helen poked, probed, and pushed every wall and ceiling she could reach until her hands were sore. She began to feel disheartened and discouraged. She hated the thought of giving up, but her strength was giving out on her. She felt ever so tired. She sat down. "I'll just rest for a moment," she thought to herself. Slowly, her eyes closed. Lulled by the eerie silence of the tunnel, her mind began drifting away into a state of semi-consciousness, but just as she was about to succumb to sleep, in the recesses of her mind, she heard something. Straining to hear, she could make out the almost imperceptible sound of trickling water. Suddenly alert, she sat straight up. She had definitely heard running water and it wasn't coming from the tunnel. The Columbia River had to be near, maybe just a few feet away. Now thoroughly awake, she crawled forward and, grabbing her wand, pointed it down and peered into the depths under the catwalk. If a person were not looking for it, he or she would surely not see the small stream running under the pipeline or the steps in the dark leading to it. Helen thought she now knew where the exit was. Being as careful as possible, she made her way down the dark stairway only to lose her balance on the last step and fall headfirst into the stream. Fortunately, it was fairly shallow. Struggling to get up, she found herself waist deep in freezing cold water. Walking against the current, she fought her way upstream until she came to what looked like a wall at the end of the tunnel. In desperation and fearing another dead end, Helen pushed on the wall with all her might. To her astonishment, the wall gave way. Helen staggered forward. When she regained her balance, she looked up and realized she had fallen through the secret opening. She was standing in the shallows on the river bank, outside the tunnel. Even now, looking back, she couldn't see where the opening was. Close examination revealed its whereabouts. It was right there on the side of the river, completely covered by a massive growth of giant ferns. If a person did not know exactly where to look, it

160

would be impossible to see the opening that led to the secret entrance of the tunnel.

Cold and shivering, Helen sat down by the edge of the river to collect her thoughts. Miraculously, she had managed to hang onto her wand and her bag that she now hugged tightly to her chest. "Thank goodness my bag was waterproof! At least my clothes will be dry," she thought.

For a long period of time, Helen just sat there, unable to move or think. Finally, like she was coming out of a trance, she became aware of her surroundings. She looked about to see if there was any imminent danger. All seemed to be clear. It was night and she found herself sitting by the river. Rolling and swirling, the river majestically made its way westward, toward the sea. To the right of the river, softly illuminated by winking stars and a full moon, was a meadow of waving grass. It looked so beautiful, it took Helen's breath away. Never, back home, had she seen anything that compared to the wondrous sights she was witnessing. Already, it seemed to her that coming outside the confines of the compound was worth the effort.

Looking across the meadow about two hundred yards inland, she sighted a line of trees. Although the meadow was beautiful, she knew it would be dangerous to stay here in the open where she could be easily spotted. She needed to get to a covered secluded area where she could hide until she was ready to make an appearance. The trees, which appeared to be the edge of a forest, would hopefully make a good hiding place. Stealthily, she made her way across the meadow. The meadow, which she had found so beautiful, now presented unexpected obstacles like deep grass that could cut and sting, stickers that imbedded themselves in her clothing, and flying insects that hovered over her head. The walk through the meadow to the trees was extremely difficult and took much longer to traverse than she had expected. Gratefully, she reached the forest and found a sheltered clearing that suited her needs. Kneeling over a convenient log, she spread open and studied a map. It was a map that had been provided her by one of her pilot friends who, on a reconnaissance mission, had charted the entire area. He had

161

spoken to her of an old abandoned house on the edge of the forest. Helen decided that was the place she could go that would provide the privacy she needed; a place where she could change her clothes, freshen up a bit, and make herself presentable to the outside world. She knew it would be difficult, but she planned to make her way from there to a spot on the map; a little town named Walla Walla. It was Helen's intention to go there, blend in with the populace, make her historical observations, and then make her way back to the compound. She realized the task she had set out for herself was an extremely difficult one, but it was one she felt she had a very good chance of completing successfully. With renewed high hopes, she set off for the old abandoned house.

When she arrived there, her first impression of the old house was one of deep foreboding. "It would take someone who was very desperate to come to a place like this," she thought. However, she shook off her anxiety, and firmly holding her stun gun in one hand and her wand and bag in the other, advanced cautiously to the old shack's broken-down doorway and peered inside. As she expected, it was old and incredibly filthy, but, apparently, as she had been told, uninhabited. It would serve her purpose. However, unfortunately for Helen, she was not alone.

Billy Bob Morris, the depraved homeless vagrant who had lived in the old abandoned farmhouse for so long now he thought of it as his house, was watching her. After the sheriff released him from the county jail, he had returned to the old house and, with the Sheriff's permission, resumed residency. He was just returning from a night's scavenging when, at the at the wood's edge, he observed the strangest phenomenon. He rubbed his eyes and stared in wonder. A strangely dressed woman headed right for the house. He wondered what in the world would a woman be doing coming here, especially at this time of night. From observing the way she was dressed, it was apparent that she was no ordinary woman and that flashlight she was carrying – he had never seen anything like that before. Billy watched in disbelief as she made her way to the entrance, peered in, and then disappeared inside. Strange woman or not, he was

162

not about to let someone move into his home. He moved toward the house.

Suddenly, a voice, hardly more than a whisper, but carrying the sound of authority, came out of nowhere. "Don't move!" it commanded.

Billy stopped, dead still. He suddenly found himself surrounded by men in military uniform who grabbed him from behind and not too gently and wrestled him to the ground where they quickly bound and gagged him. Billy was terrified. He tried to scream, but one of the men clamped his hand over Billy's mouth effectively shutting him up. Another man, one who seemed to be the leader of the group, bent down in front of Billy, stuffed a gag down his throat and signaled for silence.

"Do you speak English?" asked the leader quietly.

Wild-eyed, Billy vigorously nodded yes.

"Are you the one they call Billy Bob?" Again, Billy nodded yes.

"I want to talk to you," said the leader. "I'll take the gag out if you promise not to scream." Again, Billy nodded in the affirmative.

"If you scream, I'll shoot you," said the leader waving a big revolver in his face.

Billy, trembling in fear and eyes wide open, nodded his head. Much to his relief, the gag was removed. He didn't make a sound.

"We've been watching this area for a long time. Are you the one who lives in that house?"

"Yes, Sir."

"Who's that woman that went in there?"

"I don't know, Sir."

"She's not an acquaintance of yours?"

"Honest, Cap'n! I ain't never seen her before."

"I'm not a captain, Billy, I'm Major Chambers, a security officer from Fort Lewis."

"Yes, Sir," mumbled Billy Bob in a quavering voice.

"We were briefed about you. We heard that you're allowed to live out here in this old farmhouse, because nobody

163

wants you in town bothering the civilized townsfolk. They tell me the sheriff said if he caught you in town, he'd have his deputies bust you up. You don't exactly seem like the social type. Do you, Billy? I find it strange that you suddenly have someone visiting you. It looks suspicious. You're hardly the type that would attract anybody to come and see you unless you are providing something. We're pretty sure we know what you've been up to. While our forces were fighting an unidentified enemy, our scouts spotted you sneaking around. We're going to investigate. Why were you sneaking around the enemy's base and who is that woman we saw going in the house? We're pretty sure she's an agent from the enemy's camp. If we find out that you have in any way collaborated, aided, or provided information to the enemy, well – I'll just say you'd be in pretty big trouble. You could be considered a traitor. That's a capital offense. Do you know what that means?"

"No, Sir," whimpered Billy.

"It means you could get the electric chair. Right now, it looks pretty bad for you, so, if you know anything, you better tell us now."

"I swear! I ain't never seen her before. She just came outta nowhere. Honest, I don't know nothin' about her, and I ain't never met or even seen one of them Martians, 'cept from a distance."

"You're saying you've never talked to this woman? I don't believe you. Corporal Snipes!" called the Major.

A soldier in battle uniform hurriedly arrived at the major's side and reported. "Sir!"

"Take this prisoner back to the truck and lock him up. I want to take him back to the fort for further questioning. Gawd! He sure is a filthy looking thing isn't he?" said the Major as he wiped his hands on his trousers as if trying to rid himself any contamination that may have been transmitted to him from his encounter with the filthy-looking Billy Bob.

After the Corporal departed with his prisoner in tow, Major Chambers looked toward the farmhouse. He motioned for one of his men who moved in beside him. "Sergeant, take three men and check around the side and back of the building. If there are any other entrances, block them off. I don't want whoever is in there slipping out unnoticed. I think we're dealing with a woman. If she tries to leave, stop her. Whatever you do, don't kill her. Wound her if you have to, but I want her alive. I believe whoever is in there is from that alien base and I want her for questioning. The sergeant gathered up three soldiers and headed out for the back of the building.

The capture of Helen Mercer was without incident. Finding herself suddenly bathed in light and surrounded by a dozen soldiers, pointing weapons at her and screaming: "Put down you weapons!" left her with no choice. She dropped her bag, her stun gun, and wand, and raised her arms over her head.

Not being able to get a good look at her face, Major Chambers eyed his quarry and cautiously advanced towards what he thought was a dangerous enemy agent. With his revolver ready he shined his flashlight in her face. His immediate reaction was one of total amazement. He didn't really know what he expected, perhaps some kind of fierce looking female warrior, but he was certainly not expecting his captive to be a harmless and defenseless looking beautiful girl.

"Major," you better look at these, said the sergeant who had picked up Helen's wand and stun gun. He held them out. Major Chambers looked them over them very carefully.

"I've never seen anything like these before," said the Major.

"I don't think she's human, Sir," said the sergeant, suspiciously. "She's too pretty. Ya better be careful. She might be one of them Sireens you read about."

"Of course she's human! What do you think? She's some kind of a space vampire? No. She's human enough, however, I do believe she's from that alien base. Pat her down and search her. Make sure she doesn't have any more weapons on her. Then, we'll take her back to the fort and let the General decide what he wants to do with her."

Helen studied the two men as they discussed her fate. "I wouldn't advise your subordinate to touch me," she said almost indifferently to the man who was obviously the leader of the group. The sergeant, who had stepped forward to search her, stopped instantly and rolled his eyes from the prisoner to the Major. He was definitely having second thoughts about putting his hands on her.

"Why not?" asked Major Chambers. "Sergeant, I gave you an order! I said, 'Search her!'"

"You never know. Maybe your sergeant is right," said Helen. "Maybe something terrible will happen to him. Come on, Sergeant, if you think nothing will happen to you, just touch me. Have you ever seen a man die, writhing in pain and not even known why? Just touch me. I've watched men like you die many times." She suddenly thrust her hand out as if to grab him and laughed mockingly as he jumped back in horror. "I've never had that kind of reaction from a man before," she chuckled.

Major Chambers spoke up. "Ok, lady! Have your fun. Before I blow a hole in your head, you better tell me who you are, where you're from, and what you're doing here," he said leveling his revolver at her forehead.

"My name is Helen Mercer. I am a citizen. I don't know by what authority you are detaining me. I haven't broken any laws that I now of."

"I am Major Chambers, a security officer assigned out of Fort Lewis and I'm arresting you on charges of trespassing, espionage, and threatening the life of a soldier under my command. Also, I don't believe you're a citizen. I think you're an alien sent out from your base to spy on our defenses."

Helen shrugged and, looking as innocent and disarming as only Helen could, said, "Look at me, Major. Do I look like a threat? There's no use denying it. Yes. I am from the alien base, as you call it, but I am not a spy. I have come to your world strictly on my own, without permission or authority. My people from the base don't even know I'm here. I am a historian and I just wanted to see what the Earth was like in the 20th century. Look at the way I'm dressed. Do I look like I have any weapons on me? It's pretty obvious that I'm defenseless. Is it in your instructions to shoot defenseless people?"

166

"What about your threats to my sergeant? And what did you mean when you said you wanted to see what it's like in the 20th century?"

"I was just reacting to not wanting to be searched and your sergeant's ridiculous notion that I was some kind of monster. People usually like me and, as far as what I meant about the 20th century, it's a long story."

"What about this weapon?" said the Major, holding up Helen's gun.

"It's just a stun gun," she said. "It can't hurt anybody – just puts them to sleep. It's strictly for self defense."

"I've never seen anything like this before," murmured the Major. "Alright, Miss Mercer," he said aloud. "I don't know whether to believe you or not, but I am placing you under arrest and taking you back to the fort for questioning."

Chapter 29

A Shadow of Hope

Seated in the offices of the Colony's Command Headquarters were Doctor Friedman, Admiral Kukov, and General Varco. Doctor Friedman, for the third time in the last four days, had once again summoned his two key officers for a meeting. He needed their advice. He realized that, although he had been elevated to the position of Commanding Officer of the Expeditionary Force, he was not an expert in military affairs and tactics. They were the experts and he was not about to make any decisions without consulting them.

"Gentlemen," he addressed them. "Every day we sit here with our hands tied, unable to carry on with our mission, we are losing valuable time. We must do something. We have to come up with some kind of a plan to break out of this stalemate. We cannot forget that, back in our own time zone, our countrymen are desperately waiting for us to establish a colony. They're depending on us. They're lives are in our hands. Our situation is desperate. We want to leave this planet and this time zone so we can resume our projected voyage to the year 6000 B.C. Which is when and where we had initially planned to establish the colony. To leave this time zone, we have to dismantle and pack our base. To do this, we'll have to take down our shields. Taking down the shields would make us vulnerable to their attacks. Even as we sit here discussing what we should do, the Americans are daily pounding our base with their long-range artillery and it doesn't look like they're going to let up. As long as we maintain our shields, they can't hurt us. Without the shields, they would destroy us. So, here we sit. We've got to do something and we've got to do it now."

"What about our stun-guns?" asked Admiral Kukov.

"They're not effective for mass warfare," replied General

Varco.

"Is there some way we could adapt them to make them more efficient?" queried Doctor Friedman.

"No," answered the General, "they were designed just for self defense, to be able to render one or two people unconscious for a few hours. They won't work on a large scale and they won't work over a long distance. They only have a range of about 100 feet."

"Would it be possible to send the rest of the Armada on?" asked Admiral Kukov. "Let's not forget, we only landed eleven of our ships here; nine transporters and two battle cruisers. We still have ten transporters and one hospital ship in orbit. Why not send them on? Let them re-enter the tunnel and establish the colony."

"You mean sacrifice ourselves?" asked General Varco. "We die or surrender so the mission can go on? Who's going to lead them? That doesn't sound like a very good idea to me."

"If that's what it takes, yes! Sacrifice ourselves for the greater good," replied Kukov.

"Your plan is noble," said Friedman, "but it won't work. The master computer for the entire fleet is down here with us on the flagship, where our science officers are presently reprogramming it. The Armada's ships' computers are slaves and can't make the necessary computations to travel back in time. If they attempted the jump and failed, then all would be lost."

"What about the probe? Didn't you insist that we bring Professor Arbore's original probe along with us and isn't it already programmed for time zone travel?" asked Kukov.

"Yes it is. I brought it along only to be used in an extreme emergency, but it can't be used, either. The computer installed on the probe is an older model. It doesn't have the capability of a master computer. It could be sent out on its own, but it can't be used as a navigational control for the rest of the Armada," explained Dr. Friedman.

"Well, I've got the solution," interjected General Varco. "You talk about sacrificing for the greater good. As you said, there are a billion people back home who are depending on us to evacuate them off the planet before it is literally torn apart by tornadoes and hurricanes. The only way I can see out of this situation is to silence the American cannons. Let's do some simple math. If we sent out one of our battle cruisers, we could quite easily destroy all of their weapons in one skirmish, thus ending their threat to destroy us while we dismantle our base. The American casualties in this operation, figuring what happened last time, would be approximately four hundred men. Our casualties, using Dr. Friedman's formula, would be four hundred thousand, most of them back on Earth. Wouldn't it be a noble sacrifice for four hundred thousand citizens to give up their lives for the greater good to save the lives of one billion? I say let's use a military solution and get rid of those cannons. By then, our computers will be reprogrammed. We can leave this forsaken place and go back to our task at hand, which is to establish a colony on Earth in 6000 B.C."

"How do you know who is going to die?" queried Dr. Friedman. It could be you, or me, or President Harbill, or Dr. Steebler. So far, we've been lucky, but who knows who will die the next time we kill an ancestor."

"None of us will die," snorted Varco. "Didn't you notice from the casualty reports who mostly died in the last conflict? It was mostly people from the lower working class. The American soldiers we killed – they were all what they called, in those days, "cannon fodder". They're the sons of poor dirt farmers and laborers. Their descendents are of the same lineage. Even the people of our generation, the people that would die from my proposed operation, would be from the lower class, the common working class, and the foot soldiers. Those people, we can afford to lose. The elite, those of us from good breeding, the intelligencia of our society, would be spared."

"I can't believe what you just said!" gasped Dr. Friedman. "Surely, you're not serious! Who are you? You think you're some kind of superior being who is better that anybody else and can decide who lives and who dies? This is too much! You can't really believe that anyone would consider what you just recommended. Don't you have any feelings of compassion

170

or consideration for your fellow man? The President truly did not understand who you are and what you represent when he entrusted you to command the Expeditionary Force."

"You can't talk to me this way, Friedman! I *am* superior!" said Varco, getting to his feet and pointing his finger. "I'm too critical a member to this council. I am the key to our success. You're not even a military man. You're just a scientist, poking your nose about where it doesn't belong. The only way we can salvage this operation is to destroy those cannons. Those of us that die will pay the supreme sacrifice, but our mission will succeed. The soldiers will listen to me."

"You mean the soldiers that you would so easily let die for the greater good?" retorted the Doctor, rising from his desk and motioning. "Sit down, Varco and come to your senses before I have you escorted from the room. You are very close to being removed from this council!" Like a belligerent animal, threatened by his trainer, General Varco returned to his seat.

Seeing that Varco had unruffled his feathers and settled down, Friedman said, "I do have a plan.   You gave me the idea, Admiral, when you mentioned the probe and the stun gun. Let me run this by you and see what you think. Before I left earth on this mission, some of the projects that our engineers were working on were the development of new weapons. I wasn't directly involved in the work of any of these projects, but I do remember talk about developing weapons for riot control. It just may be possible that by now they have come up with a way to control or even disable crowds without killing or injuring them. I'm going to contact Dr. Steebler to see if any of these weapons are ready for deployment. If we had a stun gun when we left earth, I'd bet, by now, we have a weapon for riot control. If we do, we'll send Arbore's probe back to Earth, pick up the new weapons, and bring them back here. The trip there and back would take about eight days. That won't be too long to wait. From there, it would be a simple process to disable the Americans long enough for us to pack up and get the hell out of here – and no one gets hurt."

Once contacted, Dr. Steebler, in answer to Friedman's

171

request, affirmed that, indeed, a weapon for riot control had been developed that could immobilize large crowds without injuring them. The plan, as Dr. Friedman proposed, was adopted. Admiral Kukov dispatched orders for the Probe to be readied for a flight. He ordered it moored alongside a maintenance freighter and sent fleet Chief Engineer, Commander Mohamed Jamul, with his crew aboard, to service it and perform the necessary preflight inspections. The Probe had not seen service since Professor Arbore's historical flight, almost three years ago. However, over the years, it had been maintained as if it was a ship of the line and kept in flight-ready condition. The inspections being performed were double safety precautions to insure the integrity of the systems. These were standard maintenance requirements for all commissioned fleet ships on active duty. It took two days to complete the probe's preflight inspections, after which Commander Jamul declared it operational. A crew of two would be selected for the mission and would proceed with the journey as soon as the orders and clearances were received from Dr. Friedman. In the meantime, an unusual and unexpected situation was evolving aboard the hospital ship.

172

Chapter 30

Doctor Menes' Strange Request

Dr. Friedman was annoyed that, at a time when he did not have the time to give, he was asked by the administrators of the hospital ship to consider a request. He did not ordinarily interfere with the other ships' affairs and didn't see why they needed him now. However, the hospital administrators did not think that anybody aboard their ship had the authority to settle this particular and unprecedented request and asked Friedman to intervene.

It seems a Doctor Faro Menes had petitioned for permission to be a passenger on the probe and be allowed to return home. Friedman looked up Menes' personnel records and realized that the man who had made the request was a highly qualified neurologist and skilled surgeon. Friedman's first thought on the subject was, "Absolutely not!" However, out of respect, he granted the doctor a hearing. He was agreeable to at least hear what the man had to say. He was also curious to find out why.

Unable to leave his headquarters, Dr. Friedman arranged for a tele-viewer conference call between Dr. Menes, Dr. Mosley, the head of the hospital, Miss Lois Lloyd, the Hospital Administrator, and himself.

After an introductory statement in which Dr. Friedman explained the purpose of the meeting and that Dr. Mosley, Miss Lloyd, and he, due to their working relationship and familiarity with Menes, would be the judges who decided the result of his appeal. He opened the meeting by informing Dr. Menes that their initial reaction to his request was not favorable.

"Dr. Menes," started Friedman, "I have before me your file. From what I can see and from the testimony of your colleagues, you are obviously a highly skilled neurologist and neurosurgeon. For reasons of your own, you signed on to the Expeditionary Force's hospital ship and offered your skills, to what I consider the most important mission ever undertaken. You applied for this job and were readily accepted. We obviously considered ourselves fortunate to obtain the services of a doctor of your caliber. You have a great reputation and an excellent working relationship with your co-workers. You established yourself as a valuable member of the hospital staff. What the other members of this committee and I want to know is why you want to terminate your position, now?"

"First," said Dr. Menes, "I want to thank the committee for considering my request. Believe me when I say I have turned this question over and over in my mind and have always come to the same conclusion. I can serve our country and our cause better if I leave the Expedition. I have more important work waiting for me back home. Since my arrival here, I have felt unfulfilled and out of place. The truth is the hospital does not need my services. I'm like a rare spice on a kitchen shelf; available, but never used. There is no need for a neurosurgeon on this ship. I don't want to seem pompous, but the truth is my talent is being wasted. My primary job here has comprised of administering first aid and applying bandages to wounded patients. That's a job for nurses, not a neurosurgeon. I feel I made a mistake, coming here. I'm not doing what I was trained to do. My role in life is unfulfilled. I feel that, as a neurologist, I can contribute more to society back home. Here, I am not contributing, not using my skills, and not keeping up or being involved in any of the researches of my specialty. I know I'm falling behind my peers in knowledge and technique. I fear, if I do not get back to my practice, I will lose whatever skills I once possessed. My place – my work – is back home, not here. To date, I've only treated three patients, none of which required a neurologist."

"You don't believe that the goal of the Expeditionary Force is the most important task ever undertaken by mankind and that the very existence of the human race hangs in the

174

balance as to whether we succeed or fail our mission?" asked Dr. Friedman.

"There is no doubt of that in my mind," answered Dr Menes. "But I believe that my return home would actually benefit us and help us reach that goal. Research in my field of neurology is just beginning. We are just beginning to understand the workings of the mind and are developing new techniques in brain surgery that will allow us to repair injured brain cells and even cure brains that have been damaged at birth. We could eliminate the autistic and mongoloid syndromes. Cognitive disabilities could be a thing of the past. Through research, the intelligence quotient for humans could be raised so significantly that it is impossible to predict what achievements man could aspire to."

"Then why, if you had such high aspirations that could only be pursued at home, did you come here in the first place?" asked Dr Friedman.

"I was foolish. I was so taken by the magnitude of the Expedition's goal that I lost sight of my own goals. I thought I wanted to be part of the grand project; to save the world. Believe me, if I thought I could contribute to that cause, you couldn't drive me away, however, I'm not contributing. It's not anybody's fault. That's just the way it is. There's nothing for me to do here. If I stay on, it will just be more of the same. Have you ever felt completely useless? Well, I do and it's not a good feeling; not the way a person likes to feel about himself."

Dr. Friedman conferred with the panelists. "Is this true? Dr. Menes' skills are not being used and he is not needed?" asked Friedman.

Dr. Mosley pondered the question and looked somberly at Menes and then replied, "I believe Dr.Menes is understating his contributions. He has always availed himself of and assisted the medical staff whenever possible. We are very appreciative of his work."

"In other words all he does is give first aid and apply bandages?" asked Friedman.

"He has performed significantly more duties than that,"

175

replied Dr. Mosley. "However, it is true. We have had no cases, no injuries, nothing, that required the need for a neurologist or neurosurgeon."

"Sounds like we've got a high priced nurse on our hands," said Dr. Friedman. "Tell me something Dr.Mosley and Miss Lloyd. If you didn't have Dr. Menes on your staff, would it adversely affect the hospital's operation?"

"No. I don't think it would, not in the slightest," said Dr Mosley.

"What do you think, Miss Lloyd?" he asked turning to the Administrator.

She frowned, thoughtfully. "I have the greatest respect for Dr. Menes, however, I don't believe his absence would make any difference in the day-to-day operations of our hospital. He wouldn't be missed," she replied.

"Well, those are unexpected statements," said Dr. Friedman. "They certainly wouldn't help him if he were applying for a job, but does give him credibility for his petition to go back home." Dr. Friedman placed his hands on his desk and, for several minutes, quietly eyed Dr. Menes.

Finally, he spoke. "Dr. Menes, in view of what has been said at this meeting and, since there seems to be no objection from either Dr. Mosley or Miss Lloyd, I see no reason why you shouldn't be allowed to return home. I'll make the arrangements and send your transfer orders tomorrow. I hope you find whatever it is you you're looking for and, unless anyone has something to add, this meeting is adjourned."

Chapter 31

Prisoner of War

Helen Mercer sat in isolation in a filthy jail, listening to the sounds of war. The constant booms of cannon fire and the clanking of war machines seemed right outside her window. She was very frightened and demoralized. She realized that she had made a mistake. She had not only endangered herself, but probably put the entire Expeditionary Force in jeopardy. Soon, her jailers would come and take her away for interrogation. She could only imagine what tortures these primitive men would put her through to extract information.

She didn't know anything about battle plans, but she did know about the entire infrastructure of their base. Most importantly, she knew that to leave the planet, the Expeditionary Force would have to dismantle its base. To do this, they would have take down their shields. When they did that, they would be vulnerable to the shelling by American cannons. Their base could suffer terrific damage and possibly even be destroyed. She also knew the Expeditionary Force could not kill one American. If the Americans could squeeze this information out of her, it would be disastrous. The entire quest to colonize and save future mankind would be in peril.

She tried to lie down and rest on the extremely uncomfortable cot they had provided, but the pain of worry kept her fitfully awake. Finally, she heard the sound of heavy footsteps resounding down the hall. She knew they were coming for her. She shuddered with fear, not for herself, but for what horrible things might happen because of her selfish, ambitious actions.

The area Helen was taken to was a small ten by ten room with barred windows and a locked door. Two armed soldiers guarded the door. In the center of the room, was a small rectangular table where Helen found herself seated facing two menacing looking men; undoubtedly her interrogators. One of the men was Major Chambers, the man who had captured her in the old farmhouse. The other was an imposing looking man whom she knew at one glance was a man of importance. His cold eyes and superior manner gave Helen the shivers.

Helen's arms and legs were shackled to the heavy chair she was seated in. It was all she could do to keep her fears and emotions under control, but she was determined not to let her captors see her as anything but fearless and defiant.

Major Chambers was the first to speak, "This is the woman I found in the old farmhouse, Sir," he said to the other man.

"Hmm – she looks human enough."

"Yes, General. She says she is human; says she traveled here from the future," replied Major Chambers.

"You sure she's a spy?" said the General eyeing Helen.

"I'm not a spy," blurted out Helen.

"Oh, she speaks English. Are you sure she's from that alien base?"

"I'm quite sure, Sir. When we captured her, she had weapons and equipment on her that was far in advance of anything I've ever seen before."

The General sat down directly in front of Helen and, for the first time, spoke to her. "Who are you and what are you doing here?" he asked.

Helen stared into space, but did not reply.

"Let me introduce myself. I am Lt. General Nathan Ridgley, Commanding Officer United States Army. Your people, whoever they are, have invaded our country, killed our soldiers, and seized and destroyed our property. I have been ordered to use all the resources available to me to drive you people back to where you came from or demolish your entire force, whatever it takes to get rid of your presence and the dangers you present. So, don't think I would hesitate putting you to death. You can either cooperate with Major Chambers and I or face being executed as a spy! Now, let's start over. Who are you and what

178

you doing here?"

Again, Helen did not speak.

"Ok," said the general, "That's it! I don't think any information we get from this woman will change any of our plans. I think she's a spy. She's obviously not going to talk to us."

"What do you want us to do with her?" asked the major.

"Hmmm – I don't want to waste any more time with her. Arrange a firing squad."

"When?"

"As soon as possible."

Feeling for the first time that her life was really threatened, Helen spoke up. "Wait," she said. "Please! Yes. I am from what you consider the alien base, but I am not a spy. My name is Helen Mercer and I am a historian. All I do is record the travels and events of the Expeditionary Force sent here by our government, the Federation of Democratic States."

"Your government's Expeditionary Force," stated the General, "invaded our country, attacked our army, destroyed our property, and killed over 800 of our soldiers whose only goal was trying to defend their country."

"Our mission is peaceful," said Helen. "You must understand that as a historian, I am not in on or party to any of the planning committees or decision-making policies of the Expeditionary Force. I really can't tell you about anything that happened on that horrible day. I know that killing your soldiers was a mistake. Our leaders know it was a mistake and they deeply regret any loss of life or damages they inflicted."

"That doesn't make much sense, Miss Mercer."

"It wasn't supposed to happen that way."

The General, glaring menacingly at Helen said, "You mean your forces weren't supposed to invade our country and attack us? I think you're lying. I still want to know where you're from and exactly what you're forces are planning."

Helen spoke, "I can't tell you."

"Look, Miss Mercer," said the General. "You are obviously a very intelligent person, but I'm not exactly sure

179

where you're from or what you want. Your species is undoubtedly intellectually and technically far in advance of us. However, I hold the advantage. Your testimony here will not change the course of what will happen to your Expeditionary Force in the next two weeks or so, and I really don't think that withholding information from us is worth dying for, but I will have you executed, if you do not cooperate."

Helen thought long and hard. "Can I speak openly with you, General?"

"I'm not an unreasonable man," answered the General. "Perhaps, if you can make me believe that you're not a spy and your mission here is peaceful, there might room for an understanding."

Hoping that she was doing the right thing, Helen began her story. "General, I can tell you that we are from the future. We came here from Earth, the same Earth you call home. We left our homeland in the year 4555 A.D. You are our ancestors. We are your grandchildren. The Earth, where we came from, is self-destructing. We've been told in about five years, the planet will literally tear itself apart and that, if we do not find ourselves a new home, all the people living there will die. The Expeditionary Force is looking for a place to relocate our people, a place to establish a colony. That's all we want. We have not come with intentions to hurt anybody. Myself, I have no authority. I left the base without permission. They don't even know I'm gone. I just wanted to see what the world was like in the 20th century. I sneaked out of our compound."

"I'm still not sure I believe you. Your Expeditionary Force invaded our country and attacked our forces. I could rationalize that the only reason your leaders regret their actions is because they know that I have them pinned down and sooner or later my shells will penetrate those shields and when they do my artillery will destroy their base."

"No, General. You don't understand. You could bombard those shields for a hundred years and never scratch their surface and the Expeditionary Force could completely demolish your entire army in less than one hour if it wanted to.

180

But the Expeditionary Force doesn't want to fight. It wants to leave. It wants to search for a different site to set up a colony. Someplace that is habitable but not so populated."

"Well, then, why don't they leave?" questioned the General Ridgley.

"They can't."

"Oh? Why not?"

"They can't dismantle the base as long as you're bombarding the shields. They have to take down the shields to dismantle the base. When they take down the shields, the base would be vulnerable to your cannon's shells. They won't take down the shields. They can't take the chance of your forces destroying the base."

"If your forces are so powerful why don't they just neutralize our guns and then dismantle their base?" asked Ridgley.

"Because," answered Helen, "to neutralize your guns, they would have to fire on and kill your soldiers. They won't do that."

"Why not?" asked the General.

"Because," she replied, "they don't want to, they can't afford to kill even one more person."

"That's an incredible story, Miss, but there must be more to it than that. I find it hard to believe that your Generals are so suddenly righteous that they wouldn't kill a few of us to get away. Why can't they kill one more person?" questioned Ridgley.

"You must believe me. I've told you everything."

"I might start to believe you if you tell me why they can't kill one more person?" again queried the General.

"It's something they would not want me to tell you," she said.

"Lady, my patience is growing very, very thin."

Chapter 32

Zorena and Faro

Five thousand miles above the Earth, aboard the hospital ship, Zorena was packing a small bag, just large enough to carry a change of clothes and necessities for a short trip. She had been chosen for the task of flying the Probe back to the home planet. Her mission was to pick up some newly developed riot control weapons and return them to the fleet. Time was of the greatest importance. She had to make the trip there and back as quickly as possible. There would be no time for visiting. If, while there, she were to be able to see her father at all, it would be very briefly while loading the ship. Everyone knew the circumstances. The American guns had to be silenced long enough for the Expeditionary Forces to dismantle their base, pack, depart from the planet, and leave no evidence behind that they had ever been there. The riot control weapons that were going to be loaded on Zorena's ship were the weapons needed to facilitate those ends.

She wondered who would be going with her and assumed it would be another pilot. Zorena was absolutely stunned when she discovered her traveling companion would be none other than Dr. Faro Menes; the same Faro whom she had been seeing lately on a somewhat more than friendly basis. The fact was, they had become very close friends and Zorena had kept it that way, despite the appeals of Faro. He was in love with her and she, if she would admit it, was probably in love with him but she was not ready to commit herself to a full-fledged relationship. Their romance had blossomed and they spent many hours together, talking and laughing and, as much as they could within the small confines of a hospital ship, enjoying each other's company. However, their love life, if you could call it that, had developed no further than holding hands, and an occasional hug

182

and kiss. Hardly what the young doctor had in mind.

After Zorena received her orders from Fleet Command and was briefed on the details of the mission, she searched out and confronted Dr. Menes. "Faro, what on earth's going on? How did you get assigned to this mission?"

"It's a long story," answered Faro. "Come and sit with me and I'll explain." He led her to a nearby bench, where they sat down. He faced her and took her hand in his lap. "Zorena, I know I've never said it, but you must know by now that I love you very much."

Zorena removed her hand from his and said, "Faro, I don't believe now is the time for this."

"Hear me out, Zorena," he replied. "I petitioned Dr. Friedman to allow me to return home. To make a long story short, he okayed my request, so here I am. When I put in my petition, I didn't know you were going to be the pilot. I was planning to see you before I left and explain everything and say goodbye. I was hoping it would be just a short time before the Expedition would establish the colony and you would be returning home and we could be together again."

"You mean you're going home to stay?"

Faro nodded his head, "Yes".

"But why? You're happy here and we would be together. You've got your work. Don't you realize that I've really come to love the time we spend together? Being with you is about the only thing that keeps me going!" Then, Zorena dared admit what she had been denying. "Faro, Darling, I do love you. I think I've loved you from the first time we me met, after I had that stupid accident, but I didn't want to admit it. I was afraid. What if something happens? What if you go and we never see one another again? The reason I never told you I loved you was because I lost one person I loved. I don't know if I could handle it if I lose you, too."

"You will never lose me, Zorena," said Faro. "If I had to, I would search the ends of the Galaxy to be with you, but, for now, I've got to go home. If I don't go home, I'll lose everything I ever worked for. Something is calling me and the call is very,

183

very strong. I have to go. Don't forget, we'll be together on the way home."

"Yes – and then I'll come back alone. That will be a love lost trip for me."

So it was that Zorena and Faro boarded the Probe together for the journey back to the future. Before they departed, the Probe's computers had to be, once again, reprogrammed. They had been programmed for 6000 B.C. Now, the engineers had to reprogram them for 4555 A.D. and the return trip to the present. It was a tricky bit of work, but, when the engineers were finished, they were confident that they had successfully completed all of the necessary modifications. The 'OK' was given. The flight was a go. The Probe's giant engines came to life. The ship slipped out of its moorings and slowly pulled away from the mother ship and disappeared into the vast emptiness of space.

Once on their way, Zorena and Faro knew the routine. They would spend about four days en route to the tunnel at 150,000 miles per hour, accelerate to warp two, and enter the tunnel. They would then decelerate back to 150,000 miles per hour, exit the tunnel, and arrive back to their home base, four days later. If all went well, they would arrive at home on August 20th, 4555 A.D.; total elapsed time, about eight days.

Zorena accepted the fact that Faro would not be returning with her. The thought saddened them, so they did not dwell on it. Instead, they tried to be happy with the time, however short, that they would have together.

On the fourth day of their journey, Zorena alerted Faro that they were only about one hour away from entering the Aboreium Tunnel. One hour gave them time to stow away any loose gear and strap themselves into their seats. Zorena noticed that Faro was becoming very nervous as they approached the zero hour. She reached out and took his hand.

"Don't worry, Sweetheart," she smiled. "It won't be like the last time. This ship is an old warrior. It's been through this before. This time, when we enter the tunnel, all we should feel is a slight buffeting. Relax, Darling. In just a few minutes, we'll

184

be in our own time zone. Oh, my God!" she screamed. Suddenly, without warning the ship began tumbling and shaking violently. The violence was twice what they had experienced the last time they had entered the tunnel. "Hang on!" she managed to holler. Faro, who was terrified beyond words, grasped his armrests tightly.

The buffeting inside the cockpit was so vicious that their flailing arms and legs took a brutal beating against the sides of their seats. Being strapped in was not saving them from injury. Their heads rocked about, back and forth so hard that they were both knocked unconscious. The last thing they remembered was their ship was free falling out of control, apparently doomed.

Chapter 33

A Dangerous Plot

Meanwhile, on Earth, an alarmed Dr. Friedman called for an emergency meeting of the Expeditionary Council. News of the latest events was so disturbing that Dr. Friedman felt he must confer with Admiral Kukov and General Varco. In view of what had happened, new plans had to be made. Time was running short and they were not ready.

"Gentlemen," said Dr. Friedman, "Four days ago we launched the Probe. As we discussed earlier, we were sending the Probe back home to retrieve some weapons. In the interim, President Harbill had ordered us to cease all hostilities against the Americans. He said he did not want one more American killed by our hands. Dr. Steebler confirmed that he now had new riot control weapons, powerful enough to stun and immobilize the American forces without harming them. The Probe was to pick up these weapons and bring them back to us. Our entire strategy for evacuation was based on the use of those weapons. Today, we got the devastating word that the Probe has been destroyed. We've totally lost communication with it. The last we heard from it was a distress call. It apparently was destroyed while penetrating the Arboreium Tunnel. We won't be getting those weapons."

General Varco interrupted, "I knew something like this was going to happen. Well, we're right back where we started from. Aren't we, Friedman? We can't fight. We can't kill any Americans. Our mission's going to straight to hell. Isn't it, Friedman?"

"If you don't have anything constructive to say, Varco, then shut up! I don't want to listen to your whining! You've got a bad negative attitude and I don't like it," retorted Friedman.

"Maybe so, but it's something we've got to think about.

All along, you've been putting all our eggs in one basket. Now, your Probe fails and we're stuck. Where's Plan B? If we follow the orders of the President to the letter, we'll never get off this planet. Earth is doomed. I don't call that very good planning, Doctor!" snarled Varco.

"I don't like the sound of your voice, Varco!" growled Friedman, standing up.

"Ok, everybody, settle down," said Admiral Kukov, motioning to both men.

Suddenly, Varco stood up, pulled a gun from the fold of his jacket and pointed it at Friedman and Kukov. "I've had enough of your weak leadership! You two, freeze!" he bellowed. Then, speaking into a communicator, he gave the order, "This is General Varco. Due to extreme circumstances and under provisions as outlined in Section 218 of the Military Code, I am relieving Dr. Friedman from duty and am assuming control of this vessel and all Expeditionary Forces."

At once, a squad of soldiers with weapons drawn burst through the doors of the conference room and surrounded Dr. Friedman and Admiral Kukov.

"What the ...? Are you crazy, Varco? This is out and out treason! You'll hang for this!" cried Friedman.

"They'll put up a statue of me in my honor after I've saved all of mankind from extermination," exclaimed Varco, pounding his chest.

Dr. Friedman turned to the soldiers. "Do you men realize you're committing treason? You could die for these actions."

"Like I once said, Doctor. These men are loyal to me. I've had it with you, Friedman! I told you once before you were just a stupid scientist, sticking your nose in where it doesn't belong. There is a way out of this and I'm going to take it. I'm going to finish off those damn Americans. I'll kill every one of the treacherous bastards and demolish their base! Then, I'll get us out of here."

"I'll never let you get away with this, Varco," hissed Friedman.

187

"You're not gonna have that chance, Friedman. It would take very little from you for me to put a hole in your head. You have no idea how much I hate you, Doctor. You have been a real thorn in my side. You came aboard against my wishes, usurped my authority, stripped me of my command, humiliated me in front of my men, put me down at every turn, and turned the President against me. How much more can one man do to another? I can't stand it any longer, Dr. Friedman. I'd very much like to kill you, but, instead, I'll give you a fair trial, right here and now." General Varco paused and stared at Dr. Friedman, nodded his head, then finally spoke. "With all the facts in, I find you guilty of treason and cowardice in the face of the enemy. I hereby sentence you to death." That said, General Varco raised his weapon, pointed it at Dr. Friedman's head and began squeezing the trigger.

Chapter 34

Miracles

The environment, for Helen Mercer, had changed. She was no longer in prison. Instead, she was now housed in comfortable quarters and being treated most cordially. She had literally turned the very fierce General Ridgley into an ally and, likewise, captivated the heart of the combative Major Chambers who catered to her every wish. Also, after much discussion, she convinced the general that, if he stopped the bombardment of the Expeditionary Force's Base, they would leave peacefully. She had disclosed everything to him, even about Dr. Friedman replacing General Varco as Head of the Expedition and that it was Varco who was responsible for the deaths of the American soldiers. General Ridgley now believed her and wanted to know how he could contact this Dr. Friedman to negotiate a truce that would call for all hostilities to end and allow the Expeditionary Force the time it needed to prepare for departure.

A plan was adopted. Major Chambers, acting as a hostage and carrying a white flag of truce, would escort Helen to the front gate of the base. Helen, who was a high profile member of the Expeditionary Force, would, on behalf of Major Chambers, ask for a meeting with Dr. Friedman. Helen was sure she could get the two sides together. The risks for both sides were great, but General Ridgley had confidence that the plan would work. If it didn't, he could always execute Helen and start the bombardment again.

Billy Bob Morris, the vagabond that Major Chambers had captured along with Helen Mercer, turned out to be of no value. He obviously didn't possess any knowledge about anything, so General Ridgley had to decide what to do with him. Since he had not committed any crimes, did not present a threat to Ridgley's troops, and was actually the responsibility of the local civil authorities, he decided to turn him loose.

Billy was very incensed at being kept in captivity. In spite of all the questioning, the only thing they ever got out of him was, "I ain't done nothin'." Once turned loose, he wasted no time in making a hasty retreat back towards his ramshackle farmhouse. After he arrived home, he sat and sulked over the events of the last few days. He got out his old, but serviceable two barreled shotgun, cradled it in his arms, and thought about revenge and how he'd like to get even with those responsible for treating him so badly. His thoughts turned to Helen Mercer. He started wondering where she had come from on that fateful night when he was captured. He had been watching all of the grounds surrounding the farmhouse. He now seemed to recall that she had come from somewhere near the edge of the river. Overcome with curiosity, Billy, shotgun in hand, headed for the river's edge. He didn't know exactly what he intended to do, but he was going to do something. He decided to trace her travels back to where he'd first seen her appear.

There were two things Billy had; cunning and persistence. He poked and prodded and even went in the water looking and pulling at every leaf and fern. No one could have been more surprised than Billy when finally he pulled back a very large fern and found a hole in the riverbank large enough for a person to crawl through. Billy climbed through the hole and soon discovered that it wasn't just a hole. There was a tunnel; a tunnel with a catwalk running alongside a large pipeline. Billy decided to follow the walk. For five miles he trudged along the trail until he finally came to a sharp bend in the road. As he rounded the bend, a huge spotlight suddenly blinded him.

In his office, where, through the open window, he could watch both the entrance and the exit of the pipeline that delivered water to the base, the ever-present security officer, Major Max Bowers, stood guard. He was sure he heard footsteps coming down the tunnel's catwalk from the direction of the river. Grabbing his laser rifle, he quietly exited his office and stealthily crept to the front of the catwalk where he blocked the

190

passage of anyone who might be trying to gain access to the water system and the main base. He listened intently. He was now positive he heard the footsteps of an intruder. At the precise moment that Billy rounded the bend in the tunnel, Major Bowers flipped on the overhead floodlight switch. Suddenly blinded, startled, and framed by the bright lights, stood Billy Bob, shotgun in hand, frozen in horror. Major Bowers, the aging security officer, sure in his mind that the intruder was a saboteur sent to destroy the water system, raised his rifle and fired. The laser tore a hole through the center of Billy's heart. By the time he hit the ground, he was dead. Major Bowers checked his wristwatch. It read September 12, 1932, 12:05:05 PM.

Meanwhile, at exactly the same moment Major Bowers shot Billy Bob Morris with his laser rifle, General Varco was standing over Dr. Friedman with laser pistol in hand. He aimed at the Doctor's head and started squeezing the trigger.

And, suddenly, General Varco was gone! The astonished onlookers stared in disbelief. Some uttered gasps of horror. Some rolled back their eyes and fainted. Admiral Kukov looked at the clock on the wall. It read September 12, 1932, 12:05:05 PM.

Dr. Friedman was in shock. He looked around, felt his arms and legs, and then collapsed in a chair. Miracle of all miracles; he was still alive!

Chapter 35

An Uneasy Truce

The guards, stationed at the entrance to the main gate of the Expeditionary Force, were astonished to see two people coming towards them. It was three o'clock on a very quiet and unexpectedly tranquil, though hot afternoon on September 13th, 1932. It was unexpectedly quiet, because no shells or bombs were bursting on top of the compound's shields. One of the persons was readily identified. It was Miss Helen Mercer, the historian. The other person was a man in a full dress military uniform, waving a flag of truce. A call was immediately made to base headquarters, which, in turn, was transferred to Dr. Friedman.

Dr. Friedman, who was still a little shaky and recovering from the previous day's near death experience, deferred the call to Admiral Kukov.

Admiral Kukov, speaking through a televiewer, addressed the Captain on the other end of the line.

"Yes?" he asked.

"Sir, this is the Captain of the Guard, at the Main Gate."

"What is it, Captain?"

"We have two people at the main gate, asking for permission for entrance to the base. One is Miss Helen Mercer. The other is a military officer from the American forces, carrying a white flag."

"Miss Mercer? What's she doing out there?"

"I have no idea, Sir, but she says the military officer is a major with the American Security Forces and he is turning himself over to us as a hostage by order of his Fort Commander."

"He wants to turn himself over to us as a hostage?"

"Yes, Sir. We have searched him. He is unarmed."

"Alright. Have him escorted to the containment center.

I don't know what Miss Mercer is up to, but search her and bring her along, too."

By the time Miss Mercer and the American Major were escorted to the containment area, Dr. Friedman, seemingly fully recovered from his nerve-shattering experience, and Admiral Kukov were already there, waiting for them, with armed guards stationed at the exits. Dr. Friedman ordered Miss Mercer and the American Major to be seated.

"Now, Miss Mercer," said Dr. Friedman, with a disapproving frown, "the last time I talked to you, you were asking me to intervene on your behalf for an interview with Major Bowers. I think you were a bit underhanded. Now, I find you off-limits, outside the base and in the company of one of our antagonist. I don't know how you got around Major Bowers to get off the base, but you did and then, just yesterday, Major Bowers killed an intruder trying to sneak into the base. I don't know what to make of all this, but I suspect you had something to do with it. Now, I want to know what the hell is going on and why is this major waving a flag of truce?"

"Dr. Friedman, let me say I am thoroughly ashamed of my actions. My ambitions got the best of me. I wanted to, at first-hand, see the twentieth century as it really is. I wanted to visit one of their villages and actually talk to the people of that era. I sneaked off the base. I'm sorry. I was selfish and disregarded my responsibilities. The major, here, immediately captured me. Let me introduce him. This is Major Chambers, the Fort Lewis Security Officer. I'll let him explain for himself. Since you won't be able to understand each other, I will, if you permit me, act as an interpreter."

Dr. Friedman nodded to Major Chambers. "I am Dr. Jonas Friedman, Acting Commander of the Federation of the Democratic State's Expeditionary Forces. I understand you have come here under a fag of truce. We'll recognize and honor your truce. Turning yourself over to us means that you must want something. What is it you want, Major?"

"Sir, I have been given the authority to negotiate terms with you. Our commander, General Ridgley, is extremely is

193

aggravated and would like nothing better than to destroy your base and drive your Expeditionary Force off our land. We would like nothing better than to punish you for initiating a sneak attack, invading our country, and killing and wounding over a thousand of our soldiers without a declaration of war. We consider your actions treacherous and cowardly. You gave us no warning. However, Miss Mercer made us realize we could not harm you in any way. With your advanced technology; superior weapons and protective shields, we wouldn't have had a chance trying to engage you in combat. Therefore, we would like to propose a truce. We propose a cessation of hostilities between your forces and ours."

"That would be extremely satisfactory with me," said Dr. Friedman.

"There would have to be certain concessions from you for the terms of the agreement," implied Major Chambers.

"I don't see how you can ask or demand anything. You certainly don't have the upper hand. You know you're no match for us, militarily. What makes you think you've got anything to negotiate with? Why don't you just surrender? We'll treat you humanely," retorted Friedman.

"We know about your might. We also know about your limitations. We know that you will not kill us; not one of us," said the Major.

Dr. Friedman turned an angry glance towards Helen. "I see you've been talking to Miss Mercer."

"Miss Mercer is a very loyal and brave woman. It was she who convinced us that your intentions here were peaceful. If it wasn't for Miss Mercer, I would not be here trying to come to terms with you. So, what do you want from us? What kind of terms are you looking for?"

"We will stop the bombardment of your base and give you time to dismantle and pack. You must agree not to attempt not to establish a colony anywhere on this planet in this century and evacuate this planet as soon as you've finished packing," said the Major.

"How do we know we can trust you?"

194

"You will have me as a hostage".

An agreement was reached. Dr. Friedman and Admiral Kukov were elated. They could now leave the planet and travel on to establish a colony in 6000 B.C. Now, the most difficult thing they had to do was inform President Harbill that his daughter had died and they would not be able to retrieve her body. The President, mortified over the news of the death of his daughter, was inconsolable and could be heard crying in the background.

In three days, the base was dismantled and packed. The following day, the flagship, FDS Trailblazer, and its company of ships took off and headed for the Arboreium Tunnel. It would be a four day trip, but on the 3rd day out, Dr. Friedman received a joint message from President Harbill and Dr. Steebler. The usually so dignified and serious Dr. Steebler could not contain his excitement and was so gleefully animated that he appeared out of character. The news imparted to Dr. Friedman was astounding. It was the last thing he was expecting to hear. The message was an instruction. It read, "Do not proceed with the mission. Do not establish a colony. Return the entire fleet back to the home planet, immediately. Have discovered the flaw in your Reflective Magnifier that inhibited acceleration. Have made necessary adjustments. We now have unlimited space travel. Have identified a habitable planet within our own galaxy and are already in the process of transporting people to start construction of facilities. Upon your return, your ships will be retrofitted with new magnifiers and made ready for travel.

Friedman digested the news with mixed emotions. He was happy that the problem with the Reflective Magnifier was solved, but the fact that others had solved the problem made him feel a pang of jealousy. After all, it was his invention. Once again, the order was given to program the computers and prepare for the return home.

In addition, there would be a new passenger returning with them. The American hostage, Major Chambers, asked to go back to the New World with them. He was excited with the thought of traveling in space, especially in the company of Helen

Mercer. Dr. Friedman thought it would be a good idea to bring the Major along. He wasn't particularly interested in the Major's reason for wanting to go. He simply didn't believe it would be a good idea for the Major to return to the 1932 time zone. His exposure to a civilization whose lifestyle and superior technology was so foreign to him might prove to be too much of an emotional burden to bear. There was too much of a chance that he would have trouble coping with his own people because they wouldn't believe his stories. Also, Dr. Friedman did not trust the Major to be as discreet as he would have liked.

The Major, it turned out, was a very talkative fellow. Inadvertent information leaks would be bad not only for the Expeditionary Force, but could lead to untold problems for the people of that of that time period and these were risks that Friedman was not willing to take.

Helen Mercer smiled. She was pleased to hear of the decision concerning Major Chambers. She had become fond of her former captor. Also, happily for Helen, she was not going to be punished for her foolish act of sneaking off the base. After all, it had been Helen who saved the Expedition. That fact helped Dr. Friedman come to his decision. He knew his reasoning was flawed. Perhaps, he was wrong to let her go unpunished, but, on the other hand, he felt good about it. He would have not felt good to see her imprisoned and her future ruined after she displayed so much courage in befriending her captors and then negotiating a truce between the two warring parties that allowed the Expeditionary Force to leave the planet, unharmed with no more deaths to either side.

It was a grand, but sad day, on September 22, 4555 A.D., when the armada carrying the Expeditionary Force arrived back on Earth. It was with heavy heart, Dr. Friedman met with President Harbill, still mourning the death of Zorena, and the Senate and gave his final report on the details of the events surrounding the Expeditionary Force's excursion. Suffice it to say nothing had gone right. Everything that that possibly could go wrong, did go wrong. Friedman enumerated them; one: the anomaly that caused the entire fleet to enter the wrong time zone,

196

two: murder aboard the hospital ship, three: picking a bad site to colonize, four: the skirmish with the American forces which lead to the deaths of 800 to 1,000 American soldiers and 800,000 Federation citizens, five: the deaths of Lt. J.G. Zorena Harbill and Dr. Faro Menes, six: the mutiny and mysterious death of General Varco, and seven: the terms of surrender to the American forces.

The Senate wanted an inquest. Some suggested that heads should roll. What had happened to the Expeditionary Force was enough to convince many that there was a complete breakdown of discipline and the entire excursion was a total failure. Many blamed Dr. Friedman for these failures and accused him of meddling and using illegal methods to override General Varco's authority. The President defended Dr. Friedman and presented documentation and logs that proved it was General Varco who was guilty of committing illegal acts and was the person responsible for the terrible decision to use laser beams on the American forces, which resulted in the deaths of American and Federation citizens.

The President prevailed. There would be no inquest and the Federation would move forward without any more interruptions to the task of evacuating Earth and transporting everyone to their newfound planet. There was great rejoicing throughout the Federation. Even Dr. Zinn, the religious leader of The World Church, gave his approval and blessing on the move to their new home.

Chapter 36

A King Will Come

    Six thousand years and 100,000 miles away, a small space ship was descending towards the planet Earth. The ship, for the lack of a better name, was called The Probe. It was the last remnant of a once mighty armada, the goal of which was to establish a colony on ancient Earth. The mission failed and the armada returned home. The probe was believed to have been destroyed and was reported, as such, to the Federation of Democratic States. However, if one were to be able to track the Probe, he or she would have discovered that the ship was not destroyed, but was flying in a controlled pattern.

    Lt. J. G. Zorena Harbill and Dr. Faro Menes were the only persons on board. Both had been knocked unconscious, due to the violent tumbling and shaking the ship had encountered when it passed through the Aboreium Tunnel.

    As the Probe glided noiselessly in its downward flight, Zorena slowly began to awaken from her unconscious state. When her eyes gradually opened and her mind began to clear, the recollection of what happened came back to her. She remembered. She remembered that, just as they were about to enter the Aborieum Tunnel, their ship encountered violent turbulence and, just before she passed out, she vaguely remembered the ship falling through space, out of control. Now, she was alert. The fog lifted from her eyes. She felt her arms and legs. There seemed to be no broken bones. She was able to function. She had evidently not been seriously injured. Suddenly, she started to panic, but long training and conditioning helped her control her emotions. She calmed down when she realized that the ship was not falling through space out of control, but was in autopilot mode, being flown by the computer and descending towards Earth. She felt she had recovered sufficiently and, rather than risk the chances on an autopilot landing, she would land the ship herself. However, much to her dismay, when she attempted to move the controls, they would not respond. The computer evidently had committed to the autopilot and locked out the manual override. In spite of all of her efforts, Zorena could not move the flight controls. The ship continued on a pre-determined course, which had somehow, inexplicably, been planted in the computer's memory banks.

Then, she turned to Faro, to see if he was awake. She reached over and shook him. "Faro, wake up! Wake up! Are you ok?"

Faro remained slumped over in his seat and did not respond to any of her attempts to awaken him. She felt his pulse. It was strong. He was alive. Knowing that greatly relieved some of her anxieties. She looked around and then, grasping the flight controls, once more, without success, manually tried to override the autopilot. Frustrated, she sat back in her seat and watched and waited, resigned to the fact she would have to rely on the ship's computer to land them safely. She had no idea of their destination, except that it was sometime and somewhere on the planet Earth. After a period of time and watching the planet grow larger and larger, she sensed that the temperature inside the cockpit had perceptibly increased. Zorena realized they were penetrating the Earth's atmosphere. She watched from an observation window as the little ship dipped down, swinging close to the surface.

Turning her eyes to the instrument panel, she became quite alarmed when the altimeter read five thousand feet. She was afraid of the computer's program. She was almost sure it was not programmed to land on an uncharted surface. Again, she laid her hands on the controls and gently pulled back. The ship responded to her touch. It took a moment for her to realize it, but the computer had turned itself off. She had regained control of the ship. Now, to find a place to land.

On the banks of the Great River, Ahkmed and his brother Omar sweated under the hot, noonday sun. They toiled in the rich loamy soil, which had been deposited on the banks of the

199

river after the it receded from its recent flooding. Their dress, a simple loin cloth, identified them as laborers from the village. They had stopped working, laid their plows on their ground, and engaged in a quiet, but intense conversation.

"Ahkmed, you were a fool to complain to the High Priest," admonished Omar. "Look at the trouble you've gotten yourself into. And now, the guards are even watching me and my family."

"I only wanted that the priest be fair," complained Ahkmed. "Why should I get a lesser amount of grain, bread, and goats for my labor than other workers? I work just as hard as they do. I barely get enough to feed myself. I will never be able to buy a wife and have a family. You know I love Patiti and she loves me. Her father wants two goats for her. How will I ever be able to pay him? I don't even have one goat. And now, just for asking for a fair share, I am being persecuted by the priests."

"You are not only a fool, Ahkmed, you are a poor fool," replied Omar. "Patiti is a very beautiful girl and Ishmall, the rich land-owner, wants her for his very own. Her father would like a wealthy son-in-law. You have no property and no goats. Ishmall has showered the High Priest with gifts and filled his coffers with wheat and honey. You will never be able to marry Patiti. Ishmall saw her kiss you, then I saw Ishmall talking to the priest and pointing at you. To him, you are nothing but an unworthy peasant and trouble-maker. As soon as we return from the fields today, the High Priest is going to send for you and judge you for your foolishness."

"But I am a free man and Patiti and I have loved each other since we were little children. How can he judge me?"

"The priests are all-powerful."

"I am so unhappy and afraid, Omar. What should I do?" asked Ahkmed.

"When you see him, fall on your knees and beg for mercy. Tell him you don't want Patiti. Ask for forgiveness for your foolish acts. He does not want to lose laborers. He will be merciful."

"I hate the priests!" declared Ahkmed venomously.

200

"Be quiet, you fool, lest Ra hear you and report your blasphemy to the High Priest," cautioned Omar. "For this, you would surely die."

Ahkmed and Omar's conversation was cut short by the sudden, loud chanting of others. The brothers looked around and saw that almost all of the people from the village had joined the workers of the fields and were kneeling with their heads down and their arms outstretched, facing the sun in worship. A rumbling noise, faint at first, but growing louder and louder, pervaded their senses. Shielding their eyes and looking to the heavens, they beheld, emerging from the center of the sun's glare, a shining silver vessel. This could only mean one thing. The gods were coming. Trembling, Ahkmed and Omar fell to the ground, joining their fellow villagers in worship.

Flying as close as she could to the Earth's surface, Zorena circled the globe several times, looking for a satisfactory place to land. Finally, she observed a large river, whose banks embraced fertile fields with lush vegetation. There were what looked like farmers, working the fields along the banks of the river. Zorena flew closer to get a better look at them. They looked peaceful and seemed to be praying. As time and supplies were growing short, Zorena decided this to be their landing site and glided their ship to a soft landing, three hundred feet from the people kneeling before them.

It was time to wake up Faro. She was afraid he might be seriously injured. As she turned to revive him, she very carefully unbuckled his seatbelt and, trying to make him as comfortable as possible, laid him back in his seat. She massaged his arms and legs and bathed his temples with cool water. Faro finally stirred. His eyes fluttered and he faintly groaned.

"Faro! Faro, Darling, please wake up!" urged Zorena.

"Oh-ah-what? Where am I?" asked the still fazed Doctor, holding his head.

"Are you ok?" she asked.

"I think so," he answered, shaking his arms and legs and beginning to awaken from his stupor. "Where did you say we are?"

201

Zorena grabbed Faro and, hugging and kissing him, said, "Thank God you're ok! I don't know where we are, Sweetheart, but its somewhere on Earth. Looking at the ship's clock, for the first time, she whispered, in a shocked voice, "3100 B.C." She shook her head in amazement. "My God! We've landed in 3100 B.C. There's no civilization, here. We can't live here."

"That's incredible! What are we going to do? Whoa! Wait a minute," said Faro, standing up and looking out the observation window. "There are people out there."

"Yes. I know. I saw them, but they're primitive. They don't look civilized."

"Well", suggested Faro, "first, let's get out of these space suits and move around a bit to see if were okay."

After a couple of hours of exercising and limbering up their bodies, they concluded they were physically in good shape. They thought about taking a closer look and decided, if they did go out, it might be advisable to put their spacesuits back on. A look through the observation window verified that the natives were still in the fields, facing them, kneeling, and praying.

"You really think we should go out?" asked Zorena.

"Might as well, but let's take it real easy," cautioned Faro.

Zorena pressed a lever on the control panel. The ship's door slowly opened.

The natives watched in awe as a door in the silver vessel opened and a golden staircase descended to the ground. Upon seeing this, the natives were even more frightened. Some fainted right on the spot, while others fell to the ground with eyes squinched shut and arms outstretched. Those who were able to move scrambled backwards, falling over each other to get as far away as possible from the sudden appearance of their gods. As quiet descended over the crowd, whispers could be heard. "It must be Ra, the Sun God. It came out of the sun". Others said, "No. It's the Moon God. See? It's silver, like the moon."

Then, over their whispers, one of the old priests spoke up. "Fools! Can't you see the clouds of dust and dirt settling over our homes and fields? Look at the trees. They've been

202

blown down and many of our crops have been blown away. It's the Wind God whose come in person to punish you for being lazy slackers and not obeying your priests! Now, your homes will be blown away and all the fields stripped bare. We will have no food and no place to live, because you all thought your priests were just greedy old fools when we told you the gods wanted their proper share of your crops and animals, so that proper offerings could be made to keep them happy. Because of your disobedience, you've probably killed us all! Now, be quiet and show proper respect."

As the crowed quieted, there was a sudden gasp. A shadow could be seen and a round object appeared at the vessel's door and then disappeared back into the ship. Zorena, who was bursting with curiosity, wanted a better look, so she stuck her head out of the door and took a quick peek at the strange people, bowing before them. She withdrew her head back into the cockpit as quickly as she had stuck it out.

Faro asked, "What's it like out there?"

"I didn't get a very good look," she answered. "They got excited when they saw me and started that chanting and praying all over again. It was creepy. I jumped back out of sight. I can say one thing. They're more afraid of us than we are of them."

"What do you think we should do?"

"I don't know. They don't seem to be aggressive, but they won't go away either."

"We could go out there and try to talk to them and, if they attack us, we can always stun them,"

"We don't want to hurt them," said Zorena.

"Well," replied Faro, "one thing's for sure. We can't stay in this ship forever. Another thing we haven't talked about: can we take off? Can this ship fly? Can we get home?"

"I don't think so," answered Zorena. We don't have enough fuel to get home. We probably have enough food and water, but it looks like we'll never leave here. I'm afraid were stranded.

"How about our communications? Can't we contact someone? Maybe they could rescue us."

"That's a good idea. It's getting late and I'm getting tired," said Zorena. "I'll try to contact someone in the morning. Why don't you go to bed? I'll raise the stairs and close everything up."

The next day, when dawn broke and the sun poked its head over the horizon, Zorena and Faro awoke.

After a quick breakfast, Zorena smiled at Faro and said, "Honey, I have a good feeling about this. I believe we will be able to reach Dr. Friedman or even my father." Zorena then sat down to the controls, turned on the ship's communicator, and commenced trying to contact their home base. Unable to reach the home base, she tried contacting the Expeditionary Force and then the hospital ship. It was all in vain. The airways, seemingly, were dead. For hours, she worked, trying to make contact. At first, her demeanor was calm, but as attempt after attempt failed, she went from calm to worried to frustrated to being totally disheartened. There was not the faintest response to any of her calls. With tears in her eyes, she looked at Faro and shook her head.

"It's no use," she said, dejectedly.

"I know it looks bad, Darling, but even if you can't contact them today, we can try again, tomorrow. We'll be okay," said Faro, encouragingly putting his arms around her.

She shook him off. "You don't understand! We're stranded here. Do you really think we're going to be okay, trying to live here the rest of our lives with uncivilized savages?" she agonized.

"Zorena, we've got to have hope. I don't really believe they're savages. Look at them. They're farmers. They look friendly. They're waiting for us to come out. They want to meet us.

"You think so? What if they're not friendly? What if they're afraid of us and just waiting for us to come out so they can kill us?"

"We can't stay in here, forever," reasoned Faro. "We're going to have to leave the ship, sooner or later. We might as well do it and get it over with."

204

"Maybe we should wear our spacesuits and take some weapons, just in case," cautioned Zorena.

"Okay," said Faro, "but, for the way their acting, I don't believe they're any threat. I think they want to be friendly."

"I hope you're right," she said, skeptically, as she pushed the lever on the control panel to open and lower the staircase. They disembarked together and walked, step by step, down the stairs until their feet touched the sandy earth. As they looked about, they we're absolutely stunned at the sight that lay before them. At the base of the stairs, almost giving them no place to stand, were staked out a lamb, a goat, a cow, baskets of fruit, carpets, sandals, and an assortment of various other gifts, too numerous to count. They looked at each other with expressions of total disbelief.

"They are gifts for us!" exclaimed Zorena,

"Yes. I believe they are."

"These are very primitive people, Faro. The way they were bowing to us, almost like worshipers. They must think we're deities."

"I think you're right. It certainly looks that way."

The villagers, in the meantime, had moved back about fifty yards from where Zorena and Faro were standing. They were no longer praying but kneeling with their heads bowed down as low as possible, to avoid eye contact with the gods.

"Well, let's go meet them," said Faro, taking Zorena by the hand and walking toward the waiting crowd.

"Say something to them," Said Zorena, as they arrived in front of them.

"Greetings. We come in peace."

Flabbergasted, Zorena, with a sidelong glance at Faro and a hint of sarcastic humor in her voice said, "Greetings? We come in peace? Is that the best you can do?"

Faro looked at her and grinned, shrugged his shoulders, and said, "Let's take off our spacesuits and see what they do when they see who we are and what we really look like." Zorena smiled and nodded in agreement. First, they took off their helmets and as they laid them on the ground, a horrified gasp resounded in their ears. The villagers had obviously been watching the gods more closely than they had been letting on. The act of the gods taking off their heads and replacing them with human-like heads frightened them more than ever. When Zorena and Faro unfastened their spacesuits, laid them aside, and revealed themselves as humans, the simple natives, believing the gods had transformed themselves into their own image and likeness, again prostrated themselves lower and lower, if that were possible, before what they believed were gods.

One of the priests, while kneeling, spoke. "The gods have made themselves look like us. I believe they are not gods, themselves, but are a god king and queen to rule over us."

Upon this proclamation, the villagers chanted, "Oh, Almighty King and Great Queen, be merciful and forgive us our selfish and sinful ways."

Faro stepped forward. He stretched his arms out to the chanting crowd and then, pointing to himself, said in a loud voice, "Me Faro, Faro Menes." Again, only this time pounding his chest, he exclaimed and kept repeating, "Faro Menes—Faro Menes—Faro Menes." Looking down on the groveling natives, whom he saw were still purposely avoiding eye contact, he spotted one man who held his head up, briefly, just long enough for Faro to make eye contact. He motioned for the man to come to him.

Ahkmed was terrified. He had been singled out and beckoned to approach the god king. He was afraid to go, but more afraid not to go. Very painfully and slowly, he crawled to the feet of Faro, who reached down, grasped him by the shoulders, and pulled him to a standing position. Then tapping his chest once more, Faro said, "Faro—Faro Menes."

Ahkmed just stared with a blank expression. Disgusted, Faro released him and he immediately dropped to the ground, shaking with fear. Thinking that he had accomplished nothing, Faro, who was a little discouraged and frustrated, made an outward motion with his hand. This seemed to signal to the worshipers that they were released. Before Zorena and Faro knew what was happening, the worshipers fled and disappeared back towards the village, leaving them with a sheep, a cow, a goat, and the other gifts the villagers had bestowed on them.

"What the hell do we do, now?" asked a totally dumbfounded and perplexed Faro. It was Zorena's turn to shrug.

Back in the village, the High Priest summoned the people of importance to a meeting. It was time for the priests to assert their authority over them. The gods must be appeased and they had to decide how and who would furnish the gods with whatever they wanted. Ahkmed's position with the priests was greatly enhanced, due to his encounter with the gods. He suddenly went from a gravely, downtrodden nobody to the status of greatness. The priests even called upon him to sit with them before the altar, to discuss the very urgent and pressing matters concerning what to do about the gods.

"Ahkmed," said the High Priest, "the god king held you in his arms and spoke to you. "What did he say to you? What are we to do?"

"I do not know. I could not understand him," answered Ahkmed.

"But he spoke directly to you. What did he say?" again asked the High Priest.

"He just said, 'Pharaoh Menes'," answered Ahkmed, translating the word Faro to his own tongue, "that's all he said. He just kept repeating Pharaoh Menes, over and over again."

The priests conferred. "What do you think that means?" they asked one another.

"Maybe he's demanding more sacrifices," said one of the priests, maybe if we don't appease, him he will destroy our village."

"Maybe he wants another wife. Patiti is very beautiful. We could give her to him."

"He has a queen. She would kill Patiti," said the High Priest.

"I think you are all wrong," said Ahkmed. "I think he was telling us his name. Yes. That must be the answer. He was telling us his name. His name is Pharaoh—Pharaoh Menes.

The High Priest looked thoughtfully at Ahkmed.

207

"Ahkmed is right. The god king was telling us his name. From now on, he will be King Menes and will be called Pharaoh, the King of Egypt. Let us take our chariots to him and carry him and his queen to the temple, where they will rule and bring great wealth and power to our land."

And so it was. The priests and all the villagers went back to Faro and Zorena, who were still standing by their ship, and with the High Priest chariots, carried Faro, now known as Pharaoh, and Queen Zorena to the temple in the village of Memphis, where they were crowned and installed as Pharaoh Menes and Zorena, King and Queen of Egypt.

As the weeks went by, Pharaoh and Queen Zorena began to settle in their new environment and status. There was nothing they could do, but accept the roles given them. They decided they could help these people and talked about teaching them means and ways to improve their lives. Zorena, however, did not give up the hope of being rescued and, every day for two weeks, went out to their marooned spaceship and tried to make contact with her father or anybody else who might be monitoring the airways. In spite of her efforts, she could not establish even the slightest contact. The airways were dead.

After a period of grieving over the loss of her home and family, she gave up and stopped her daily trips to the ship. She resolved to do her best to help Faro, the man she had grown to love, rule these people and accept them as her new family.

Ahkmed, the former serf, once considered the lowest of the low, reached immense heights and eventually became the High Priest. He married is life-long love, Patiti.

Chapter 37

A Soldier's Secret

The date was September 25th, 1932. Two officers; a three star and one star general, sat back in their easy chairs in the officer's quarters in Fort Lewis, Washington, smoking, and obviously enjoying, their Cuban cigars. They sat there quietly. Neither had said a word for half an hour.

Finally, Lt. General Nathan Ridgley spoke. "So you're going to retire. Huh, Starling?"

"Yeah. It's about the only option I have. Nathan."

"It's a damn shame. You're a good officer, Harold."

"You're about the only one who thinks so. Thanks to you, I didn't get court marshaled."

"That's the least I could do and I don't think I misrepresented the facts. I think you really did have a nervous breakdown. You were certainly in bad shape when I walked into your office that day."

"Yes. I remember," said General Starling. "That's the day you relieved me of duty."

"I had to. You were in no position to command. On the other hand, I had no idea what kind of hell you and your men had gone through. In the annals of military history, you and your men experienced and suffered one of the weirdest and most horrible events ever to happen. The rest is history," said Ridgley. "I reported that, when my troops moved in on the old farmhouse, it caught on fire and killed everybody inside. Now, Washington is happy. Everything is back to normal and I'm waiting for new deployment orders."

"What did happen to that old farmhouse?" asked Starling.

Ridgley looked thoughtfully at his old friend. "Don't tell anybody, Harold. This is strictly between you and I. I burned it down myself and destroyed all the evidence."

Starling asked, "And the President and the Secretary of Defense; they really bought your entire story?"

"Lock, stock, and barrel. No questioned asked."

"No Spaceships or men from Mars. Huh, Nathan?"

"Not on your life," said General Ridgley, taking a big draw on his cigar and watching the smoke curl over his head. Then, murmuring to himself, he said, "Besides, if I had told the truth, nobody would have believed me, anyway."

Epilogue

Six months had passed since the Expeditionary Force returned to the home planet. Its ships, by this time, had all been retrofitted with new Reflective Magnifiers and the evacuation of Earth was complete. The citizens of Earth were now en route to their new home, on a small habitable planet, at the opposite end of the galaxy. They named the planet New Earth. Joy and anticipation of the new mingled with tears of sadness, as they reflected and mourned the loss of their beloved homeland. The last to leave was The President and his entourage. The engineers and construction crews, who had preceded the main body of immigrants, had almost completed building the facilities on the new planet. They described the new planet as beautiful beyond belief. They said it was probably much like Earth, before it was besieged by the onset of men's wars which caused the pollution and terrible storms that followed.

The President's thoughts were mostly always on the direction the government would take after settling in their new homes. That changes would be made was inevitable and went without saying. The circumstances New Earth would be in were entirely different than those that had faced them in the past. It was then that he remembered Zorena. He still mourned the death of his beautiful daughter and always found it difficult to hold back the tears whenever he thought of her.

On this day, however, his reflections were cut short. His old friend, Dr. Steebler cut short his reverie. "Sorry to bother you, Sir, but we're getting some very strange transmissions from deep in space that I think you will be particularly interested in."

"Something wrong?" asked the President.

"No. It's not the colonist," answered Steebler. "Wait 'til we get to the Communication Center. I don't want to speculate on what I think these transmissions are. I want you to hear them and judge for yourself."

211

The President was ushered into the Communication Center and seated at a receiver station.

"Just listen for a while," said an operator, who, as he spoke, kept turning the dials on a huge console.

Soon, a voice was heard through one of the speakers. It was so faint, it was hard to make out. "Can anybody hear me? Please come in," came a female voice. "This is ...," and then, the voice faded out.

"We've been receiving these transmissions for about two hours now, but haven't been able to get a good read or a fix on them and I haven't been able to identify who's talking, either," said the operator.

The President had turned ashen white. He was visibly shaken. "That was Zorena!" he exclaimed. "I would recognize her voice, anywhere."

"We sent for a power booster," said Dr. Steebler. "That should help our receivers. These transmissions are coming from millions and millions of miles away. It's a miracle that we're receiving them at all.

"Where are they coming from?" asked the President.

"We don't know, but we're trying hard to get a better fix on their location. We've got to make contact, soon. If these ethereal clouds break up, we could lose the contact forever."

Shortly, the booster arrived and was added to the power supply. "Okay," said the operator, "let's give it a try." Again, he worked the dials on the console.

With the aid of the boosters, a clear voice came through the speakers. "Can anybody out there hear me? Father? Dr. Steebler? Dr. Friedman? Anybody? This is Zorena Harbill. If you can hear me, please answer. I am shipwrecked and stranded. Dr. Menes is with me. Our ship was thrown off course when we entered the Aboreium Tunnel. We have landed on ancient Earth, in the year 3000 B. C. The date is October 24th. We're safe, but stranded. I've been transmitting, trying to reach somebody for two weeks. I guess it's no use, but, if anybody receives this message, if you can't help us, wish us well. Father, if you can hear me, just remember, I love you and Mom. Tell all my friends

I love and miss them. Like I said, I'm safe. The people here are very friendly, but primitive. Dr. Menes and I will be okay. If you can locate his family, tell them he's well and give them his love. For the hundredth and last time, I'll sign off now. Goodbye."

"Get her back!" yelled President Harbill. "Tell her we got her message."

"Sir, we can't get her back," said Dr. Steebler. "We can't make contact. She transmitted that message on September 24th. That was six months ago. She has quit transmitting and, by now, with the equipment she has, she won't be able to receive our transmissions."

"But she is alive. Thank God for that! You must know, my first instinct is to go after her, but I have a feeling that's not possible. Is it, Dr. Steebler?"

"You know I loved Zorena as if she were my own daughter," said Steebler, "but, from our position, it would be impossible."

"My wife and I mourned the death of our daughter. Now, I know she's out there safe and alive. It's hard to console myself with the thought that we'll never be able to see or talk to her again, but I am grateful and give thanks, knowing all is well. That is a great gift of comfort to my wife and I. Our prayers have been answered. Maybe now, we can both be at peace."

213

The End

This is a fictitious story

OR IS IT?

About The Author

Harlen West was born in Akron, Ohio, September 22, 1928.
When he turned 18 he joined the Air Force where he served for
28 years. Harlen never regretted his choice of career and
relished the assignments and responsibilities given him, which
included maintenance superintendent for four different munitions
storage areas two overseas in combat zones, one at Nellis AFB,
Las Vegas Nevada, and one At Howard AFB in the Panama
Canal Zone. Another assignment placed him at Edwards AFB,
California, where he was assigned as maintenance
superintendent in charge of the flight line where future astronauts
flying modified F104 fighters were trained. His military training
and experience is what led him to write his novel – The Dome
Wars.

About the [First] Editor, Emily Ann West Jan., 1932 – June, 2011

As a sergeant in the U.S. Air Force, I met and married Emily Ann West. I had no idea of what a brilliant woman I had wed. She astonished me with her accomplishments. There seemed to be nothing she couldn't do and she was not afraid to try anything. Here are a few of her accomplishments:

Shortly after we were married, our country became involved in the Vietnamese Conflict, which resulted in me being transferred almost every other year, between the U. S. and Thailand. This resulted in Emily constantly having to move. First, she moved to Sacramento, California, to live with her parents. Not one to sit at home, Emily immediately secured two jobs; one as the writer and editor of the Sacramento Legal Press and another writing a column in the local newspaper, the Sacramento Bee. After a short stay at home, I was, again, shipped overseas for a one-year tour. While I was gone, Emily volunteered to work for the MARS (Military Affiliated Radio Station). She was one of the key ham operators at the station, that linked military families with their loved ones during wartime. On my last overseas assignment, I was assigned to Albrook AFB, in the Panama Canal Zone. Emily and the kids, five of them by now, came with me. During her four years there, her activity only increased. She became a journalist and analyzer for Copley News Service and interviewed such notables as Panamanian President General Omar Torejos, after he put down an attempted coup, and the Chinese Ambassador to Panama, General Huang. She also wrote a column for the Southern Command News, which served Central and South America. Southern Command News also had a television Station, where Emily was an anchor woman on the Friday night news. Last, but not least, Emily edited my book.